THE LAND GIRL ON LILY ROAD

Homefront Hearts #3

Jillianne Hamilton writes delightful historical fiction and historical romance featuring rebellious women and happy endings. Her debut novel was shortlisted for the PEI Book Award and her debut historical fiction novel was longlisted for the Historical Fiction Company Book Award. She lives in Charlottetown on Canada's east coast.

OTHER BOOKS BY THE AUTHOR

The Hobby Shop on Barnaby Street
The Seamstress on Cider Lane

The Spirited Mrs. Pringle

The Lazy Historian's Guide to the Wives of Henry VIII

Molly Miranda: Thief for Hire
Molly Miranda: Thick as Thieves
Molly Miranda: Honor Among Thieves

The Land Girl on Lily Road
By Jillianne Hamilton

www.Jilly.ca

ISBN: 978-1-7381992-2-8

Published in 2024 by Jillianne Hamilton and Tomfoolery Press.

Book and cover design by Jillianne Hamilton.

the Land Girl on Lily Road

A HOMEFRONT HEARTS NOVEL

TFP

one

Elsie

"Alright, girls," announced our overly enthusiastic instructor, hands on her hips. "That wraps up our very last class together. You've all done a tremendous job. Britain owes you a debt of gratitude for your service."

Several ladies in the class whooped in celebration while I glanced at the clock.

"The lot of you will make great farmers. Remember your training and recognize that you are serving your country as much as any infantryman."

"Oy, does that mean we get guns too?" quipped one of the girls in the back of the class.

"You can barely 'andle a pitchfork, never mind a rifle," one of her class clown friends chided, her thick cockney accent strangling the words.

I rolled my eyes. I couldn't wait to get away from these blatherers.

The instructor smiled serenely, now used to the jokes and jabs from some of the London girls in the class. "*We* don't need guns. The Women's Land Army fights the enemy with strength, determination, and dedication." She held up a slim stack of papers. "Please collect your certificate before you leave. Class dismissed."

After picking up my paper and saying goodbye to our immeasurably patient instructor, I headed straight for the dormitory to pack my belongings. One of my classmates, Sheila, sat on her bed next to mine and watched me curiously as I pulled my brown leather suitcase out from under my cot and flipped it open.

"You're packing? You're not coming to the pub with us?"

Sheila Buckley's chestnut spiral curls were never quite under control, no matter how much she tried. Her nose was just a little too pointed, her freckles were just a little too prominent, and her eagerness was just a little too earnest. She was one of those girls who was friendly with everybody, even if they showed absolutely no sign at all of wanting to reciprocate—myself, for example.

"I'm hoping to catch the last train to London. If I hurry, I can make it." Looking over my shoulder, I checked the clock at the end of the long room lined with single beds and trunks. I did *not* want to spend another night in this room, hearing the snores and whispers of twenty-three other women, if I didn't have to.

"Oh, come out with us, Elsie," she said. "It'll be jolly. Don't you want a chance to say goodbye to the rest of the girls?"

I did not. Our Land Army training had only lasted a month. I didn't even learn all their names—I certainly didn't need to say goodbye to them over a poorly made cocktail at the musty local. Besides, I had nothing in common with any of these girls. They all spoke loudly, laughed boisterously, and came from working class backgrounds. Plus, I'm quite certain they loathed me. I believe they mistook my complete disinterest for snobbishness.

"You can take the train back to London in the morning with the rest of us," Sheila added, leaning in.

"No, that's alright. Thank you for the invitation though, I appreciate it."

I did not.

"Oh, alright then," she said, the corners of her frown sinking deep into her chubby pink cheeks.

She continued watching me pack, looking glum.

"Did you say you already know where you're going to be assigned?"

"I'm going to my family's country estate in Suffolk," I said, tucking the last of my things into my suitcase. "I expect it will be a lot of hard work, but at least it's a place I'm familiar with."

"You're lucky," she said. "I'll probably end up sleeping in a hayloft in Dover somewhere and get bombed every other night."

I winced. Because of its location right on the Channel, Dover had been raided countless times. Although the London bombings had basically stopped in May 1941—about nine months ago—people from poorer boroughs of London, like Sheila, still felt the effects of the attacks every single day. You could see the flames from the incendiary bombs in their eyes as they spoke of their homes getting destroyed in a split second.

I fastened the buckles on my suitcase and fetched my coat from my trunk. "Well, good lu—*oomph*."

Sheila threw her arms around me and squeezed me. "Goodbye Elsie. It was so nice to meet you and get to know you. Good luck."

"Thank you. You too," I wheezed.

She slid her arms away and I swear I saw a tear in her eye. I nodded and headed out.

"I have your address," she called after me, "so once I'm settled at wherever I end up, I can write to you. Byyyye Elsie!"

As I turned the corner and retrieved my Army-issued winter coat from one of the hooks in the front hallway, I wondered how on earth Sheila had my mailing address since I certainly had not given it to her.

Relieved and out of breath from running most of the way to the train station, I sat back in my seat and let out a long, slow breath. I gave a little shiver as the frigid February air sneaked in through the train car door.

The lady in the seat next to me took notice of my red and green Women's Land Army armband and smiled at me. "Are you one of the new land girls in training?"

"I finished the course today actually," I said. "I'm just on my way back to London for a few days and then I'm off again to Suffolk."

"What a lovely part of the country to be assigned to. Have you ever been there?"

I almost laughed. Channel House, our Suffolk property, was where I spent every summer as a child and most summer months during my adolescence. I had grown up skipping across the nearby beach and splashing in its frothy waves, lounging in the garden, and reading in the lovely conservatory until sunset.

"A few times," I said, not boring her with the details.

My taking WLA training was my father's idea. I was soon to be drafted into some kind of war work anyway and he cleverly suggested I become a land girl and spend the rest of the war in Suffolk.

Most of the women of my social class had found jobs working in offices so many of the Women's Land Army recruits came from London's…well, less privileged, shall we say? By going to Channel House, I could go to London whenever I liked, I wouldn't have to lift a finger unless I wanted to pick some wildflowers for my bedroom, and the War Office chaps would think my father was some kind of a hero for having his socialite daughter working hard in the fields as a member of the WLA. It was ingenious really. My biggest concern was that it might get lonely out there in the country.

"How was training?" the woman next to me asked.

"Ghastly," I admitted. "I'm so happy to be done with it. They made us get up at an unholy hour in the morning, and these boots are terribly uncomfortable."

She lifted an eyebrow at me. "It's not going to get easier when you're out on a real farm, you know."

"Yes, of course." I faked a laugh. "Right."

She didn't need to know I was heading into an extended country holiday. Channel House already had a full staff for caring for the crops. I supposed I could help out if I got tremendously bored but as far as I was concerned, my farming days were over.

"The Army has acquired Channel House," my father announced, his nostrils flaring with great abandon. "I got a call from some Corporal So-and-So this morning. He said the location is strategically advantageous so the British Army will be moving troops into our home within the week." He shook his head and puffed his cheeks out. "I've never heard such outrageous poppycock."

"No," I said. "No, no, no, no. No, they cannot do this. They can't just *decide* to move into our house because they want it. *I'm* going there next week to—" I hesitated as we both knew very well what I was going there to do "—work in the fields."

He gave an exaggerated huff and the hairs of his thick mustache fluttered. "I called the War Office and they said there was nothing to be done." He shook his head again. "The bloody nerve of those bastards."

I considered what a manor full of troops and handsome officers might be like.

"I could still go—"

"No, you could not," he thundered.

"Well, what is she supposed to do, Robert? She can't go to some farm and live with-with-with strangers in the middle of nowhere." Mother laid a protective hand on the gold chain at her throat.

An enormous portion of British Army uniforms were made at Father's textile factories and this gave him some influence at the War Office. Evidently, it had not been enough to keep Channel House untouched by the war.

Sighing, Father lowered his eyes. Robert Foster-Quinn hated a lot—and I mean a *lot*—of things but he hated disappointing my mother most of all.

"I'll make some calls," he said quietly. "You may have to go to a farm temporarily while I sort this out and get you reassigned somewhere more appropriate."

My mouth fell open. "Go to a farm? A *real* one? That was *not* part of the plan."

"I knew it," Mother added. "You should have taken a secretarial job and we could have avoided this whole situation. You would have stayed in London and slept in your bed instead of…instead of…" She shuddered and threw her hands up in the air.

"I'm sorry," Father said, almost whispering. Apologizing was also high on his list of things he hated. "I *will* see what I can do."

"Thank you," I murmured, giving a Dutiful Daughter nod and leaving his office.

My suitcase was gone from the foyer. George must have already taken it up to my room. I wondered if it was against Women's Land Army regulations to bring a butler with you.

"Elsie, darling?" My mother still looked distraught as she lifted a slender finger and gestured. "Those trousers are terribly unflattering on you."

The high-waisted brown corduroy trousers were roomy around the thighs and backside, letting the wearer move around to work. They weren't nearly as unflattering as the army-issued dungarees though.

I clenched my jaw. "They're part of the uniform."

My mother's hand went to her cheek. "Oh, God. It keeps getting worse."

two

BEN

"No, no, no. Absolutely not. I'm not putting up with any more bloody land girls."

Vera crossed her arms over her chest. "You need to be practical. You can't handle everything on your own."

I glared at her over my empty lunch plate. "I'm *fine*—"

"But you won't be come spring," she snapped. "You're going to work yourself to death. You need help. You only have two hands and so many hours in a day."

"I told you I would take on some of those POWs—the German ones if possible—but not the land girls. That one girl we had here before was useless. All she did was complain."

"To be fair, she *was* very sick—"

"Farm work didn't *give* her asthma," I said. "And there was that other one! The one I caught kicking Dottie." My blood boiled just thinking about that rotter.

"When I talked to the chap with the War Ag this morning," Vera continued, "he said they couldn't provide us with any POWs right now but he'd let us know when some came available."

"And you told him we're definitely not taking any more land girls, yeah?"

"Yes, that's what I told him."

I sat back and gave a firm nod. "Good. Maybe he'll get it through his thick skull."

Vera took my empty plate and my teacup and busied herself in the small, cozy kitchen. I shrugged my coat back on as Sam, my Border Collie, rose from his napping spot in the corner by the fire and stretching his back legs out behind him. Together we went back outside to continue the never ending list of tasks to tend to.

Honeyfield Farm felt so peaceful that day, like it was still asleep under a thin layer of glittering white snow. Soon bits of gold and green would begin to peek through the frost as the world began its cycle once again.

And I would be plunged into more work than I could possibly handle alone.

Yes, of course I knew Vera was right. I just didn't want her worrying about me.

I thought I'd lucked out in December when I found a pair of brothers from the next village who couldn't serve because of some shared health issue. Turns out the British Army was more desperate for men than I thought as both were called up to serve in noncombat roles, and they were gone the next week. The older one was around twenty, I think, about the same age as my younger brother Walter was when he signed up back in '39.

I checked in on the ladies in the barn. Dottie, one of my best milkers and always one of the most vocal of the herd, mooed in greeting as I ran a hand down the side of her black and white neck. She bumped my chest with her nose, and I scratched behind her ear until she snorted in approval. My friend Amos, another dairy farmer, said I shouldn't pick favorites.

But maybe if Amos had Dottie, he wouldn't feel that way.

Next, I collected a hammer and some nails from the toolshed and strolled down the path to the front gate. A bit of fencing nearby had come loose during a winter storm, and I hadn't gotten around to fixing it yet. I noticed two silhouettes at the front gate and I put a hand to my forehead, shielding my eyes from the sunlight glinting off the surrounding snow.

"Oy," I called up the lane. "Can I help you?"

Sam went to go investigate the figures, but I whistled sharply and he instantly laid down in front of me, staring straight ahead.

"Is this Honeyfield Farm?" the taller of the two said.

As they neared, I recognized their matching armbands—a crown and the letters 'WLA' in red on a green background with a red border. My shoulders sagged.

"Aye, 'tis," I said hesitantly.

"We're dreadfully sorry to be so delayed. We lost our way," said the shorter one in a posh accent as she put her two suitcases on the ground and flexed her fingers.

Her companion smiled wide. "We got directions from one of your neighbors. Never thought I'd miss signposts so much."

Fairbury was one of the many English villages that were signpost-free since the beginning of the war. The government couldn't provide us with protection against a potential Nazi invasion so getting the Germans lost and irritated was apparently the next best option.

Thankfully no German army ever arrived, so it was mostly tourists getting lost instead.

And two land girls.

I frowned at the suitcases on the ground before looking back up at them. "How can I help you?"

The two young women exchanged glances. The shorter one spoke up.

"We're from the Women's Land Army." She gestured weakly to the armband, bright against the brown of her coat. "We're assigned to your farm."

I sighed loudly. "There's been a mistake. I told the War Ag I don't want any land girls. I don't have time to teach a pair of city girls about farming. This isn't dress-up or playtime. It's hard work."

The land girls looked at one another again, this time with a shared look of concern.

"Sir, we have come a very long way," the shorter one began,

speaking very slowly, as if to a child, "and we are here to assist you. We have completed our agriculture certification course and—"

"How long was the course?"

"A month," the taller one said.

A loud laugh escaped me. "A month! And you studied in February? That's just perfect. You must know everything there is to know about farming then." I shrugged. "I'm sorry you traveled here for nothing, girls."

The shorter one narrowed her eyes and took a step forward. "Sir? We were sent here. We're going to do our duty, and you need to make peace with that. If it helps you feel any better, we don't want to be here either."

"I'm actually happy to be here," the other woman said quietly, moving out from behind her blunt friend. "It's a lovely part of the country."

"Quiet, Sheila," the shorter one snapped, throwing a quick look over her shoulder before glowering back at me with fire in her eyes. She widened her eyes at me directly, indicating she was waiting for my reply.

Before I could argue with the angry little woman, we were interrupted by the sound of horse hooves on the road. I took a step back and shoved my hands in my pockets, knowing I was about to get a scolding. Sam looked over his shoulder at me, still waiting for his release command.

"Ladies, you're here!" called Rosetta Watkins from atop her impressive rust-colored thoroughbred. She dismounted with the ease of a seasoned rider and smiled wide at the shorter of the two younger ladies. "Darling, it's been too long!"

The two embraced and kissed cheeks in the way that rich people do. Now it was my turn to exchange a look with Sheila.

"So nice to see you again, Rosetta," the Angry Little Woman said, her wrath melting away in an instant. "How are the boys?"

"Well, the two older boys are serving as officers and our youngest just began a new position at the War Office. He's about your age. You've met our Clement, haven't you?"

Neither of them even looked up at Sheila or me as they caught up, these two old chums reuniting. I wanted to suggest they go have lunch so I could get back to work.

"Your dear mama gave me a call and mentioned you were sent to Fairbury for your WLA work and she asked me if I knew who the local WLA district representative was and I had to laugh because it's me," Mrs. Watkins said quickly. "She's terribly worried about you. She's devastated about the Army taking over Channel House."

Angry Little Woman hesitated. "It certainly complicated plans."

"Not to worry, girls," Mrs. Watkins said, finally gracing Sheila and me with brief eye contact. "Mr. Grainger is an upstanding young man and will be a good coach to you as you get settled into your duties."

Angry Little Woman dragged her gaze over to me. "Unfortunately, Mrs. Watkins, Mr. Grainger here has just explained to us that he is refusing to accept any members of the Women's Land Army at his farm." There was a wicked little grin in her voice as she spoke.

Mrs. Watkins blinked at me. "Mr. Grainger? Is this true?"

"It's nothin' personal," I blurted. "I just haven't the time to, er, coach, as you say, people who don't know the everyday workings of a farm—"

"They completed their training. I'm sure they'll be fine." Mrs. Watkins smiled sweetly but there was nothing truly sweet about it. "Perhaps they'll even teach you a thing or two."

Sam looked up at me again, likely hearing the scraping of my clenched jaw.

"I don't think it's a good idea," I protested. "The land girls here before turned out to be bad apples. Besides, I have some German POWs coming over to work the fields in the spring, and it doesn't seem right to have two young ladies around those bast—er, those brutes."

Angry Little Woman arched an eyebrow at me.

"I can vouch for Miss Foster-Quinn personally and I'm sure Miss Buckley will prove to be just as hardworking. As a matter of fact, many farmers have had nothing but positive things to say about land girls. Many say they work harder than the POWs." Mrs. Watkins' smile remained but she narrowed her eyes slightly. "I'm sure Miss Buckley and Miss Foster-Quinn will prove to be positive additions to your farm."

I rubbed the back of my neck. "Well, perhaps Vera could use their help around the cottage—"

"Land girls are to be used for agricultural purposes only, Mr. Grainger." Mrs. Watkins tutted at me. "You know that."

She simply wasn't going to let me send them away, I realized.

I let my shoulders drop. "I'll agree to keep them here on a trial basis."

"You won't regret it," Sheila piped up.

Mrs. Watkins bid us farewell and mounted her horse, puffs of dusty snow rising as its hooves landed on the ground.

"Well, that'll be enough of that Mr. Grainger nonsense," I said. "My name is Ben. This is Sam."

Sam gave a little whine and finally put his head down between his front paws.

Sheila immediately dropped to her knees and rubbed Sam behind the ears and over his neck causing Sam's tail to thump against the ground.

"Oh, I'm Sheila," she said, looking up at me before resuming her scratches and pats.

I let out a quiet snort-laugh from my nose. "Now he'll be following *you* around all day instead."

I turned my attention to Angry Little Woman as she picked up her two suitcases again.

"You may call me Miss Foster-Quinn," she said, her nose lifted slightly.

"Right. I'm not calling you that," I said. "What's your first name?"

"That won't be necessary. Miss Foster-Quinn will do."

"Very well," I said. "I will call you 'Norman.'"

"Fine." She rolled her eyes. "My name is Elsie."

"No, no, no," I said, raising my palms. "You were very clear—you don't want me calling you by your Christian name, and I will respect your wishes. 'Miss Foster-Quinn' is a bit of a mouthful though and I'm but a simple farmer." A smirk tugged at the corner of my lips. "So, I'll just call you 'Norman.'"

As Norman puffed her cheeks out and huffed in a rage, Sam flopped over on his back to receive a belly rub, his tongue lolling out one side of his mouth.

"Come on then," I said, nodding towards the cottage. "I'll show you where you'll be living while you're here." They followed me and

Sam trotted at my side.

"Do you have a telephone?" Norman asked from behind me.

"No telephone. The nearest telephone box is at the end of the road just as you get to the village," I said. "And we're not on the grid either."

"You are joking," she exclaimed. "Tell me you're joking."

This sent me chuckling. "Oh, you're going to love it here."

three

Elsie

If I had been at Channel House as planned, dinner would have been brought up to my room on a little tray. A jazz record would have been playing quietly in the background as I finished up my latest reread of *Persuasion* by Jane Austen. I would have eaten something like Beef Bourguignon or perhaps vegetable au gratin. Maybe I would have had a biscuit after dinner with a mug of cider or cocoa. Then I would have relaxed in a hot bubble bath. It would have been lovely.

Instead, I was staring down into a sparse bowl of vegetable stew, drinking very weak tea, and trying not to cry in front of Mr. Grainger. I would rather die than show weakness in front of that blighter.

"I'm off then," Vera said, wrapping a thick knit scarf around her neck. "See you all tomorrow at breakfast."

Mr. Grainger plucked a piece of thick bread from the plate in the middle and dipped it in his stew before stuffing it in his mouth. He nodded his goodbye to Vera as she flew out the door.

Sheila reached for a piece of bread. "Vera seems a fine cook. Is she your missus?"

Mr. Grainger nearly choked on the crust he chewed. "Christ, no!

She's my sister."

Sheila flushed. "Oh, goodness. I'm so sorry. I didn't realize—"

"Since I'm an old bachelor, she keeps house for me. She lives up in the village." He took a slurp of tea.

For an 'old bachelor,' Mr. Grainger didn't seem *that* old. Maybe thirty. There were no signs of silver whiskers among the black stubble on his cheeks or in his thick, tousled, dark hair.

He looked out of place in this small, tidy country kitchen. He had to duck under the wooden beams that crossed the ceiling, and his wide shoulders barely fit in the slightly uneven doorway frame. It was like the whole room—possibly the entire cottage—was too small for him. But he likely had never lived anywhere else, I realized, so probably didn't even notice.

Not to say that the kitchen wasn't charming in a quaint sort of way.

I was mostly just relieved we weren't sitting in total darkness or forced to exist by candlelight. The petrol-powered generator lighting was, however, a bit dimmer than what I was used to.

Sam, the sweet black and white Border Collie, lay by the stone fireplace in the corner of the kitchen. A black patch covered one half of his otherwise snow-white head. Every so often he would raise his head and check for any scraps that had fallen to the floor.

Mr. Grainger cleared his throat. "The cows need to be milked twice a day, every day. No matter the weather, the holiday, the day of the week, or how you feel that day, the cows *have* to be milked."

We obviously learned that during our training course, but he thought Sheila and I were simpletons. I speared a vegetable chunk in my bowl as he continued.

"We start our day milking at five o'clock. Don't be late." He rose from his chair and set his dishes in the sink. He leaned against the wooden shelf well-stocked with preserves and canned goods and crossed his arms over his chest, causing the few holes in his well-worn cable knit jumper to shift in shape. "You can have Sunday afternoons off but otherwise you'll need to be here, working."

"Yes, sir," Sheila said.

I nodded in agreement.

"Any questions? Or at least any questions that can't wait until tomorrow morning?" He glanced between the two of us.

"Just the one," Sheila said shyly. "If the cottage doesn't have hot water, how are we to…bathe?"

My eyes darted to Mr. Grainger. I hadn't even thought of that.

Mr. Grainger's eyebrows went up slightly. "Right. That. Did you see where the pump is just outside? There's a wee room through there with a tub." He gestured vaguely to what I had previously assumed was a pantry door. "You'll want to boil water to fill the tub. There's a cauldron in the tub you can use for that. Just hang it over the fire on that hook. It takes a while to heat up enough water so we'll take turns."

He didn't bother commenting on Sheila's slightly ajar mouth.

"Alright. Until the morning then." He nodded and left the kitchen. The ceiling creaked as he went upstairs and down the hall.

Sheila looked at me. "I forgot to ask him where the toilet is."

"There's an outdoor privy," I said glumly. "I saw it when we were coming down the drive."

"Oh," she said. "I suppose I just won't piss until the war is over."

I bolted up in bed the next morning as Sheila poked her head into my bedroom. "Morning."

Blinking hard at her, I felt my pulse slow in my chest as I gradually realized where I was. I let myself fall back on the pillow.

"Morning," I mumbled, reaching a hand out from under the covers to touch my ice-cold nose.

As Sheila shuffled back to her room at the top of the stairs, I forced myself out of bed and into my uniform as quickly as I could move. Once I had my fawn shirt, deep bottle green jumper, and tan breeches on, I pulled back the gingham curtains over the window and looked over the farmyard. A shimmering border of frost had built up on the window overnight, and I scraped some off with my fingernail.

I slid my armband on, pinned my blonde curls into place under my WLA-issued felt hat, and met Sheila in the hall. She was beaming.

"Ready for our first day?"

"Not in the slightest," I said.

When I'd boarded the train in London the day before and spotted Sheila frantically waving to me, I couldn't quite believe my luck. My very, very bad luck.

She slid over and manically gestured to the empty seat beside her. Sitting elsewhere seemed rude, so I made my way down the aisle with my two suitcases.

I frowned up at the crowded overhead storage before smiling sweetly at the middle-aged man in the seat behind Sheila. "Sir, would you mind…?"

"Of course!" He leapt to his feet and quickly began shifting things around to fit my belongings.

"Thank you," I said, adding a bit more syrup to my voice. "That's very kind."

I took my seat next to Sheila and wished I was literally anywhere else on the planet at that moment. Occupied Poland? Siberia? Manchester?

"I thought you were going east, not west," Sheila said, her enthusiasm practically spilling out of her.

"My plans were unfortunately ruined when the Army took over my family's estate. I was devastated. Now I've been assigned to a farm outside of Bath."

My stomach dropped as Sheila's face lit up somehow even more. "Honeyfield Farm in Fairbury?"

Oh, please no.

"That's the one," I said with a fake little chuckle.

"We're going to be working together!" Sheila squealed with delight. "Isn't that wonderful?"

Yes. She squealed. She *actually* squealed.

"Brilliant," I said, trying to match even an eighteenth of her zeal.

At least we didn't have to share a bed at Honeyfield Cottage, or even a bedroom. During our training, we had been warned that sleeping arrangements were likely to be rough for the land girls living with the farmers they worked for.

Our rooms were tiny, the beds creaked loudly, and the windows rattled with every breeze but I was so incredibly grateful to have even a hint of privacy in this new, strange world. Some of the ladies went to shared dormitories—this seemed like a fun prospect to some of my classmates but certainly not to me. Sharing one big room with those girls for a month during our training had been enough for me.

Sheila and I reached the barn at five o'clock sharp. I inhaled sharply as the smell of the barn hit my nose, and I slapped a hand over my face. Sheila wrinkled her nose slightly but shook it off. Meanwhile, I tucked my face into the collar of my coat to hide from the odor.

Perched on a little stool that looked comically small for him, Mr. Grainger was already milking when we arrived and only peered up briefly.

"Don't care for the smell?" He smirked as he continued milking.

Sheila cleared her throat. "I'm sure we'll get used to it."

"Speak for yourself," I added, wincing as I took small breaths through my mouth.

Ignoring me, Mr. Grainger gestured to the buckets behind him as he stood. He dipped a cloth into one bucket.

"Wash the udder with warm water first. Make sure it's good 'n clean before you start milking," he explained. "Did they teach you how to milk a cow?"

"Yes, sir," Sheila and I said in unison, neither of us mentioning that we used fake udders made of rubber.

I didn't know about Sheila but I'd never been this close to a cow before. I had certainly never touched or milked one before.

We nodded as he advised us which pails to use, when to pour the pails into the larger canisters, which cows were too pregnant to be milked, and which cows had the most 'spirit' and might give us a hard time.

"Any questions?"

Sheila and I looked at one another.

"You…" I glanced at Sheila again. "You milk by hand?"

Mr. Grainger's mouth twisted into a scowl.

"Not that there's anything wrong with that method," Sheila blurted. "We were just told a lot of dairy farmers switched to milking machines."

He gave a sniff of derision. "The ladies didn't like it."

"The ladies?" I repeated.

"Yes." A burst of fog appeared as he huffed and nodded to the stalls next to us. "The ladies."

Sheila leaned closer to me. "I think he's talking about the cows—"

"Yes, Sheila, thank you," I hissed. My eyes narrowed slightly as I studied Mr. Grainger. "Did they…*tell* you they didn't like it?"

He crossed his arms over his broad chest. "I know when my own cows are upset."

"But you *have* tried one? Do you own one?" Sheila hesitated as she spoke. "Maybe we could try it?"

He rolled his eyes. "It's in the cabinet over there but it needs to be cleaned before you can use it. We don't have time for that right now."

He moved the stool over to the next cow down the row and dipped the cloth in the bucket of warm water before cleaning the next udder. I watched carefully as he firmly squeezed the milk out of each teat, studying how the flow of milk slowed as the udder gradually emptied. Our rubber udders in class certainly hadn't done that. Likely sensing he was being watched, Mr. Grainger glanced up at me and I looked away at once, grabbing a small pail and the warm wet cloth.

I took a deep breath and reminded myself that if this complete philistine could milk a cow without trouble, I could certainly handle it.

Mr. Grainger cleared his throat. "Unless you want to get a hoof to the face, I'd suggest you not start with that one." He pointed to the two cows next to it. "Try Matilda first. Sheila, you start with Harriet over there."

As a matter of fact, I did not want a hoof to the face so I did as I was told. I rubbed my palms together briskly to warm them up before brushing dirt away from Matilda's swollen udder. I passed the cloth on to Sheila and tried to recall exactly the hand motion Mr. Grainger had used—holding the top of the teat between his index finger and thumb, then moving the milk down the length of the teat by wrapping his fingers around it and aiming the stream of milk into the bucket. He didn't pull, he just squeezed and held onto the pail with his other hand.

Mr. Grainger and Sheila watched as I sat on the floor on Matilda's right side and tried to replicate what Mr. Grainger had done.

A strong stream of milk hit the bottom of my pail and made a pleasant metallic chime on contact.

"Ha!" I smiled wide at Sheila. "It worked!"

"You sound surprised," Mr. Grainger said. "I thought you knew everything there was to know about farming."

"Yes, well, I thought perhaps your cows might have…unique teats."

His eyebrows went up. "Did ya now?" He went back to milking his own cow. "Carry on then, Norman. You've got four teats and a lot of cows to go."

I shot him another look. I knew objecting to my new nickname would just amuse him.

Sheila had a few false starts but quickly got the right grip and rhythm down, although I don't believe Harriet appreciated being her test subject. By the time we completed milking the entire herd, I had a cramp in my hand and a sore lower back.

"Your hand'll get used to it soon enough," Mr. Grainger said. "Next time, you should probably use one of the milking stools. We have a few in the cabinet."

I glared at him. "Why didn't you say you had more stools before?"

He fought back a grin. "You didn't ask."

After a quick breakfast of bread and margarine and eggs made from a powder mix, Mr. Grainger announced the next challenge of the day.

"Sheila, you and I are going to feed the cows and hopefully get the tractor up and running," he said. "Did you work with tractors during your training?"

Sheila nodded. "And some basic repair stuff."

"Good." He turned to me. "Norman, you're going to deliver milk."

"All by myself?" I nearly spilled my tea as I put it down on the table.

Vera looked up from her ironing board nearby. "Did you just call her 'Norman'?"

"I don't know where anyone lives," I continued. "There are no road signs!"

Mr. Grainger gave a weak shrug. "Ask for directions."

Sheila, Mr. Grainger, and I finished lugging the crates of milk bottles onto a cart about forty minutes later. The biggest horse I had ever seen stood patiently as Sheila and I harnessed him and hitched him to the cart.

"Will you be alright?" Sheila whispered when Mr. Grainger was out of earshot. "I asked if I could go with you, but he said you could handle it."

"He's trying to make me quit." I lifted my chin defiantly. "He doesn't know how stubborn I can be."

She studied me for a moment. "You're quite intimidating sometimes. You know that, right?"

Mr. Grainger inspected the harness and the hitch and nodded in approval. "Sherlock is old and can't see as well as he used to but he knows the route just fine."

I gave Sherlock's salt and pepper mane a quick brush. "I hope so."

Patting the pocket of his coat, Mr. Grainger pulled out a small notebook, well-worn with age and accompanied by a pen clipped onto the cover, and handed it to me. "This is all our customers and how many bottles their household gets. Make sure you get the same number of empty bottles back as well."

I nodded and put it in my coat pocket.

Vera joined us and put a lunch pail into the back of the cart. "This horse goes at a snail's pace so I made your lunch."

I thanked her and climbed into the cart, taking a seat on the little bench at the front. Before I could even uncoil the reins and command him to move, the gigantic horse began his slow trudge down the drive to the road.

After a few minutes, I regretted not bringing my book with me.

I gave a gentle tug on the reins; Sherlock flicked his ear and snorted in reply. I let out a long sigh and let my eyes wander over the rolling white hills and serene meadows on both sides of Lily Road. A well-maintained rock wall lined both sides of the straight stretch of mud road, and farms dotted the picturesque landscape. Besides the sound of Sherlock's hooves and the creaking of the rickety, bouncing cart, all was silent and still.

When we finally reached the outer edge of the village, Sherlock slowed and stopped in front of a small cottage with a front garden that was home to six raised vegetable gardens, all glittering with frost. An older woman came out of the cottage, wiping her hands on her apron, and narrowed her eyes at me.

"Goodness," she said. "You must be one of the new land girls."

"Good morning," I said. "Yes, we just arrived on the train yesterday. I'm so sorry, can you tell me what your name is?"

The woman chuckled. "Mavis Seaton, dear. Might be under my Albert's name."

I felt silly having to ask every single customer their name but Mr. Grainger left me no choice. I took notes on the few empty pages at the back of the notebook so I could recall their names next time: what their cottage was called or looked like, something memorable about the customer, and what buildings their home was near.

Almost every customer asked me about myself, likely curious about this newcomer to their village.

"What's your name, love?"

"Where are your people from?"

"Are ye likin' the work?"

There were two bottles of milk left when we stopped in front of a tidy little cottage belonging to the only name left in the book, someone named Herb Collins.

I had barely finished knocking on the door when it was opened by an older woman with round spectacles perched on her button nose.

"Good morning," I said. "Is this the home of Mr. Collins?"

"'Tis. Come in, dear," she turned around and headed back into the house. "I already have the kettle on."

"Oh. That's very kind but I-I mustn't stay," I said, stammering a little. "Mr. Grainger is expecting me back as soon as I'm finished making deliveries—"

The lady looked at me over her rounded shoulder. "You'll get back when you get back. I'm not giving you the empty bottles until you have a brew with me." She looked at me over the top of her glasses. "If he gets cross with you, you can blame me."

I frowned. "Alright then." I looked back at Sherlock. "I should probably tie—"

"He's not going anywhere. Come in, girl, you're letting out the warm air."

I did as I was told and stepped inside the cottage, shutting the door behind me.

If that horse wanders off without me, I am in so much trouble.

I slid the two bottles of milk onto the table already set up for serving tea as the woman retrieved the kettle.

She gestured to a chair and I quickly sat, folding my hands in my lap.

"Are you Mrs. Collins then?"

She snorted. "Heavens, no."

As much as I had protested, sipping the fresh, hot tea was quite soothing.

"So, city girl, how is farm life so far?"

"What gave it away?"

She gave a quick eye roll. "The whole village knew there were two Londoners at Honeyfield by sunrise. Nothing stays quiet here for very long."

I should have known.

"We milked the cows this morning. That was an experience," I said. "I managed not to get kicked or lose any milk to a stray hoof which was nice."

She nodded as she tipped her tea. "How is working for Mr. Grainger? He can be a bit of a grump sometimes."

"Sometimes? Are you suggesting it's not permanent?"

Her shoulders shook as she laughed, and she raised a wrinkled hand to her mouth. "Perhaps."

"Forgive me. I shouldn't have said that."

"Between us, he takes himself far too seriously. He wasn't always like that." Her gaze wandered away to the window overlooking one of the two main roads of the village.

"I suppose you've known him for many years."

She considered this and nodded. "Since the day he were born." Her mouth spread into a mischievous grin.

I carefully placed my tea upon its saucer and winced. "You're his mother, aren't you?"

Her shoulders vibrated with laughter again.

Placing my hand to my flushed cheek, I sat back in my chair. "He is going to have me sacked."

"Oh, hush," she said with a dismissive wave. "I won't say a word, I promise. Besides, I know what Ben is like."

"I'm mortified," I said with a small chuckle. "What a clever trick."

"I'm sorry, love. You just looked so serious. It'll be alright." She wiped a stray tear from the corner of her eye. "I'm Dora, by the way."

"Elsie Foster-Quinn." I tilted my head slightly. "Wait, then who is Mr. Collins?"

"Herb is overseas. He's married to my daughter, Vera," she explained. "She keeps house for Ben. I live with her and do my best to keep house for her." A deep crease formed between her brows. "That girl works too hard. Both of them do. When Vera gets home from making Ben's supper, she comes home and takes care of June, the young evacuee we have staying with us."

Shortly before the war officially began, thousands of city-dwelling children and pregnant women were packed onto trains and sent to live in the country since cities were expected to be bombed by the Germans. Their poor parents had no way of knowing where their children would end up until after they arrived and sent them a postcard. Many families hadn't seen one another for months or even years.

When Dora finally let me get back to my duties, Sherlock blinked at me slowly.

"Did I interrupt your nap, old boy?"

I gave his broad neck another smooth pet before depositing two empty bottles into the last crate, climbing up into the cart, and taking my seat on the bench. I was finished eating my sandwich by the time we reached Honeyfield Farm again. Sheila wore a worried expression.

"How was it?"

"It was fine, actually," I said, lowering my voice. "I met Mr. Grainger's mum."

I told Sheila about her impish charade as we freed Sherlock from the harness and hitch.

"How was the rest of your morning?"

"Not bad. We fixed the tractor." Her face still seemed pinched.

"What's wrong? What happened?"

"Nothing," she said. "It's just…he wants you and me to…"

"Sheila?"

"Deal with some used rat traps."

My shoulders fell. "Of course he does."

four

BEN

Amos took a long swig from his pint glass and sat back in his booth seat with a loud, exaggerated sigh. "I tell ya, Ben. I hate this time of year."

I raised my pint in agreement and gulped greedily, finishing off the glass and wiping the foam from my lips.

Looking around the pub that night in mid-March, Amos and I were far from the only farmers sharing a drink and commiserating about the upcoming busy season.

"What, you don't like working all day and then staying up all night with the cows? What's wrong with that?" I rolled my eyes.

"You joke but when you get to be my age, that shite gets old but quick." He shook his head. "The wife knows not to ask me anything important during calving season because me brain doesn't work half the time, I'm so dead tired."

I'd known Amos Osborne my whole life. His family's farmlands were located beside Honeyfield Farm, further down Lily Road. He was a decade older and like a brother, always looking out for me. When I was forced to make the transition from sheep to dairy at the start of the war, Amos guided me every step of the way and made sure I knew all I needed to know.

"Good thing I'll never be your age, old man," I said with a grin, raising from my seat.

"Hey now," he warned with a chuckle.

I ordered two more half-pints for us at the bar. While I waited, I spotted Pauline Pritchard strolling in with a friend. As always, she looked polished in a modern wide-shouldered blouse and pearl earrings, her dark hair styled just so. Noticing me, she gave a small wave before sliding into a booth. Two golden glasses appeared before me on the bar, rallying my attention.

"I see your friend just came in," Amos said as I retook my seat across from him.

I silently sipped my beer.

"You best be careful with that one, lad," he said, lowering his voice slightly. "She's grieving."

"It's not like that." I shrugged.

"As long as you're both on the same page is all." He sent me a meaningful look across the table.

This wasn't Amos' first warning to me about Pauline. I guessed it wouldn't be the last.

"Speaking of ladies," I said, desperate to change the subject, "you don't need a pair of land girls on your farm by any chance, do ye?"

Amos snorted. "No, I don't reckon. Although my cousin John over in Box Hill told me his land girls work ten times harder than the Italian POWs he's got."

I raised an eyebrow.

"The POWs, ye see," he continued, "they get special treatment because of wartime rules and all that. Land girls don't get that kind of treatment 't all."

Maybe I lucked out, I thought but certainly didn't say.

"Are your girls not working out then?"

"Well, I can't get either of them to quit, no matter what I tell them to do. It's been almost three weeks and they're both still at it." I shrugged again. "The one I told you about, the rich girl, I thought for sure she'd be done by the third day."

"She's probably just trying to spite ye now," Amos said, laughing. "She seemed nice enough when I've met 'er in the village and such. A right pretty little thing."

I studied the few bubbles floating to the surface of my glass of beer. Of course I noticed she was pretty. She was living under my roof and working with me every single day. It was hard *not* to notice.

Just then Pauline sauntered by our booth on her way to the bar, dropping a napkin on the table in front of me without making eye contact. It wasn't terribly subtle but she didn't need to be—I'm sure most people in the pub already knew about our, er, friendship. That sort of thing was hard to keep a secret in Fairbury.

"I suppose that's my cue to go home to the wife," Amos said with a yawn, eyeing the napkin with amusement before looking back at me. "Take care, lad."

I nodded my goodbye and lifted the napkin to read the note: *Mine in 20?*

Pauline lay on her side on her bed, her long elegant arm draped over her hip. Her mouth curved into a small contented smile, and she had tugged the sheet up over her bare form.

I pulled my trousers up and zipped before retaking my spot beside her, rolling over to face her. "And how was your day?"

She giggled and a piece of her dark hair fell over her face. "Better now."

"Glad I could be of service, ma'am."

Smirking, she flipped over on her back and sighed at the ceiling. "Do you think the war will just keep going forever?"

"Everyone seems more hopeful now that the Americans are in it," I said. "But I don't know."

On a quiet Sunday morning three months before, 350 Japanese planes flew into an American naval base in Hawaii and blew up four battleships and several other ships. Over 2300 people died. Everyone was glued to their wireless sets for days after—it was god-awful. The Americans weren't even *in* the war at that point! They certainly were the next day though.

Pauline yawned. "Have you heard from your brother recently?"

I shook my head. "Not since Christmas. He better start writing more often or Vera will track him down and have a go at him in front of his regiment."

She giggled again. "She would, wouldn't she? It *would* be very funny."

I peered at the clock on the bedside table. "I should probably get home. I have a few cows due any day now so I probably won't see you again for a while."

Pauline rolled over on her side again, watching me as I slid my shirt back on. "How are the city girls?"

I worked the buttons of my shirt. "They're alright. They're working a lot harder than I ever expected."

"I see one of them doing milk deliveries." Pauline smirked. "She's very pretty."

"You sound like Amos," I said before squeezing my eyes shut. "I just remembered a man from the bloody newspaper is coming over tomorrow to interview her."

"What?" She laughed. "Why?"

"I have no idea." I leaned over the bed and gave Pauline a quick peck on the lips. "Good night."

"Night. Lock the door on your way out please," she called after me as I slid my arms into my coat and began the late-night walk back to Honeyfield Farm.

I'd taken that walk many times in the past year or so. Pauline's husband didn't come back from Dunkirk and about a year after Pauline and I ended up sharing a few too many pints at the pub together one night and I ended up in her bed for the first time. Neither of us took the relationship too seriously—she was a lonely widow and after the war started, I was, well, I was one of the only men left in Fairbury under the age of forty. And I was lonely too, I suppose. We kept our arrangement quiet—as quiet as can be in a close-knit village like Fairbury anyway.

I cleared my throat and adjusted my position on my milking stool. "So, why is there a newsman coming to my farm?"

"I told you," Norman/Elsie said, not looking up from her cow's udder. "I'm going to discuss the work of the WLA and talk about the sacrifices we're making all over the country."

Glancing over my shoulder at Sheila, I raised an eyebrow. "Is he interviewing you too?"

Sheila rolled her eyes and continued connecting the milking machine to her cow. "No."

I frowned. "Hm."

"What is *that* supposed to mean?" Norman/Elsie scowled.

"I didn't say anything. I just said 'hm.'"

Norman/Elsie stared straight ahead and suddenly her cow let out a warning moo. Elsie quickly pulled her hands away from the udder.

"Try not to take out your mood on the cow," I warned. "Why isn't the newsman talking to Sheila? She's a land girl too." I carefully poured my pail into a canister.

Elsie shook her head, the colorful rags tied in her hair swinging slightly. "I have no idea."

Sheila and I exchanged a look behind Elsie's back.

Before Elsie was back from delivering milk, the man from the weekly Bath newspaper arrived at the farm, beeping the horn on his little car as he parked in the farmyard.

I wiped my hands on a rag from my pocket and inspected the man. He fetched a camera out of his boot and slung its strap over his neck. He was likely in his fifties, wore a bow tie and a fedora, and had one of the largest mustaches I had ever seen. Perhaps he and Stalin exchanged styling tips.

"What a lovely piece of land you have here, Mr. Graham," he exclaimed, propping his pudgy hands onto his hips and scanning the surrounding fields and hills.

"Grainger."

"Sorry?"

"It's Grainger, not Graham."

He chuckled. "You must have misheard me. Either way, it's very nice to meet you. I'm Ned Norbury from the *Chronicle and Herald.*"

Sheila raised a flat hand over her forehead and squinted up the road. "There's Elsie now. She's just coming back from delivering milk."

"Brilliant." He fetched a notebook from inside his coat.

I peered down at the man as he used a chewed-on pencil to take notes. "Why are you only interviewing Elsie and not Sheila?"

Sheila winced. "Ben—"

"Sheila does as much work as Elsie does," I added. "Surely having two land girls quoted in your story would make it more interesting for readers."

"Well, I-I-I think it's important that readers get to know a specific person in a feature story. It's easier to make that happen with just one person." He shifted his nervous gaze to Sheila. "It would get too long for the newspaper if we interviewed both of you. You understand. Our newspaper has lost pages already because of shortages."

Sheila nodded in an effort to calm the anxious man. "It makes sense."

Elsie and Sherlock rounded the corner into the drive. Elsie climbed down and greeted Mr. Norbury with a wide and friendly smile.

I raised an eyebrow at her and she quickly glanced my way before focusing on Mr. Norbury again. Her lips were bright red with lipstick and her eyelashes seemed longer and darker than usual. The rags were gone from her hair but instead of tucking her perfectly styled blonde waves under her WLA hat, they framed her round, angelic face.

She must have done her hair and makeup at Mum's, I realized.

Sheila's eyes widened as she assessed Elsie's appearance. "Where's your hat?"

Elsie let out a small laugh. "I didn't want the WLA hat to put a shadow on my face for my picture," she explained to Mr. Norbury. "It's fine."

"But—"

"It's fine," Elsie repeated, shooting a warning look to Sheila. "Maybe you can unhitch Sherlock and get the bottles from the cart while I talk to Mr. Norbury?" It wasn't so much a question as an order. "Would you care for some tea, Mr. Norbury?"

Sheila gave a tight-lipped forced smile and nodded. I followed her to the cart but not before overhearing Elsie apologize to Mr. Norbury.

"I must apologize for the smell," she said as she directed him to the door leading into the cottage kitchen. "We're fertilizing the upper fields where the crops will be grown."

I gave a quiet grunt of annoyance under my breath. As if anyone in Somerset wouldn't know what a farm smells like in the spring.

Sheila and I hauled the crates of empties into the barn to be cleaned.

"It's because her father owns a bunch of uniform factories," Sheila said, "in case you were wondering."

"Does 'e now?"

"Yes. She's some kind of socialite back in London. Posh clothes, finishing school, all that."

"Those types don't usually go in for land girl work."

"She was supposed to go to her family's country estate but the Army snatched it up before she got there," Sheila explained.

It was all finally beginning to make sense. "She wasn't expecting to have to actually work and now she's stuck."

"That's what I figure, yeah." She shrugged and then threw me a warning look. "Don't tell her I told you, eh?"

"Mum's the word."

After we finished unhitching Sherlock and put him back in his stall, Elsie—now wearing her wellies and carrying a pitchfork—and Mr. Norbury appeared and suggested that we take a walk up to the upper fields where we'd been working the last two weeks.

"My editor is insisting on a field photo to show the hard work these young ladies are doing," Mr. Norbury said.

"I suggested a photo with a cow," Elsie said weakly, "since they're closer than the fields and it's a bit smelly and messy up there and you probably have places to be—"

"I've got time," he said with a chuckle. "The editor didn't want any cow photos since we featured a dairy farmer in last week's paper. Plus, I can ask you some more interview questions on the way."

And ask more questions he did—the entire way up the hill. He hardly even took notes. Most of his questions didn't even relate to farming or the WLA.

"What do you do for fun, Miss Foster-Quinn?"

"I love organizing charity events. That was always my thing back in London," she said. "I like going to the theater and the cinema. I love reading too."

I glanced back at her quickly but then put my eyes front again. I hadn't taken her for a reader.

"Do you have a beau back home?" Mr. Norbury grinned. "Or maybe you've got some handsome chap in a uniform serving overseas."

"No, I don't have a boyfriend."

If I didn't know any better, I would have sworn she was beginning to sound irritated with the line of questioning.

When we finally reached one of the freshly fertilized fields atop the hill, Mr. Norbury directed Elsie where to stand and how to pose.

"Must I stand right in the—"

Suddenly Elsie's boot slipped in some fertilizer and she landed with her hands and knees in the muck. She groaned loudly. Sheila turned around, slapping her hand over her mouth to cover her giggle while I laughed freely.

Elsie glared up at me and pushed herself up, her pants smeared with brown sludge. "This isn't funny."

"It's a bit funny," I said.

"Sheila, please stop laughing," she added, wiping her hands on the back of her trousers and picking up the pitchfork again.

Sheila bit her lip, tears in her eyes.

Elsie released a long, slow breath and smiled wide, posing with the pitchfork like she was just a happy farm girl, doing what she loved most—standing in shite.

"You look great!" His camera clicked as he snapped away.

I wondered if he really needed to take as many photos as he did, the lecherous old goat.

The following Sunday evening, my mother, Vera, and six-year-old June came round for dinner. Elsie and Sheila had Sunday afternoons off but usually ate with us anyway. Sheila couldn't likely afford to eat a meal out and I think Elsie just enjoyed my mother's company.

"Elsie, dear, I saved that article in the paper for you," she said, reaching for her bag and pulling out the newspaper clipping. "It was in the paper yesterday."

Elsie gave a little squeak of delight and unfolded it quickly. "I haven't seen it yet!" Her face fell immediately. "Oh, no."

"What is it?" Sheila leaned over her shoulder to look at the clipping. "Oh."

Elsie folded the article and slid it under her dinner plate.

Mum blinked at her. "What's wrong?"

"Nothing," she said quickly. "Thank you for saving it for me."

I took a sip of tea. "Are you mad because Mr. Norbury didn't tell you there was manure in your hair when he was taking your picture?"

Elsie's eyes widened to about the same size as her plate. "You could have said something." She threw a look at Sheila. "Why didn't *you* say anything?"

"I didn't see it, I swear," she said. "You *know* I would have said something."

Mum pinched the edge of the article and slid it out from beneath Elsie's plate. She unfolded it while Elsie looked at her pleadingly.

"Oh, goodness." Mum winced. "That is certainly something. Maybe people will think it's just a spot of ink, that it's just a bad photo?"

June strained to get a look at the photo over Mum's arm but quickly returned to her dinner.

"Oh, it's a bad photo alright," Vera chimed in, laughing behind her hand.

Elsie crossed her arms over her chest, her nostrils flaring. "I wonder if I could get Mr. Norbury fired."

This sent the rest of us around the table laughing even more. Eventually Elsie let out an exasperated sigh and released a little chuckle too.

five

Elsie

"I've started seeing sugar beet seed in my sleep," Sheila said, her unfocused gaze hovering over the middle of the dinner table. "I blink. More seeds."

"That's not a dream," I pointed out. "That's a bloody nightmare."

Mr. Grainger's eyebrows raised. "I never took you for a sailor, Norman."

"Hardly." I finished off my piece of Woolton pie and reached for my tea, wincing slightly. Everything ached. "Do you want me to work on the back of the tractor tomorrow?"

She narrowed her eyes. "No. I started this fight with the seeds. I'll finish it too."

Mr. Grainger and I exchanged concerned looks.

"You just wait until the sugar beet grows in. That's when the *real* hard work starts. Weeding and picking by hand and chopping the tops off." His eyes sparkled with mischief as he spoke. I remembered learning about harvesting sugar beets in our course and he wasn't making any of it up. "Maybe you'll lose a couple fingers and get to go home." He flashed a Cheshire cat sneer.

"I wouldn't give you the satisfaction," I said, raising my chin defiantly. "It'll take more than a few missing fingers to get rid of me."

He considered this. "A hand? Half an arm? Whole arm?"

"Why, are you planning something?"

Looking amused, Mr. Grainger lowered his gaze to his tea before taking a gulp.

I looked back at Sheila. "I think I might order some new boots from London. The boots the WLA gave us are so uncomfortable."

She blinked at me. "You can't do that. You have to wear the uniform they give us."

I pursed my lips behind my teacup. "I'm sure Mrs. Watkins won't care as long as we're doing the job."

Mr. Grainger snorted. "Not that she checks up on you girls anyway."

He wasn't wrong. In fact, Rosetta hadn't been back to Honeyfield since the day we arrived. I'd seen her in the village a few times but she had yet to pay us a second visit. I wondered how often other WLA representatives checked up on the land girls in *their* districts. Perhaps Rosetta was right on track.

Anxious to change the topic, my eyes wandered the little kitchen. Already having departed for the evening, I gave Vera credit for keeping the place so tidy. She managed to cook meals, clean the house, tend to the large veggie patch by the front gate, do the shopping, *and* take care of her mother and June when she returned home.

My gaze landed on a small framed watercolor painting hanging on the wall closest to the living room. Delicate brush strokes of pale greens, golds, and oranges combined to create an ethereal garden teeming with lilies against a subdued backdrop of a rock wall. The initials *DG* were visible in the bottom right corner of the painting.

"That's quite lovely." I pointed. "Did your mum do that?"

"Yeah." Standing up to take his dishes to the sink, he cleared his throat. "You two should get some rest. I thought for sure Gertie was going to start calving today but you watch, she'll start in the middle of the night."

Sheila sat up slightly straighter in her chair. "Does that mean you'll be checking on her through the night, or do you want us to take turns?"

I thought about kicking her under the table just then. Why would she volunteer us for *that*?

"No, no." He waved a dismissive hand. "I'll take care of it. No use in all of us having a terrible sleep."

I sat at the long, elegant table in the dining room, watching as my parents bickered about whether or not we should keep a cow in the back garden.

"We can't possibly keep a cow in the garden," my mother insisted, shaking her head. "It will eat all the flowers!"

"Well, we have to get milk somehow," my father grumbled.

George, the butler, arrived at Father's side, and instead of waiting for attention per usual, he pounded his fist on the table so hard I thought he might crack it.

"Get up," he barked. "It's time."

Inhaling sharply, my eyes flashed open and my fingers curled around the edge of the quilt. At first, I wasn't sure if I really had opened my eyes or woken up since everything around me was so dark. A flicker of light appeared under my door from the hallway and I released a quiet groan.

"Elsie, Sheila, come on," Mr. Grainger said. "Gertie's havin' trouble."

"Be right there," I called back, pulling back the blankets and letting the chilly air give my body a bit of a shock to wake up.

The stairs creaked under Mr. Grainger as he went downstairs. I changed into my uniform as quickly as I could, stumbling around as my eyes adjusted. Torch in hand, I met Sheila out in the hall.

I covered a yawn with the back of my hand. "What time is it?"

"Not quite half three." She blinked hard and rubbed her eyes. "Gertie better have that damn calf quickly, that's all I can say."

The gloom hid my grin. It was actually kind of nice to see her be shirty for once.

We met Mr. Grainger out in the barn, kneeling beside Gertie in her pen and stroking her back to try to calm the beast. Wide-eyed and huffing, Gertie lay in the straw, mooing loudly.

Sheila glanced at me, looking as unsure as I felt. "What can we do?"

"This is 'er first calf and she's havin' trouble gettin' the job done," he said. "I just hope it's not in there backward."

Gertie gave a sudden jerk of her hind legs and mooed again. A few of the other pregnant cows watched us curiously from their nearby stalls.

"Shh, girl," Mr. Grainger cooed, brushing her neck. "We're here to help." He looked back up at us. "Sheila, you and I are going to try to keep Gertie as calm as possible. Elsie, there's some gloves in the back room—"

"Oh, no, no, no, no. You are not serious—"

"We don't have time for this," he snapped. "You have the smallest arms. We need to get the calf out or we might lose both o' them. D'ya understand?"

Panic squeezed my chest as I looked down at Gertie. I swallowed hard.

"I can't—"

"Yes, you can," he said. "You have to."

Sheila grabbed my hand. "You can do this. Just like they showed us during our training."

I almost laughed. We hadn't *touched* a real cow during our agriculture course. We hadn't milked a real cow and we certainly had helped a real cow give birth. We just saw diagrams on how to help a cow with a difficult birth. A textbook was nothing like the real thing.

Mr. Grainger went to the back room and brought out a crate of supplies. I took off my coat, rolled up my sleeves, and pulled on a pair of arm-length gloves. Mr. Grainger gave me a bottle of sanitizing liquid and I coated the gloves with it. He directed me to add lubricant to the gloves and then returned to his spot beside Gertie. Sheila sat with the cow, talking to her gently and running a hand over her side.

I lowered myself to the floor at the cow's rear and stared at the open birth canal. I had never felt more awake before in my life. I wanted to throw up. I gave Gertie a few gentle pats on her rump and she looked back at me, likely wondering why it was me and not Mr. Grainger about to stick a hand into her body.

I let out a long, slow breath and guided the tip of my middle finger in. Gertie responded by mooing loudly and kicking a hoof out at me.

I whipped my arm back and raised my hands in the air. "I can't do this! I can't!" My throat ached and tears pricked the backs of my eyes.

Mr. Grainger frowned. "Alright."

I scooted further away and sat on the floor of the barn, watching as Gertie snorted and strained.

"I shouldn't have asked you to do that," he continued. "It's just not something your people do. My apologies."

I shot him a look. "My people?"

He shrugged. "High society types. Your folk don't like getting their hands dirty. Why tackle a dirty job when you can just pay a poor person to do it for you?"

Sheila's eyebrows went up, her gaze darting between Mr. Grainger and I.

"I know what you're trying to do," I said. "You're trying to manipulate me into proving you wrong. I would *love* to do that but I just...I can't do this. I can't..." I looked at the ceiling instead of at him. "What if I hurt her or the calf?"

I lowered my gaze again to meet his and found his expression had softened. His condescending know-it-all smirk had faded. He studied me for a moment, focusing on my face so intensely that I looked away again, suddenly feeling like he was becoming too intimate with me just by scrutinizing my expression.

"She's already in pain. Giving birth hurts. Or so I've been told," he quickly added. "She needs you to try. Her calf needs you to try."

I took another deep breath and scooted closer to Gertie again. She looked back at me, and the pace of her breathing quickened slightly.

"I'm so sorry about this," I whispered as I slid my hand inside.

Trying to ignore the pressure of her muscles condensing around my arm, I closed my eyes and tried to picture the diagrams from our textbooks. My frenzied mind went blank.

Mr. Grainger's voice was calm and quiet. "Do you feel a wall directly in front of your hand?"

"No."

"Okay. That's good," he continued. "Put your arm in a little further and feel for hooves."

I adjusted my sitting position and focused on the shapes. Suddenly my fingers curled around two small hooves. A surprised laugh escaped my lips.

"I feel them," I said, opening my eyes. "I feel the feet."

"Good. You'll need to reach in a bit further and find the head."

I closed my eyes again and concentrated on what I could feel. I leaned forward a bit, reaching further inside. Gertie mooed again but didn't try to kick me. I traced my hand down the hooves and fetlocks until my hand met a large hard surface. Once I ran my fingers over its various bumps and grooves, I realized what it was.

"I found its head," I said, "but it's sideways. I think it's wedged."

Mr. Grainger nodded. "That's why she's havin' trouble. Do you think you can get your hand around to the other side of its head and straighten it out? You may have to push it back down a bit if it's too stuck."

Locating its facial features, I slid my hand to the other side of its head and carefully nudged it clockwise so its nose faced me instead of the side of the birth canal. Gertie lurched slightly as the head shifted into place and Sheila rushed to calm her, brushing her and humming a sweet song.

"Oh my God, I have it," I said, releasing a loud breath. "The head is forward."

The cow mooed and I felt the calf's hooves slide forward. I pulled my arm out of the space as Gertie took over.

"Looks like she's got it under control," Mr. Grainger said, giving Gertie a congratulatory chin scratch. He nodded at me. "Good work."

We backed off to give Gertie some space. Within two minutes, two slimy hooves and fetlocks emerged. With a couple more strained moos, the calf was sliding onto the floor. Mr. Grainger knelt again, quickly checking its nose, mouth, and eyes before Gertie went to work licking the calf clean.

"It's a male," Mr. Grainger said, standing back up.

"Can I name him?"

He glanced down at me. "I suppose you could but—"

"His name will be Brandon."

Mr. Grainger snorted. "Brandon? For a cow?"

"Yes," I said. "Named after Colonel Brandon." I would have

crossed my arms over my chest with smug satisfaction if my gloves weren't covered in blood and about fifteen other types of fluid. I had to be satisfied with a wide grin.

"Friend of yours?"

"You could say that."

Mr. Grainger looked at Sheila and she shrugged.

Not wanting to interrupt the early bonding of mother and baby, we watched the calf blink up at us with big dark eyes and enviably long lashes. His entire head was black except for a nearly perfect white circle on his forehead.

"Kind of a unique looking little thing, isn't 'e?"

Exhausted, I nodded and smiled. "He's perfect."

Two days after, Sheila was working in the field and I was sent to clean the barn. I didn't even mind since it gave me an excuse to check on my favorite handsome little man. It almost made up for having to muck the stalls in the first place.

While taking a break, I leaned my mop against a wooden beam and watched as Brandon—or Colonel Brandon as I called him—greedily fed at Gertie's udder. He couldn't seem to get enough.

"You are going to get so big and strong, aren't you?"

Kneeling down, I held onto one of the metal bars of Gertie's stall to steady myself. Brandon finished his feeding and warily came closer, sniffing my fingers before sucking on the side of my hand.

"Pardon me, you can't eat that," I said. "That's mine, I need that."

Hearing a snort of laughter from the barn doorway, I looked over my shoulder. Mr. Grainger leaned against the doorframe, arms across his chest. I wondered how long he had been watching me.

"Oh, hi," I said, a bit startled. "When do we start bottle-feeding him?"

He lowered his eyes and rubbed the back of his neck.

"You should, uh, probably try not to get—" He cleared his throat. "—too attached."

"Why, am I fired?"

"No."

I gestured to Brandon. "Is *he* fired?"

I think my joke took him by surprise because I caught the corner of his mouth nearly curl up.

I stood. "What do you mean then?"

Mr. Grainger set his jaw and watched as Brandon, still a little wobbly, lowered himself into the straw and yawned.

"I'm, uh, takin' him over to the Osborne's tomorrow," he said, referring to another dairy farm further down Lily Road.

"Oh." I frowned. "You don't keep bulls, I suppose."

"No, I don't."

"Do you think they would mind if I visited Brandon? He's such a sweet thing."

Mr. Grainger finally met my gaze. His Adam's apple bobbed as he swallowed and stepped inside the barn, a bit closer to me.

"No." His voice was almost a whisper. "You won't be able to visit him there." He studied the floor again.

I hesitated when I saw his knit brow. Staring at him, my whole body tensed.

"What happens at Mr. Osborne's?"

His mouth formed a tight line as he finally made eye contact again but he didn't speak.

"What happens at Mr. Osborne's, Ben?"

He released a shallow sigh. "He will put the calf down."

"What? Why on earth—"

"This is a reality of dairy farming," he said slowly. "I don't like it either but that's just the way it is. They didn't mention *any* of this during your course? Why do you think farms are full of cows and there are maybe one or two bulls?"

"I-I-I hadn't thought about it." I shook my head. "You need to keep him. You can keep a bull."

"This country barely has enough food for its people let alone bulls we don't need. I can't keep a bull—"

"But you have to!" I exclaimed. "He's just a baby. I'll pay for his food myself. Please!"

"It's not possible." His eyes hardened. "You need to understand that this is the way it is."

"But—"

"Sheila could use a hand in the fields. Go on."

I stared at him for a moment, willing him to look me in the eye again. My hands clenched into fists at my sides and my eyes narrowed. When he refused to look back at me I stormed out of the barn, lowering my head slightly as I passed him so he wouldn't see the tears in my eyes.

A person can only stare at the ceiling for so long before they realize it's just not going to happen. By three o'clock the following morning, I knew I couldn't just go to sleep. If I waited any longer to do something, it would be too late.

My brain was too sleep-deprived to stop me from sliding out of bed, putting my uniform on, grabbing a torch, and creeping downstairs. If Sheila or Ben heard me on the creaking stairs, I hoped they would just assume I was off to the loo in the dead of night.

The night air was cool on my skin as I made my way to the barn. The big barn door screeched as I slid it open and I winced, glancing back at the farmhouse and waiting for lights to appear in the windows, but none did. I turned on the lights in the barn and a few cows blinked sleepily at me.

"My apologies," I whispered before going to the back room to locate an empty bottle.

As I brought a stool up to Gertie's side and aimed the milk from her udder into the bottle, she watched me curiously, Colonel Brandon sleeping peacefully in the straw beside her.

Sliding the full bottle into the big pocket of my overalls, I found a rope and tied it loosely around Brandon's neck. He shook his head as he woke.

"I am getting you out of here," I said quietly before looking at Gertie. "I'm going to keep him safe."

Brandon got to his feet and I tugged him gently out of the stall he shared with Gertie. Thankfully she didn't put up a fight because I certainly didn't know how to handle an angry and protective mother cow.

I led him just outside the barn and slid the giant door closed again, slower this time to lessen the screeching a bit. I lured Brandon into a wheelbarrow with the bottle of milk and groaned as I lifted the handles, sending the calf's body sliding further in. He didn't seem to mind the cramped conditions of the wheelbarrow as long as he had the milk bottle in with him.

We made our escape into the black night, the light of my torch leading the way.

six

BEN

"Have you seen Elsie this morning?"

I blinked hard at Sheila as we met in the hallway. "I've only been awake for two minutes, so no."

Sheila, still in her pyjamas, furrowed her brow. "She's not in her room. Her coat and boots are gone too."

"Maybe she—" My sleepy mind sluggishly drifted from excuse to excuse. "—wanted an early start on the day."

She frowned at me and I knew what she meant—that wasn't it. Elsie never left the comfort of her bed a moment earlier than she had to.

I shrugged. "Toilet?"

I immediately regretted saying something so…private. And about Elsie in particular.

"I thought I heard someone get up in the night," Sheila said, her eyes wide with worry. "I should have got out of bed to see if she was alright—"

"Elsie is not your responsibility. She's an adult." I paused. "An annoying little adult."

Sheila followed me to the barn and I huffed when I saw the lights had been left on the evening before.

Or maybe during the night.

I cursed under my breath and promptly checked on Gertie's stall. The male calf was gone.

Sheila joined me at my side and gasped. "She didn't."

"Oh, yes, she did."

Cursing again, I stormed back out to the farmyard.

"Get started on the milking," I called back to Sheila. "I gotta go find her royal highness and the cow she stole."

Riding in on her bicycle, Vera slowed to a halt in front of me. "What's got you lookin' so grumpy already?"

"Elsie took off with Brandon last night."

She tilted her head slightly. "Is that a boy from the village?"

"It's a male calf she helped Gertie deliver," I explained. "I told Elsie yesterday that she couldn't get too attached, and she didn't know what happens to most male calves and she got upset. Now I gotta go find 'em."

Vera bared her teeth as she cringed. "She didn't know?"

I rolled my eyes and headed for my pickup. "Unbelievable." I slammed the door shut behind me a little harder than necessary and took off down the drive. I looked up Lily Road towards the village and considered. I doubted she would have gone that way, although the idea of Elsie walking from door to door in the village asking for anyone wanting a free calf made me smirk. No, she wouldn't have gone that way.

Maybe she took the cow to Amos's to offer to pay for his upkeep herself?

I decided to try that direction first, just hoping she wasn't hurt or hadn't injured the calf or wandered into a bull's paddock or something.

I didn't have to drive far. The sun was barely peeking over the hill behind me, but I still managed to make out their silhouettes by the lake, about halfway between the entrance to Honeyfield and Amos's farm. I slowed the pickup to a halt and turned off the engine, keeping my eyes on the both of them in case Elsie made a run for it. She didn't move. She remained laying in the grass, her head propped against the calf as he slept. An empty milk bottle lay in my wheelbarrow a few feet away. She had to have been quite cold by then, assuming she'd been there for a few hours. She merely looked up at me and, really, didn't even seem surprised that she'd been discovered.

My steps were quiet on the cool dewy grass as I neared them. Crossing my arms over my chest I looked down at her, mentally preparing myself to fire that spoiled, entitled mischief-maker.

But then she looked up at me with bloodshot eyes, her hair disheveled, and her face blank.

She looked...undone.

That defiant, confident, cheeky, stubborn, intelligent woman looked entirely defeated.

A memory of the first time I held a bolt gun flashed in my mind. It appeared at the worst times and more often than a person would ever want.

Quickly blinking away the memory I lowered myself onto the cool grass, watching as the early morning sunrise dropped dancing fragments of orange light onto the surface of the lake. We sat in silence for a moment, Elsie, Brandon, and I.

"What was the plan exactly?" I finally said.

"I didn't have one. I figured that was obvious." She crossed her ankles, staring straight ahead at the water. "I suppose I'm to be shipped off to another farm then."

I scoffed. "Nobody would take a cow thief."

"Shame," she said. "Maybe after the first dozen or so, I might actually figure out how to save them properly."

I allowed myself to smile at her joke. I knew I should be furious. I knew I should yell at her, fire her, report her to Mrs. Watkins, something.

"This is a reality of farming," I said. "Nobody feels good about it but this is how things are done. During a war is not—"

She turned to me. "How can you be okay with it?"

I wasn't prepared for that question. Nobody had ever asked me that. And she didn't shy away from asking it either. I stared at her for a moment, my mind racing.

When I couldn't stall any longer, I let out a loud sigh. "I never said I *was* okay with it."

Elsie studied me and waited for my explanation.

"Honeyfield used to be a sheep farm before the war. I've been around farm animals my whole life and when one of our sheep died, it was from illness or old age. I was used to that," I said. "Then the War Ag ordered us to convert to a dairy farm instead of keeping sheep, and it became my responsibility to deal with male calves and…I…well, I simply couldn't do it. Amos takes care of that part of dairy farming for me because I just…I can't do it myself. I've tried and I-I just can't. Some of the farmers in the area like to give me a hard time because they know Amos deals with my calves because I can't bring myself to…to do it."

I hadn't meant to say that much but the words just tumbled out.

"I tried to keep a few young males before to see if they could be used for veal so their death had *some* purpose but the shortages just make it impossible," I added, trying to make myself look slightly less pitiful.

Elsie's brow pinched as she took this all in. "What happened to your sheep?"

I winced. "We had to send them to slaughter. All because of this bloody war. Broke my heart."

My jaw clenched at the realization of what I'd just said. I'd never told anyone that before.

She looked back at the lake. "I'm so sorry you had to go through that."

"Yeah."

Elsie let out a breath and stood. Brandon looked up at her, his black ears twitching, before getting to his feet. She held the rope out to me to take before kneeling down to scratch behind the calf's ears. She gave a little sniff, picked up the handles of the wheelbarrow, and wordlessly headed back in the direction of Honeyfield Farm.

I frowned at the calf before leading him to my pickup. I lifted him up into the bed and drove him to Amos's. Amos and his sons were working on the morning milking, as I should have been in my own barn by that time.

Amos smiled weakly as I lead the calf into the barn. "Mornin.'"

"Mornin.'" I cleared my throat. "His name is Brandon," I mumbled.

seven

Elsie

The first half of April flew by in a blur of milk, soil, seeds, fertilizer, and weeds. By the time Sunday afternoon came round, I usually didn't have the energy to try to get to Bath to have fun—I just wanted to eat a good meal and lay very still in bed with a book.

Although Sheila and I were free to do as we pleased on Sunday afternoons and evenings—our one free afternoon off per week—we regularly joined Ben for his weekly family dinners.

On that particular Sunday Vera cooked a cheese, tomato, and potato pie and we all enjoyed every bite. Even so, I promised myself I would avoid potatoes for the rest of my life once rationing ended.

Dora, seated next to me, smiled sweetly at her daughter. "It was delicious, dear." She peered at June, the young evacuee, across the table. "Did you like it?"

She gave an exaggerated nod, a glob of cheese sauce visible on her frock.

Sheila, always eager to help, collected the empty plates and fetched some water from the pump outside so the long process of heating up water could start. I never thought I would miss indoor plumbing and instant access to hot water so much.

Ben finished his tea and pushed his chair back. "I should go check on that calf," he said as if we all knew exactly what calf he was talking about. "Thanks for supper," he called back over his shoulder as he escaped into the farmyard.

I looked to June. "How is school?"

"Good," she said. "We painted."

"Oh, that sounds like fun," I said.

Vera rolled her eyes. "Now, did you get any of the paint *on* the paper or did you and your friends just paint each other?" She glanced at me. "She was a rainbow when she got home, head to foot."

"So, *extra* fun then," I added, winking at June.

She gave another excessive nod in agreement.

Vera joined Sheila at the sink and June scampered off to the living room, stretching out on the rug with a coloring book and crayons.

"That reminds me," I said to Dora as we finished our tea, "I've been meaning to compliment you on your skills with watercolors." I pointed to the painting in the hall with the lilies. "That's lovely."

"Oh, thank you, dear." Her eyes lingered on the painting. "That garden, those lilies, used to be just out here at the end of the drive, just before you get to Lily Road."

I caught Vera shooting a subtle warning look at her mother.

Dora went on. "Ben and Vera's father, he knew I loved lilies. On our first wedding anniversary, he planted that garden for me. That's where the road got its name in the first place."

"I didn't know that," I said. "That must have been a very impressive garden."

"It was beautiful." Her radiant smile faded and she looked back at Vera.

"Unfortunately," Vera continued where her mother left off, "when the war began, the War Ag inspector ordered Ben to take out the garden and replace it with a veggie patch. The more land that can be used for the production of food, the better."

Her eyes growing cold, Dora's jaw tightened. "He didn't even try to argue with him."

Vera winced. "Mum—"

Dora waved a dismissive hand. "I know, I know. I shouldn't bring it up."

I wanted to tell Dora she was right to be angry. I wanted to tell her Ben was cruel for destroying something that meant so much to his mother. Most of all, I wanted to march out to the barn that very second and slap Ben across the face for not even trying to save his mother's lilies.

How could he be so inconsiderate?

"I will give you ten pounds to let me use the tub tonight."

With the empty cauldron in hand, Sheila frowned at me. "Please don't do that."

"Don't do what?"

"Offer me money for something just because you don't want to wait your turn." She left me in the kitchen so she could fetch more water from the pump just outside.

It was the following Thursday and it had been a long and exhausting day. My arms were terribly sore, my back ached, and my skin felt sticky. I *needed* a bath.

"You'll just have to stay up and heat up water when I'm done," Sheila added.

I dropped into a kitchen chair and sulked, crossing my arms over my chest.

The heat of the hearth fire in the kitchen was certainly not helping with my perspiration situation so I went upstairs and threw the window open, letting in the evening breeze and watching as the curtains swayed.

The moon was half full, throwing just enough light to let me see the farmyard, the drive, the road, and, in the distance beyond that, the lake.

The lake!

I grabbed my caddy of bath necessities, a towel, and a torch and made quick work of going back downstairs, grinning at Sheila as I appeared in the kitchen again. She glanced at my caddy and then up shook her head at me.

"I already told you—"

"I'm going to the lake," I announced before sliding my feet into my shoes on the small shelf by the door.

Her eyebrows went up. "You're going to freeze to death."

"It'll be refreshing," I said, trying to encourage myself as well. "Invigorating."

"You're mad," she said with a laugh. "Who even are you?"

"I'm…" I hesitated. She was right.

This isn't an Elsie Foster-Quinn thing to do. Elsie Foster-Quinn doesn't swim in lakes.

"I'm desperate," I finally said, letting myself out.

Crickets sang to me as my caddy bumped my thigh with each step. Uncertainty crept up on me. Perhaps swimming alone in the dark in an unfamiliar lake was a very bad idea. I lowered my head to subtly sniff under my arm, and I recoiled as I realized exactly why I needed to get into the water that night.

Then I realized I had just sniffed myself in public.

What is happening to me?

When I reached the far side of the lake a few minutes later, I took one last look around, scanning for the lights or rumbles of any vehicles traveling down Lily Road. That side of the lake was far enough from the road that any motorcars going by would likely not see me anyway as long as my torch was off. A small wooden dock on the other side of the lake served as a good omen—the lake was obviously used by someone for swimming and so was hopefully not teeming with nasty things.

Perching behind some tall reeds for some sense of privacy, I slid my shoes, socks, trousers, and blouse off. My undergarments would serve as my bathing costume, I decided.

Taking a deep breath, I stretched a foot out from behind the reeds and dipped a toe into the water. I let out a high-pitched squeak and whipped my foot back to the safety of the bankside.

"You can do this, you can do this, you can do this," I whispered. "If you can help birth a calf, you can certainly get into a lake."

Bracing my hands on the grass behind me, I lowered myself very, *very* slowly into the water. When I was submerged up to my knees, one of my fatigued arms gave way and my whole body went plunging in. The cold felt like knives against my skin, and I flailed my arms to reach the surface again. Once my head was above the water, my teeth chattered, my shoulders shook, and my breaths came out in shaky streams. I pulled myself out of the water and shivered on the bankside, reaching frantically for my caddy. I lathered up quickly and put a dollop of shampoo in my hair, working it to a frothy foam.

Suddenly the road lit up with the lights of a pickup.

I snapped my torch off and got behind the reeds again as I waited for the pickup to go by. Instead it slowed to a stop. I could hear my pulse pounding in my throat.

It was Ben's pickup.

Through the reeds I watched as the lights on the pickup went dark and Ben got out. He stepped out onto the dock, taking a moment to stare at the sky.

The light of the moon lit up his silhouette—his nose, his broad shoulders, and his beard—as he stood before an endless backdrop of stars. He took a seat on the edge of the dock and untied his boots. He unbuttoned his shirt, shrugged it off, and let it fall to the wooden planks behind him before yanking off his undershirt and adding it to the pile. Next he ran a hand through his dark hair before reaching for his belt buckle.

I lowered my eyes, my cheeks suddenly going from icy cold to flaming hot in an instant. It was too dark for me to see much but knowing that all of those *things* were right there in front of me made me think of things I should not have been thinking about.

There was a loud splash and I jerked my head back up. The moon's reflection teetered on the upset lake before Ben broke through its surface again. He gasped and cursed from the cold before lazily backstroking.

A cool breeze licked at my damp, bare arms and legs, and I crossed my arms over myself. My fingers brushed up against something slick on my skin. A black leech clung to my arm, its body plump.

I screeched. Quite loud.

"Bleedin' wounds o' Christ," Ben yelled, halting in place. "Who's over there?"

"There's a leech on my arm," I squealed. "It's *so* disgusting!"

"Elsie? Why are you out here?" He shook his head. "Why are you *never* where you're *supposed* to be?"

"How do I get this thing off of me?" I gave it a little tug, pinching it between my fingers, but it stuck firm. I shuddered and let out a drawn-out whimpering whine.

"Don't yank on it," Ben said, swimming over to the edge of the lake and effortlessly hoisting himself out.

Water dripped from his defined arms and chest and, well, other areas. I averted my gaze away from him, feeling a flush spread over my face again. He grabbed the torch off the ground and shone it at my arm. I whipped away from him, remembering I was still only in my underwear, before sticking my arm out to him.

"Is that shampoo in your hair?"

"Yes."

Ben snorted. "That lake is near freezing—"

"Says the man who was *just* swimming in it," I snapped. "I was perfectly fine until you arrived—"

"Do you want me to get this leech off you or not?"

I looked at him over my shoulder. "Yes, please."

He thrust the torch at me. "Hold this."

I held it, still facing away from him.

Ben sighed loudly. "I need you to actually point it at your arm."

Glancing back, I adjusted my aim.

He grabbed one of the reeds from the bank, folded it in half, smoothed it down, held it in his mouth, and took my arm in his large hands. I couldn't easily tell what he was doing since I was facing away from him.

His hands were rough but he was careful with me as he pressed down on the skin on my arm.

"First, you pull the skin around the sucker taut. I'm just sliding this reed under this bastard's mouth so it'll let go," he explained, his voice almost a whisper before I felt a quick swipe against my skin. "There. It's gone."

I shone the torchlight on my arm, highlighting the tiny red 'x' where the leech had been.

"Thank you," I said quietly, shutting off the torch to give both of us some sense of privacy.

"You'll want to wash that and put a bandage on it," he said. "Might bleed a bit." He cleared his throat and made his way around the lake to the dock.

He was a lot less shy about his underwear than I was.

"It wasn't my turn to use the tub but I needed a bath," I blurted, speaking loud enough so he could hear me.

He pulled his trousers on and snickered. "Carry on then." He pulled his undershirt on over his head and it clung to his damp torso. He headed for his pickup but paused to yell back at me over his shoulder. "When you're done rinsing your hair, you should probably deal with the four leeches that are on your legs."

"What?!"

He was still laughing as he got into his pickup and left me alone, screaming in the dark.

eight

BEN

Stop staring at Elsie.

I lowered my eyes to the soil directly in front of me where pesky weeds had risen up around the sugar beet and I gave my head a subtle shake, hoping to snap myself out of it—whatever *it* was.

Not that there was much to admire easily anyway. Her dungarees hid all signs of any sort of womanly shape as she knelt, yanking weeds from the dirt.

I'd seen Elsie in her knickers the night before, soaked and clinging to her after her late-night dip in the lake. The flair of her hip under the thin fabric and the curve of her perfect heart-shaped ass had haunted me since then. I felt like a dodgy old man, leering at her and thinking about her.

I'd even dreamt about her the night before.

Before my mind wandered back to the dream, Amos' mint green pickup sped up the hill toward us, a cloud of dust in its wake.

I stood up and winced into the sun as Vera whipped open the passenger side door before the pickup had even come to a full stop.

"June went off alone after school," she shouted, her voice tinged with fear. "She's somewhere in the woods by the school."

Elsie and Sheila stood, exchanging worried looks.

The driver of the pickup, Amos' wife Doreen, peered out the driver-side window. "She told my boy she goes walking alone in the woods all the time, and I knew that weren't right."

We hopped in the back of the pickup and sped down the hill to the farmyard.

I whistled sharply and Sam leaped into the back of my pickup, Elsie and Sheila climbing in after him. Vera got in the front with me while Doreen raced down the drive to go fetch Amos and meet us at the school.

"Has she ever run away before?" I turned out of the drive and headed in the direction of the village.

"We don't know she was running away," Vera snapped. "Maybe she just felt like—oh, I don't know, exploring or something. Children do silly things." She waved a dismissive hand at me, chewing mindlessly on her thumbnail as she stared out the window.

Little June's arrival in Fairbury had changed my sister. A train packed full of city children just showed up and they poured out onto the platform, some curious but most looking terrified or wailing for their mothers. Farmers from the area quickly picked out the older boys who could serve as free farm labor. Since I didn't have a wife at home, I wasn't assigned to take an evacuee. Vera was irritated when she got her notice but didn't fight it, accepting it as her patriotic duty. I went with her to the train station that day.

June was so young and so small, standing off to the side of the platform, her chubby cheeks stained with tears. I watched as Vera's wrinkled brow relaxed and the tension in her face softened. Without a word, she squeezed through some older kids and knelt down in front of the little girl with the ribbons in her pigtails. After a moment she picked up the girl's suitcase, June took Vera's hand, and that was that.

It was a shame she and Herb weren't able to have kids of their own. As much as I wished the war would end, that meant June would go back to Manchester and my sister's heart would break.

The girls hopped out of the back of the pickup as I switched the engine off and we gathered in front of the village school—the same school Vera and I had gone to as children and our parents before us.

"I just…" Vera let out a loud breath as the four of us headed for the wooded area behind the school. "I don't know why she would just wander off into the woods."

I shrugged. "Did you do something to upset her this morning?"

The three women stopped walking and, in unison, turned slowly to stare at me. Even Sam gave me a curious look, the traitorous mutt.

Elsie frowned and shook her head.

"Ben," Sheila hissed.

Vera scoffed, "Don't be such an arsehole." Reaching the edge of the woods, she nodded at the girls. "We'll cover more ground if we split up. Sheila, you come with me."

"Vera, don't—"

She pointed back at me as she started down the path to the right, Sheila in tow. "Get moving."

I knew sticking me with Elsie was my sister's way of punishing me for saying the wrong thing. Marching down the left path, I rolled my eyes. Sam sniffed at the trail as he beelined in the path in front, Elsie behind us.

"June!" Elsie called out suddenly, startling me and making me jump. "June, are you here?"

"Christ almighty, you coulda warned me," I grumbled.

"There's no point in us just walking in silence," she said. "I know silence is kind of your whole *thing* but—"

"What do you mean by that?"

"You just don't talk very much, that's all."

"I talk enough." I held a branch up so she could walk under it. "Maybe you just talk too much."

"That is an incredibly rude thing to say," she exclaimed.

"Is it any ruder than suggesting I'm too quiet?"

"Yes, it is!" She sighed heavily. "Society cherishes a quiet woman while women who actually have many interesting things to say are admonished for sharing them. Meanwhile, men are allowed to be quiet or talkative and society labels them as 'stoic' or…"

While she was distracted by her explanation of gender stereotypes, I stopped following her and changed directions. Sam let out a small whine as he trotted at my heels.

"Don't worry," I said. "She'll notice we're not behind her soon."

"Ben! Ben, where are you?"

I watched as her blonde head swiveled in all directions, looking for me through the trees. Spotting me, Elsie shot me a glare so powerful it could shatter glass. She struggled through the underbrush to join me, shielding her eyes from stray twigs.

She panted as she reached me. "Do you want me to get lost in the woods too, is that it?"

"That wouldn't do me any good, would it? I'd have to go back to delivering milk myself."

Elsie narrowed her eyes, planted herself directly in front of me, and placed her hands on her hips. I swallowed and edged back a bit, caught off guard by her close proximity.

Though she be but little she is fierce.

She stared up at me, letting the silence linger in the limited space between us.

Without warning, she bellowed, "June!"

I slapped my hand to my chest. "Bloody hell, woman! Stop doing that."

Cackling to herself, she whirled around and continued down the path.

A few minutes later Elsie stopped suddenly and I nearly bumped into the back of her. She carefully untangled a tiny pink bow out of a prickly branch. She looked back at me, her green eyes wide.

"This is June's. She must have come this way." She slid it into the pocket of her dungarees and went back to calling June's name into the thicket.

We carried on walking for another ten minutes in silence, other than calling for June and Sam woofing at every suspicious sound—crows cawing, woodpeckers hammering away on tree trunks, and squirrels chasing one another in the canopy above.

"Thank you," Elsie blurted suddenly, "for showing me how to remove a leech. I would have just pulled the thing off." She kept her eyes down, focusing hard on the trail.

I waited for a saucy remark but it never came.

"You're welcome." I rubbed the back of my neck. "You washed the bites after, right?"

"Yes, thank you."

"Good," I said. "My brother got an infection that way once."

"You have a brother?" She glanced up at me. "I didn't know that."

Was she…was she actually making conversation?

"He signed up as soon as he could." A twig snapped underfoot and Sam sniffed it warily.

"Wouldn't he be exempt as a farm laborer?"

"Yeah, but he didn't care. He wanted to do his patriotic duty as an Englishman."

"Isn't providing food for your fellow countrymen a different type of patriotic duty?"

Assuming she was being snide I surveyed her as she walked beside me, but she didn't smirk or even look up at me.

"I think so, yeah. We wouldn't last long without food. A man can't live on American tinned Spam alone." I cleared my throat. "What about you—any siblings?"

She looked at me before answering, she too checking my sincerity. "I have two older brothers. Jack is a history teacher in London and Archie is serving in North Africa."

After a few minutes of silence Elsie spoke up again.

"Last night," she said shyly, "you didn't…*see* anything, did you?"

I bit the inside of my cheek, fighting a grin. "What do you mean?"

She rolled her eyes. "You *know* what I mean. I was in my," she quickly scanned the area and lowered her voice to a whisper, "underthings."

"Why are you whispering?" I cocked an eyebrow and quickly peered around. "No, it was dark. I didn't see anything."

Except for that perfect, plump, round—no, not going to think about that.

"Am I hearing a river?" Elsie stopped, her eyes widening with fear. "Oh, God. What if she fell in?"

We quickened our pace toward the sound of the water, stopping at the water's edge. At least a foot deep, the river tumbled down roughly onto two levels of rocks, creating a waterfall in miniature and frothing around the polished stones.

I pointed slightly further up the riverside. "She could have crossed up there."

Getting closer, we could see three small footprints in the mud on the opposite riverbank.

Elsie put her hand on her forehead. "She is fearless."

"If we manage to get her back, I'm going to tell Vera she needs to keep her on a lead."

"Perhaps put a bell on her too." Elsie pointed to the rocks. "Those look slippery."

They were only big enough for one pair of adult feet each but, thankfully, they were close together. I stepped off the riverbank and onto the first rock, measuring its slickness underfoot. I carefully moved to the next stone and then the next.

Looking back at Elsie, I gave an encouraging wave. "Come on."

Sam, tail wagging, plunged into the river and waded through the rough waters, not bothering with a silly thing like walking on stones. He shook himself off at the other side of the river and barked in celebration at his triumph.

"Good boy, Sam," I called over my shoulder.

She stepped back. "No, I think I'm fine here."

"The kid did it. You can do it."

Brow furrowed, she assessed the foam collecting around the rocks further down the river.

I quickly hopped back to the second stone and stretched my hand out to her. "June needs us."

She blinked at me a few times. Finally she stepped onto the first stone and clutched my hand. My gaze landed on her graceful hand in mine. It was small and delicate, but not as soft as I'd expected; a few months of farm work had fixed that. But it was the most beautiful hand I'd ever seen.

When I looked up she too was studying how our hands fit together, but I couldn't read her. When she slowly lifted her eyes to meet mine, my breath hitched in my chest. Elsie had never looked at me like that before; there was no longer any hint of suspicion or malice in her gaze. Was that…was that trust?

She tightened her grip and nodded. "Let's go."

I was thankful for the volume of the gurgles and splashes of the river as it rushed around the stones at our feet. If not for that, I thought she might hear my heart pounding through my rib cage.

Elsie and I reached the other side of the river and I reluctantly dropped her hand. Neither of us said anything as we continued our search.

"Wait," Elsie said a few minutes later, holding up her hand. "Do you hear that?"

I did. It was the sound of June crying.

"June!" I shouted into the forest. "Sam, find her. June!"

"June, sweetheart," Elsie called. "It's Elsie and Ben!"

The sobs stopped as we located her, sitting at the base of a giant oak. Her cheeks were streaked and damp from tears and her shoes and dress were caked with mud. Sam immediately went to her side and laid down, his head resting on her feet, and June wiped her dripping nose into his furry neck.

Elsie pulled the ribbon from her pocket. "Look what we found."

June stood up and clung to Elsie's leg, crying fresh tears. "Is everyone mad at me?"

"No, of course not, sweetie," Elsie said, petting June's hair. "We were just very worried."

June looked up at Elsie, her little mouth quivering. "Sometimes me and Mama would walk in the woods and I thought I could find her if I came here." Her tiny frame twitched as she sobbed.

Elsie gathered June up in her arms and the child wrapped her arms around Elsie's neck, resting her head on Elsie's shoulder. Elsie looked at me, tears in her eyes.

"Let's get you home," I said.

That night I stuffed my hands into my pockets as I waited for Pauline to answer my knock. After peeking through the blackout curtains, she opened the door. Wearing a dressing gown and slippers, she crossed her arms over her chest and let a sly smile linger on her lips.

"Hello," she said. "I wasn't expecting you this evening." She opened the door wider but I didn't follow her inside. She looked back at me, curious. "Something wrong?"

"I've been thinking…" I cleared my throat, "it might be time for us to…" I forced myself not to look at my feet as I forcibly yanked the words out of my throat, "part ways."

Pauline's eyebrows went up as she tipped her chin. "Part ways?"

"I was lonely, you were grieving. You *are* grieving still, of course." I wanted to kick myself for babbling. "We agreed it would never be serious and when it was time to move on, we would." I swallowed. "And I think it's time for us to do that."

Pauline tilted her head, her eyes narrowing slightly. "Is this about that pretty blonde land girl you've got working for you? The one who was in the newspaper?"

"No, don't be mad." I snickered.

"You're a terrible liar."

I laughed. "I'm not lying."

"Oh, maybe it's the other land girl," she said with a chuckle. "The one with the frizzy hair?"

"It's not about either land girl." I shrugged. "I just think you can't grieve properly while we have this, er, thing. It's not fair to you."

"That's so selfless of you." Her smile turned coy but there was something darker behind her eyes.

After an awkward goodbye, I walked back to the farm while considering the various ways I might try to end my stupid little fascination with Elsie and get back to normal, uncomplicated life.

nine

Elsie

My eyes flashed open.

At first I didn't know if I was still dreaming or where I was. Light from a torch flooded into my bedroom as a faceless figure in the darkness flung open my door. I held my hand over my eyes and winced in its direction.

"Get up *now*!" Sheila shouted before disappearing.

I blinked away the blurry spots in my vision and sat up. "What time is it? What is happening?"

Surely the birth of a calf wouldn't warrant this level of extreme behavior.

Suddenly I heard it—the siren. It wailed in waves, slowly up and then slowly back down. I'd heard the sirens so often in London that their distinct howl became part of my everyday routine. I never expected to hear it all the way out in Fairbury.

Is this a nightmare? This can't really be happening. Can it?

"We need to get the cows from the pasture back to the barn before the planes get here," she shouted from her bedroom. "Ben is waiting for us. Come on!"

I grabbed my trousers from the chest of drawers and wriggled into them as quickly as I could before yanking on a blouse. With a torch held between my teeth, I continued to struggle with the buttons on my shirt as I rushed downstairs and slid my toes into my boots.

The siren grew louder as I stepped outside into the darkness, running after Sheila towards Ben's pickup. We hopped in the back and Ben floored it, sending a spray of dust behind the pickup as we peeled out of the farmyard and to the lower pasture.

"Why would the Germans come *here*?"

"They're probably going to Bristol," Sheila said.

Bristol was one of several British cities Germans raided on a regular basis. London was their leading target because of its dense population, industrious dockyards on the Thames, and well-known landmarks. Birmingham, Manchester, Liverpool, Southampton, Plymouth, Cardiff, Portsmouth, and many other cities were bombed by the Luftwaffe because of their industries related to the war effort—naval yards, plane manufacturing, that sort of thing. Poor Coventry, home of munitions factories, was reduced to rubble in 1940.

"Exeter was bombed last night and the night before," Sheila reminded me. "They were talking about it on the wireless."

"Exeter? What's there?"

"No idea," she said. "A friend from back home went there to stay with family because it was supposed to be safe."

The pickup screeched to a stop at the gate to the pasture and we hopped out.

My stomach turned and my pulse raced as I looked back at Sheila, trying to study her expression with only the light of the waxing moon. "What if they're *not* going on to Bristol?"

"Then we're in for a long night," Ben said, holding his door open.

Sam leaped out, bounded over the stone fence, and lowered himself to the ground, waiting on Ben's command.

Most of the herd cuddled together on one side of the pasture. A few of the cows in the pasture slowly raised their heads, surveying us curiously as we unlatched the wooden gate and let ourselves into the pasture.

"You two, come with me." Ben explained the plan as we followed him across the field. "Sam is going to stay on this side of the pasture and herd them toward us, to that gate on the other side." Ben pointed across the paddock with his torch, its light fading before it even reached the other side of the field. "You probably can't see it but it's there. You two will try to herd them down the path and into the barn from there. We have to do this quickly."

When we were halfway across the meadow, I took a sharp intake of breath. The droning from above—I'd heard it before. All three of us looked over our shoulders and to the sky, towards the sound.

Everything happened in a flash. I saw only stars overhead and heard only the moaning of the air raid siren and the loud hum of plane engines. Suddenly a shower of shots rained down into the pasture and loud, frantic moos erupted from the herd.

"Get down!" Ben hurled himself at me, landing on me, and shielding the top of my head with one arm.

I clung to Ben's shoulders, my fingers pressing into his skin as hellfire streaked past us, striking the earth around us and sending sprays of soil and grass into the air. With my face buried in his neck, his weight on me, and our chests pressed tight together, I slammed my eyes shut and held my breath. The world went silent other than a steady high-pitched ringing coming from inside my own head. Hearing the shots from the sky was scary enough—not being able to hear anything was even more terrifying.

Ben shifted, raising himself off my chest slightly. He said something but I couldn't hear him. He sat up and palmed one ear, checking the skies as he tried to regain his hearing.

"Are you hurt?" The ringing subsided just enough for me to hear Ben's yelled question.

I shook my head, tears stinging my eyes. "Are-are you alright?"

"I think so." He stood, helped me up, and grabbed his torch from the ground.

I clasped my hands firmly together in front of myself and Ben pointed his torch at them. "What's wrong with your hands? Are you sure you're okay?"

"I'm fine," I said quietly. "They're shaking, that's all."

Heavy footfalls on the grass behind us caught our attention and we spotted Sheila running toward the frenzied herd.

"Sheila, don't get too close!" Ben shouted, racing after her. "Sam, here boy!"

My stomach twisted at the thought of Ben's constant companion getting hurt. I flexed my hands a few times, trying to rid them of their shivers, and dashed after Ben.

Sam sprinted out of the darkness, sitting obediently at Ben's side and letting out a soft whimper. Ben knelt down and gave Sam a quick check-over, running his hand over the dog's sides, back, head, belly, and chest.

"You're alright, boy," he said, rubbing Sam's neck. "You're alright. Good boy."

The cattle had stopped sprinting about madly but their moos were still low and agitated. Ben's eyes darted from one cow to the next, accounting for each one, in between nervous glances at the night sky.

"Over here," Sheila yelled. "I think this one's hurt."

Ben and I hurried to her side to survey the cow—a calf we named Madge. The light from my torch landed on a bloody wound where a stick had pierced her right back leg.

"Oh, no," I said, taking a step back.

Madge's chest raised and fell rapidly and she released long, miserable moos.

Ben surveyed the sky again quickly. "Another plane could come by. We need to get the rest of the herd in the barn—"

Just then, several faraway booms made us all look to the west. The explosions continued and my shoulders fell.

"Oh, my God, no," I breathed. "They're bombing Bath."

Ben growled a curse.

Sheila brushed a calming hand over the cow's neck before looking back up at Ben. "Should one of us go to the village to see if Vera and your mum are okay?"

He rubbed his neck hard and took a moment to decide what to do. "We would have heard the bombs if they dropped any on the village.

They're…" he paused and let out a breath. "They're fine. Herd into the barn first and check the other cows once we can actually bloody see them. Then we try to call the vet to get him here and *then* we check on Vera and Mum."

Sheila frowned. "Where does the vet live?"

Right on queue, another string of thunderous rumbles sounded from Bath.

"Over there," he said quietly.

We hated to leave Madge in pain but we knew if we lost just one cow that night, we were lucky. Getting the herd into the barn was the best way to save it from a second aerial attack.

Ben gave a sharp whistle and Sam bounded into action, racing at top speed to the far side of the pasture.

"Come by," Ben shouted, causing Sam to begin herding the cows into a smaller area to better control their direction.

Sheila and I unlatched the gate on the other side and waited for them to get on the path toward the barn. Every ten seconds we checked the skies or looked in the direction of Bath as the sky above it lit up from the incendiaries.

After only a few minutes Ben and Sam got the cows over to the right side of the field, moving toward the open gate. Sheila and I placed ourselves along the short path between the enclosure and the barn and quickly moved the entire herd inside.

"Good boy, Sam," Ben said, giving him a quick pat before beginning his checks on the cows.

Sheila's brows were knit with worry and she kept glancing at the ceiling as if she could see intruding planes through the barn roof.

Ben released a loud sigh. "You two better go check on Madge. These ladies look okay. We got lucky." He brushed Dottie's neck.

I jogged after Sheila, out to the field. It wasn't hard to find Madge again in the darkness, her mournful moos leading us right to her. I held two torches above so Sheila could take a closer look.

"Careful," I warned. "She might kick you."

"No," Sheila said, keeping her tone soft and relaxed even though her worried eyes told a different story. "This little lady is fine. She's just fine.

She knows I won't hurt her."

Behind us, Ben's pickup pulled out of the farmyard and sped down Lily Road towards the village—the location of the nearest phone box *and* his mother and sister.

Sheila sat back up again, resting her hands on her thighs and getting bloody thumbprints on her trousers. "I don't think it's that bad," she announced. "I think if we clean the wound, stitch up the wee hole, and wrap it up good, it'll probably be fine." She let out a long breath. "We just have to pull the stick out first."

"I'm *not* pulling it out," I said firmly. "I've already pulled enough things out of a cow for the time being, thank you."

Sheila wiped the sweat from her forehead with the back of her arm. "Do you remember seeing a first aid kit anywhere in the house? I wonder if Ben has a roll of gauze somewhere—"

"You're going to do it?! You're not going to wait for the vet?"

Sheila frowned at me. "The vet isn't coming. Not tonight. The longer we wait, the more blood she'll lose and the more likely the wound will get infected."

We searched Ben's house and finally found a dusty emergency supplies box with a gauze roll and a bottle with a small amount of rubbing alcohol inside.

Sheila nodded. "It'll have to do."

As we returned to the farmyard, Sheila carrying the box under her arm, the headlights of Ben's pickup went out and he shut his door behind him.

"Did you check on Vera and Dora?" I asked.

"Mum is a bit shaken up but they're fine. They're down in the cellar now," he said. "I didn't tell them about us getting shot at by a Nazi plane and I beg you not to say anything about it either, at least not to Mum." He eyed Sheila. "What's that?"

"Medical supplies," she said, matter-of-factly. "The vet isn't coming, is 'e?"

"Phones are down," he mumbled.

I looked at Sheila. "How do you even know how to treat a wound?"

She smiled weakly. "I've got five younger siblings. I've seen my share of cuts and bruises."

"No, you're-you're not going to operate on Madge. No. No." Ben crossed his arms and pushed his shoulders back. His tone contradicted his rigid stance though.

"Ben," she said. "Leaving her like that is cruel. I had a look at it already and I can do this. If I didn't feel confident I could deal with it, I wouldn't give it a thought."

I raised my eyebrows at Ben. I only knew Sheila as more of a "Yes, sir!" type of person and I was impressed by the assertive and confident woman before me.

Ben's shoulders lowered. "Alright. I don't want 'er to suffer."

"Good. Let's go."

We made our way back to Madge and I took my position holding two torches above as Sheila worked.

"Ben, are you ready? You need to keep her still," she said sternly.

"Yes, I've got her," he said, basically laying on top of the mooing calf, her enormous dark eyes darting between us.

With one clean motion, the stick was pulled from the cow's leg and she let out her loudest, most frantic moos yet. Ben's knees and the heels of his shoes dug into the mud as he strained to keep the calf still. Sheila, calm and focused, expertly cleaned the puncture and bound her leg tightly in gauze.

Ben scooped up the calf in his arms and carried her to her stall in the barn, despite her loud, upset protestations.

He looked at Sheila and nodded in approval. "Good work. And thank you."

She nodded, suddenly looking worn out.

"I'm still gonna get the vet over here as soon as I can," he added. "Just in case."

"I'd be upset if you didn't."

My gaze drifted to the open door of the barn and in the direction of Bath. The sirens had long since gone quiet but the thunderous echoing coming from the historic city persisted. An orange glow appeared over the city as fires spread between homes and streets.

"They're still at it," Ben said, moving to stand beside me. "It's been two hours."

Sheila and I exchanged knowing glances. We were unfortunate enough to know just how long the Nazis could continue their nighttime assaults. Two hours was nothing for them.

"When the second siren sounds, I'm going to Bath to help." Ben's eyes were hard as he stared straight ahead, his jaw set.

I knew that look and I certainly knew that feeling. It was a feeling of hate for the destructive and murderous miscreants in the night.

Fearing a German bomb landing on the top floor of the farmhouse, Ben and I opted to sleep in the living room, me in the armchair and Ben on the couch. Sheila slept in the barn with her young patient.

Not that I actually slept much. I mostly just stared into the darkness, worried about world events I had no way of impacting and thought about my brother fighting overseas. What would Archie do if he were here?

"I'm going to Bath with you," I announced at half-two after the all-clear siren blared, signalling the departure of the German bomber planes.

Ben sat up and rubbed his eyes with the heels of his palms. "That's not a good idea."

I grabbed our coats from the kitchen and tossed Ben's to him. "I wasn't asking permission."

His frown tightened as he pulled his coat on. I could tell he was preparing his argument, his mind slowed by fatigue. Thankfully I already prepared mine instead of sleeping.

"We can't fight fires and we can't tend to wounds," I said, "but we *do* have a vehicle. We can help get people to hospital or a shelter."

His face brightened slightly. "Let's go."

The city, aglow with fire and grey with dust, was a nightmare. Bath's famous golden stone architecture was now a collection of smoldering wreckage. Entire rows of houses were reduced to rubble in the streets. Storefronts were ripped wide open and rooves were obliterated. Some row houses had their lovely gold Bath Stone facades peeled away, revealing charred brick underneath.

There were sirens everywhere. And crying. And frightened screams.

"Reminds me of home," I said.

Ben, both hands tight on the wheel, carefully maneuvered the pickup around great craters in the earth.

"I can't believe Londoners dealt with this for months and months. Maybe they're tougher than I thought," he said quietly, wisely keeping his eyes on the road. "Why didn't you and your parents leave London?"

"My father needed to be there for his job and my mother wouldn't leave without him and I…" I was briefly distracted as we drove past a multi-home building with its entire front wall missing. "I suppose I just wanted to stay with them. North London got hit but nothing as bad as Central London." We slowed to a crawl as we neared a whole half block of row houses, three or four homes violently plucked out from the middle of the row.

A man carrying a crying child, a woman carrying a wailing baby, and two slightly older children ran down the pavement. Ben stopped the pickup as I whipped my door open and shouted to them.

"Are you all alright? We can take you to hospital."

Once they were all settled in the back and the gate was up, I got back in and Ben crept the pickup towards the hospital, avoiding heaps of debris and any streets where firefighters were battling blazing buildings.

Once at the hospital, the family carefully unloaded from the back. The woman, exhausted, smiled at me. "God bless you."

I shut the gate on the pickup and took my seat beside Ben again.

"They didn't have shoes."

Ben looked at me. "What?"

"That family." I stared straight ahead, blinking. "None of them had shoes on."

Sighing, Ben snapped his fingers beside my face. "Keep it together. We've got work to do."

"I'm fine," I insisted.

It was a very long night. I lost track of how many people we delivered to the hospital. I endeavored not to look at the gashes and scorched flesh of our passengers as they climbed into the back of the pickup—I've never done well with the sight of blood.

We were on the way to the hospital again, a full load already in the back, when Ben stopped the pickup and got out. When he knelt down beside a little boy sitting by himself on a step in front of a ruined house, I fought to keep the tears from my eyes. He simply stared into the middle distance as Ben calmly spoke to him before scooping him up and carrying him to my side of the pickup. His shivering little body clung to my arm as he sat on my lap. The boy didn't utter a word, even as I asked him his name and age. I didn't dare ask him about his family.

"We should probably get back to the farm," Ben said softly as we pulled away from the hospital. "It's morning."

With weary eyes, stinging from the smoke and the grime of the devastated city, I looked to the sky. "So it is."

Seemingly seconds later Ben was gently waking me up to tell me we were back at the farm. Raid or no raid, the cows still needed milking.

ten

BEN

I was grabbing a very quick, *very* strong cup of tea before returning to work when Elsie came in, fresh from her milk delivery. Her eyes, underlined by dark shadows, were dull and lifeless.

"You alright?" I leaned against the countertop, steaming hot cup in hand.

She nodded wearily and slid her boots off. "I have never been more exhausted in my entire life."

It was the day after the Bath raid. I half expected Elsie to pass out into her porridge that morning.

"No, I mean, are you…alright?" I gave her a meaningful look.

She and I had seen some horrifying things the night before while whisking wounded Bathonians to the hospital and shelters. Anyone might feel a little shell-shocked after the night we had.

"I'm fine." She smiled weakly. "Thank you." She hung up her coat.

"There's still some hot water left in the kettle if you want a cuppa."

"No, thank you," she said. "I'm going to spend my free afternoon sleeping and I could not be happier."

I chuckled. "Did you happen to meet up with Mrs. Watkins in town?

She came round to check on you and Sheila."

"She did," she said. "She commented on how terrible I look."

My grip on my teacup tightened and my jaw clenched. "Well, that was nice of her."

Elsie waved a dismissive hand. "She asked me to help her organize a fundraiser for those who lost their homes in the Blitz." She covered a yawn with her palm. "Oh, pardon me."

I nodded. "I'll let you go to bed now."

Her eyes brightened a bit and she disappeared around the corner, the stairs creaking under her feet.

In that moment I would have given anything to carry her upstairs in my arms, lay her down into bed, and tuck her in. My bed, specifically.

My eyes widened and I gave my head a little shake. *None of that.*

I downed the rest of the tea and returned to the farmyard to see Mr. Linden's car driving down the lane. I'd only managed to get in touch with him by word of mouth through Amos since the Luftwaffe took out the telephone lines with their bombing campaign.

I nodded at him and smiled wide. "I'm glad to see you made it out alright, Mr. Linden."

"As am I." He didn't smile back, likely too exhausted to make the effort. He pulled his bag of medical tools and salves from his car. "I heard the Nazis gave your herd a good scare last night."

My anger flared. "I spent half the morning digging ammo out of the ground. Thankfully they didn't manage to hit anything but they came damn close." I nodded to the barn. "The wounded calf seems to be doin' well but I wanted you to check on 'er."

He followed me and I was only slightly surprised to find Sheila still in the barn, keeping a close eye on her patient like a protective mother hen.

"Mr. Linden, this is Sheila, the land girl that did a proper job saving this calf's leg, probably its life."

"That's very kind," Sheila said.

"Sheila, this is Mr. Linden. He's the best animal doctor in Somerset."

Mr. Linden raised an eyebrow at me. "You're just full of compliments today, aren't you?"

I shrugged. "It's exhaustion. Don't get used to it."

"Alright, let's take a look." He knelt down and carefully unwrapped the dressing from Madge's leg.

Sheila brushed the calf's back, keeping her calm. "Is your clinic in Bath?"

He nodded, keeping his eyes on his patient. "'Tis."

"I hope your clinic and home are alright," Sheila said.

Mr. Linden finally allowed a little light into his eyes. "I was one of the lucky ones." He laid the dressing aside and inspected the wound closely. "It was a puncture right through the leg?"

I nodded.

The doctor looked back at Sheila. "Did you take nursing training?"

Sheila blinked, surprised. "No, nothing like that." She laughed nervously. "I just have five younger siblings."

"You did a fine job," he said. "The wound is healing perfectly. Well done."

Sheila beamed.

"Keep wrapping the leg and cleaning the wound the same way until that wee hole is covered up and ring me if it looks infected or if the calf seems uncomfortable. Well, try to ring me. I don't know when the phones will be back." He gave these directions to Sheila, and she seemed happy to oblige.

"Of course!"

I nodded to the side. "Alright, go get some rest."

As she neared the open door of the barn, Mr. Linden stopped her. "When the war is over, you should look into animal medicine if that's something that interests you. We need more women in the field."

Sheila's eyes glowed as her cheeks flushed. "Thank you, Mr. Linden. Maybe I will."

I looked back to Mr. Linden after Sheila departed. "We were in the city last night, helping get some folks to hospital and…it was awful."

He fetched a bottle and a roll of gauze from his kit and began cleaning the wound. "You're not the only farm around that got shot at last night. But the city…it's a catastrophe. The house across from mine and the people who lived there are just gone now. All gone. The planes dove down and shot at people in the street." He looked back up at me.

"I spoke with one constable who said it might happen again, and soon. So keep the cows in the barn at night, at least for a while."

I nodded as fear ran down my spine.

A second attack? People 'round here never expected the Nazis to hit Bath once, let alone twice.

The Germans returned late that night just like Mr. Linden had warned, this time at one o'clock. I was in such a deep sleep that I didn't even hear the siren.

"Ben!" Sheila called through my bedroom door and knocked hard. "Ben, the Germans are back!"

I bolted upright, blinked hard into the darkness, and seriously considered just flopping back down on my pillow before swinging my legs out of bed with a grumble. I grabbed a blanket and a pillow from the bed and unsteadily joined Elsie and Sheila in the hall as the distant rise and fall of the siren's moaning crescendo blared its warning.

In the dim light from our torches I managed to catch Elsie's gaze lingering on my bare chest and shoulders—or maybe I just imagined it in my sleepy fog.

Like three children sleeping at their grandparents' house, we piled into the living room with our blankets and set up camp.

I settled into an armchair and was about to prop my feet up on a side table when Elsie lifted an eyebrow at me.

"You look absurd. You're too big to sleep in the chair." She pointed to the couch. "It's *your* couch, take it."

"I took the couch last night."

"And? You're six and a half feet tall. You can't possibly be comfortable."

"I'm not *that* tall." I stared up at her. "And this is a great chair." I spread the blanket over myself and hid my smirk under it.

"Fine!" Sheila exclaimed. "I'll take the bloody couch." And she did.

Elsie sighed dramatically and dropped into the second—although not quite as comfortable—armchair and tucked herself under her blanket.

As booms sounded from the west, Sam whimpered and scurried under the kitchen table.

Within minutes of the all clear siren sounding around four o'clock, the three of us were dressed and rushing for the pickup, Sheila hopping in the back. Elsie leaned forward in her seat, watching the sky fade from black to red as we approached the burning city.

"It's like driving into Hell," she said.

I glanced at her. "You don't have to go. I can take you back to the farm."

Say yes so I can take you home. Say yes so all of us will be safe. I wondered if there had been a hint of fear in my voice.

"No," she said. "I'm fine. We're fine."

We didn't have to go far into the city to find buildings lit up with flames, thick towers of black smoke pouring out of their rooves and windows. We crawled through the streets, weaving around the gaping pits left by bombs and mounds of rubble. Sheila kept her mouth under her sweater as she rode in the back, occasionally coughing as the smoke reached her lungs.

"Are you alright?" Elsie yelled back to her. "Do you want to switch for a bit?"

"I'm fine," Sheila said between coughs. "Carry on."

After we'd made four trips to shelters and hospitals, all while trying to stay out of the way of emergency crews, Sheila shouted to get me to stop the pickup. She flung herself out of the flatbed before we were even fully stopped, rushing to the aid of a family in front of a smoky, fire-blackened building. Elsie jumped out as I parked nearby.

A small child was crying into her mother's nightgown, her mum's face and hair coated with soot. A smaller child sucked on her thumb in her mother's arms, her dirty face streaked from streams of tears.

Her mum tried to take the girl's hand. "Sweetheart, we need to get to the shelter with this young lady—"

"I'm not going without Clyde," she wailed.

Hearing his name, a dog barked from one of the upstairs windows.

"The firemen said we can't go back in, that the walls are unstable but we can't get him to come out on his own," the mother said, her whole body quivering with shock. "I don't know what to do. I don't want to leave him here."

Before I could suggest they come back later to see if he'd come out,

Sheila was already on her way into the burned-out home, yanking her sweater over her mouth and nose.

"Sheila, no!" Elsie screamed as Sheila disappeared into the smoky front hallway.

"Oh, God," the woman slapped a hand over her mouth.

Her daughter watched their charred family home, her little chest heaving and her eyes darting from window to window.

We heard something crash inside and my stomach lurched. I knew I should go in after her but my feet were glued to the pavement. I couldn't move, think, or breathe.

"Sheila!" Elsie shouted before coughing into her sleeve.

I should be in there. I need to get Sheila out of there.

But I couldn't.

Suddenly Sheila burst from the door, a scruffy little terrier wriggling in her arms. Clyde escaped her grasp and bounded to the little girl who tearfully scooped him up, holding him tight to her chest.

With a hand on her chest, Sheila tried to catch her breath between coughs and gasps. Ignoring her need for oxygen, Elsie threw her arms around Sheila.

"You foolish girl," she said, releasing Sheila from her grip.

"Thank you," the mother said. "Thank you!"

"Proper job, Sheila," I said with an approving nod.

The family of three loaded into the back of the pickup and Elsie forced Sheila into the cab with me since she was still coughing. Elsie pulled the gate closed and we made for the nearest shelter. Sheila's coughing eventually calmed as we drove back to the farm a while later, just as the sun's early morning rays snaked through the grey clouds over Bath.

As we milked the cows in silence, too tired to speak—and Sheila's throat too sore—I wondered where she had found the courage to dash into a precarious building to save a stranger's dog without a moment's hesitation. Meanwhile I couldn't even make myself follow her to help.

I glanced at Elsie as I poured my pail of milk into a larger canister. I winced.

Now she knows I'm a bloody coward.

eleven

Elsie

Only a few days had passed since the second bombing raid in Bath. Riding into the traumatized city on Vera's bike, I carefully avoided pits in the streets and piles of debris.

In London it was routine to go on your merry way while strolling by ruined homes and devastated lives. Carrying on was what the government and the King asked of us, so we obliged.

But things felt so different in Bath.

As I slowed the bicycle at the corner of two busy, relatively intact streets, I heard an older lady ask her friend the same question that had been on everyone's mind for days.

"Why Bath? Why us?"

Londoners always knew their city would be a prime target. Children were sent away, and many adults left the city as well. Those of us who stayed braced for impact and simply got used to the nightly barrages. But Bath was different. It was *supposed* to be different. Bath was supposed to continue on, its famous architecture untouched and unscathed by Nazi bombs.

A possible reason for the raids was briefly discussed on the BBC.

Because our chaps bombed the beautiful historic German city of Lübeck, the Germans retaliated and blasted several of our historic cities right back—first Exeter, then Bath, Norwich, and York.

It was all so very pointless.

I grabbed the stack of flyers from the bicycle basket and pulled a sheet out, slipping into a greengrocer's. The place was jammed with customers—I guessed some other stores in the city were unable to serve their regulars at the moment or simply no longer existed.

Squeezing in, I found a noticeboard and added a flyer. The wall was already busy with posters about food conservation and saving your kitchen leftovers for the local pig clubs but I managed to find a space for our event flyer off to the side. I hoped perhaps its bright white paper might make it stand out against the colorful government posters.

I stopped into every little shop and business I could find without wandering too far into the hardest hit areas of the city. Vera heard from a friend that many destroyed homes belonged to poorer families living in tightly-packed neglected Georgian row houses. The last thing those poor souls needed to see was a flyer for a fundraiser.

My last stop was at a tobacco shop, the glass of its front windows blown out and swept into a neat pile off to the side of the front step.

While pressing the tack into the flyer on their noticeboard inside, I was startled by a deep, American voice.

"A dance, eh? That sounds swell."

I looked up at the young man beside me, and he flashed me a smile fit for a film star, square jaw and all. His officer uniform fit him perfectly, particularly across his broad chest.

"You're American," I said, stating the obvious like a fool. "I didn't know there were Americans stationed nearby."

"We just set up camp a few days ago." He nodded to a few other uniformed men nearby. "A few of us decided it was a fine day to come in and visit the city."

"Poor timing, I'm afraid," I said. "It was much nicer about a week ago."

He frowned. "Don't worry. We're here to make sure the Germans get everything they deserve."

"Well, we certainly appreciate the assistance."

Finally, I couldn't help but add silently.

He raised his hand to his forehead in an American-style salute.

"Second Lieutenant Garrett Miller." He dropped his hand and nodded to my armband. "I see you're serving as well."

"Yes, Women's Land Army. My boss let me quit early today so I could put up flyers." I smiled up at him, trying not to smile too wide and betray my eagerness. "Elsie Foster-Quinn, lovely to meet you."

Garrett's eyes brightened. "That name sounds familiar." He took off his cap, revealing a head of dark, slicked-back hair, and tucked the cap under his arm. "Were you in the Bath newspaper recently?"

"Yes, I was," I said. "How did you know that?"

"The only reading material at our barracks was a bunch of old newspapers. I remembered seeing your picture and your name and thought you seemed familiar."

"I was mortified when I saw that photograph. I have never looked worse in my entire life." I let out a little laugh.

"Nonsense," Lieutenant Miller said matter-of-factly and without a hint of shyness. "I thought you looked beautiful."

Heat crept up the back of my neck. "You're too kind."

Lieutenant Miller followed me outside where I fetched my bike.

"It would be wonderful if you and your friends could join us at the dance," I said. "It's for a good cause after all and I'm told there will be plenty of alcohol."

The handsome officer nodded. "If I'm still here, I'll make sure I can come. I might be shipped off somewhere before then. Hard to say." He paused to consider. "I think it would be a terrible shame if you and I didn't have a chance to get to know one another before then. Can I take you out for dinner?"

"Oh," I said, genuinely surprised but impressed by his confidence. "Well, yes. Certainly. That would be nice."

We exchanged contact information so we could arrange a time and a place for our date and I cycled back to Fairbury with a big smile on my face and butterflies in my stomach.

That Friday, Ben, Sheila, Vera, Dora, and I boarded a shuttle in Fairbury bound for Bath. Sheila and I wore our WLA overcoats, armbands, and deep green ties while nearly everyone else on the tram wore dark clothes. It was cold that day but sunny as the country shuttle made its usual stop in central Bath, cautiously weaving between deep pockmarks in the streets, before continuing up the hill to Haycombe Cemetery. It didn't seem to matter what route the shuttle took; there were damaged buildings and piles of rubble everywhere. The dust had settled and the fires were out, but it would be a long time before Bath recovered from the crushing blow.

A crowd had already gathered by the gravesite where the victims of the two nights of the Bath Blitz would take their eternal rest. It was a grave like I had never seen before: the usual depth and height but at least fifty meters wide. It looked more like a deep ditch than a hole for a casket. Through the mass of mourners I could just see glimpses of the collection of plain wooden coffins laying in a tight, neat line. None of the coffins had markings beyond a black number. The only difference between the many, many coffins was the flowers brought by loved ones—a single flower lay atop some while elaborate floral wreaths adorned others.

Sheila and I didn't know any of the deceased but Vera, Ben, and Dora knew a few families who lost loved ones during those two nights of terror. We stood further back to give the devastated families their space.

I wiped a stray tear off my cheek and Sheila put her arm around my shoulder, leaning the side of her head against mine.

Dora patted her eyes with a handkerchief and shook her head. "This bloody war needs to end."

A man in a grey wool suit joined us, nodding somberly in greeting. Perhaps in his late twenties, he folded his hands and watched the service.

"Did you lose any loved ones, Mr. Linden?" Sheila asked quietly.

"No, thankfully. My parents' house needs repairs, but I'm very grateful it's *just* the house that got hit." He turned to her. "How's the patient doing?"

"Quite well, thank you." She looked at me. "Elsie, have you met

Mr. Linden? He's Ben's veterinarian."

I nodded, fighting the urge to make a remark about Ben needing a veterinarian because he was so pigheaded.

"Nice to meet you," I said instead.

When the service ended and the huddle of mourners separated, I spotted a few chaps in American officer uniforms, one of them waving to me from across the green. Lieutenant Miller jogged over, his smile wide.

"I wondered if I might see you here," he said. "How are you?"

Out of the corner of my eye I saw my companions exchange a quick glance. I hadn't told them about Lieutenant Miller yet. I hadn't seen a reason to. It was none of their business.

"I'm fine, thank you." I gave a little wave to his mates. "It was very nice of you to come to the funeral today."

"This town sure did take a beating," he said. "All these buildings look old as dirt. It might have been time to replace some of 'em anyway."

I opened my mouth to defend Bath's famously beautiful architecture but thought better of it. *Perhaps classic architecture isn't as respected in America as it is here.*

"That reminds me," Lieutenant Miller continued, "we just found out we won't be shipping out for at least a little while so me and a few of the guys can come to that shindig you're planning for next weekend. But I'm still taking you out to dinner on Sunday night as planned."

Once again I caught an exchange of looks between Sheila, Ben, and Vera. I turned to them.

"I would like you all to meet Lieutenant Garrett Miller," I said, proceeding to introduce everyone else, even Mr. Linden who was still hovering about for some reason.

"It's great to meet all of you," Lieutenant Miller exclaimed. "Any friend of Elsie's is a friend of mine." He draped an arm around my shoulder and gave me a squeeze before planting a quick peck on my cheek.

Ben's eyebrows shot up and Dora pursed her lips slightly.

Lieutenant Miller peered back at his friends again. "I'm getting the signal that it's time to go. I'll see you tomorrow!" He lifted my hand to his lips, kissed it, winked up at me, and threw a grin at me over his shoulder as he and his fellow officers left the cemetery.

Cheeks burning, I avoided looking at Sheila and Ben. I hadn't expected that much show of public affection from him and I was a bit embarrassed.

"He's a handsome lad," Vera said, breaking the silence of our group.

Sheila and Dora nodded in agreement.

That evening during the second milking of the day, the only sounds in the barn were the mooing of the cows, the hiss of milk hitting the pails, the quiet chug of the milking machine, and the rustling of the hay in the stalls. I considered what clothing options I had for a dinner date. I began doing the mental math of when I might make it back to Bath to buy something more formal for the fundraiser or if I could make do with the formal dress I brought with me.

I was trying to recall how many clothing ration coupons I had left when Sheila moved her stool to the cow next to mine.

"I did that one already," I said.

Sheila smiled weakly, glancing at the deflated udder. "Ah, yes. Seems you did." She didn't move on though. She bit her lip and wouldn't meet my eyes.

"Is everything alright?"

"I didn't want to say anything in front of the others…" She winced. "We're friends, right? So, I feel like I *have* to say something."

I raised an eyebrow. "Are you quite alright?"

"I could be very wrong about this but," she hesitated again, "are you sure about your new American friend?"

"What do you mean?" I chuckled.

"You don't think he was a bit…inappropriate today?" Her face melted from uncertainty to seriousness. "It was a funeral but he acted more like it was, I don't know, a party or something."

I felt my lips tighten.

"I just got a bad feeling from him, that's all." She picked up her stool and pail and moved down to the next cow needing milking.

"You don't even know him," I said, carrying my pail to one of the bigger canisters and carefully pouring it in. "You know nothing about him."

"True," she said. "But how much do *you* actually know about him? You've met him, what, twice? And he's already acting possessive of you."

"Goodness, Sheila," I said, letting out a surprised laugh. "I'm going to dinner with him, not settling down immediately."

"I know. I'm being silly." She gave her head a small shake. "He just reminds me of a boyfriend my sister had—"

"I'm sure nobody in your family could land a catch like Lieutenant Miller." I moved my stool down to my last cow of the evening. "It's understandable that you're jealous."

Sheila stared at me. "I'm *not* jealous."

"You are," I scoffed, "and you're embarrassing yourself."

She sat up straight on her stool and blinked hard. "*I'm* embarrassing myself? You're only interested in him because he seems posh and you're ignoring the fact that he's an arsehole."

"He is not," I snapped.

"Oh, these buildings are old as dirt and need to be replaced anyway," she said, lowering her voice to mock Lieutenant Miller. "Smiling like a twit at a bloody funeral."

I released a slow breath. "I was going to set you up with one of his friends but perhaps that wouldn't be a proper fit—"

She cackled. "No, thank you."

My body tensed as I glowered at her. "No man wants a green-eyed monster. Enjoy being a spinster."

I dumped the rest of my pail in the canister and stormed out of the barn. I couldn't stand to be anywhere near her for another moment.

twelve

BEN

I'd never been inside Watkins Manor before—to their farm to talk business, sure, but not inside the grand house with its glittering chandeliers, polished staircase railings, and plumbed toilets. I suppose I really wasn't their type of company on an average day. I'd shared a pint or two with a few members of their staff down at the pub, but Mr. and Mrs. Watkins were more of the champagne class.

I carried two pints from the bar to the table where Sheila and Vera sat. Vera took one of the glasses off my hands and took a grateful gulp. Sheila, still working on her cocktail, gently bobbed her shoulders along to the band playing from the corner on an elevated stage area.

"That figures," I mumbled. "Mrs. Watkins *would* hire a band from outside of Fairbury."

Vera arched an eyebrow. "Who was she supposed to hire, Frank and Leonard?" She rolled her eyes. "She probably wanted the band to sound *good*."

I chuckled. She had a point. "What's wrong with Frank and Leonard? They always make sure people have a good time."

"Are they the brothers that play down at the pub?" Sheila glanced between Vera and me. "The tone-deaf ones who can't keep time with one another?"

"Aye, those two," Vera said before nodding to the five-piece swing jazz outfit in the corner. "These chaps are doin' a proper job."

Of course they were. Mrs. Watkins would only hire the best. I wondered if they were from Bath or if she'd shipped them in from London for the night.

I sipped from my glass of beer. Bloody hell, even the beer somehow tasted better at this place.

"Amos didn't stay very long," Vera added. "I guess that means you're stuck with us for the evening."

"Don't ever mention that bastard's name to me ever again," I said with a smirk. "He was supposed to stay for at least an hour, not five minutes."

"Not really his style," Sheila said teasingly.

"It's not mine either but I'm still here."

Vera tilted her head at me. "Why *are* you here anyway?"

I swallowed. "Elsie asked me to come and I said I would."

"I'm surprised you haven't made your excuses and left by now," Vera said, sitting back in her seat. I didn't like the all-knowing big sister look she was giving me. I was used to that expression but it usually didn't come with cherry red lipstick and mascara.

Restraining myself from looking at Elsie across the parquet floor, I shrugged. "I'm a man of my word." I took another sip. "Unlike that bloody traitor, Amos Osborne."

I cast my gaze around the busy room so I could catch a glimpse of Elsie and the American. Surrounded by his army officer chums and their dates, Miller rested his hand on the small of Elsie's back. She laughed at something he said and leaned into him and he slid his hand further around her narrow waist.

I pulled my eyes back to the glass on the table in front of me and took an eager gulp. This was so stupid. Why was I even there? Just to torment myself apparently.

"He's such an arse," Sheila grumbled before finishing off her drink.

"Did you tell Elsie that? Is that why she's so quiet?" Vera asked.

The tense silence between the two of them for the past week was hard to miss, especially when they spent so much time working together in the barn and the field. Any required communication was limited to single word answers with no eye contact.

"I may have mentioned it." Sheila pressed her red lips firm. "I probably shouldn't have said anything. It was none of my business."

Vera sighed. "You were being a good friend."

Sheila smiled gratefully.

She was right though—Miller was a git. He'd come by the cottage to pick Elsie up for dinner earlier in the evening.

"I suppose *some* of the younger men around here have to stick around while the brave ones go to fight," he'd said—in my kitchen, in my home—to my face.

Thinking about it again made my blood boil. I'd plastered on a friendly—well, friendly enough—expression when Elsie came downstairs, incandescent in a wine-red dress, her blonde curls gleaming and styled perfectly. Waving goodbye, she beamed as she left with Miller and all I could do was watch them go.

Vera nodded to the bar. "Oh, look at that. Your other best friend made it."

I scowled at her. "Alcohol doesn't agree with you, Vera. It makes you think you're amusing."

Sheila leaned in conspiratorially. "Who is that and why do you suddenly look like you want to punch something?"

"It's the local War Ag rep, Glenn Watkins. He's Mr. Watkins' nephew so you can just about guess how he got the job as a War Ag inspector," I said in a hushed tone. "Bloody fool doesn't know a thing about farming."

"He hasn't been too popular around here since he told a farmer in one of the nearby villages that he wasn't taking full advantage of his land," Vera explained. "The War Ag took half his land from the farmer and gave it to one of his *own* relatives."

"They can *do* that?" Sheila's eyes popped. "Just take away a farmer's land?"

"Happens more than you think," I said. "There was a Hampshire farmer who was ordered by the War Ag to give up his land and he refused. There was a shootout with the police and, well, the farmer didn't make it."

Sheila sunk back into her seat. "Goodness."

As if feeling our eyes on him, Glenn scanned the room and gave our table a wave. Vera and I waved back cheerfully, acting as if we were old friends.

I took the opportunity to glance Elsie's way again, just in time to see Miller's hand slide down to rest on Elsie's backside. I felt my muscles stiffen, my whole body preparing to leap from my seat without my mind getting involved in the process at all. Elsie simpered up at Miller and delicately slid away from his hand to face him, shaking her head at him. With a stupid, innocent look on his face, he shrugged. He threw his arm around her shoulder and pulling her close again.

I heard my molars grinding together in my head as I watched the exchange.

It was none of my business, I reminded myself.

I finished my lager and headed for the bar again. While waiting on the busy barman, Elsie crossed the floor in front of me, the frills at her hem hitting her milk-white calves as she floated. She threw me a shy smile and a nod on her way by.

I nodded back, hoping my smile didn't look too dopey and lovesick, as Elsie continued down a hallway deeper into the Watkins' home.

I don't know if it was the music or the beer or the way she looked in that dress but I was very close to walking home. I wanted out of there, I wanted out of my uncomfortable suit, and I wanted to go to bed.

"Nah, she's not the princess she pretends to be. I can tell," I heard Miller say behind me. "Girls like that? All they want is a man to tell them what to do."

Miller and three of his officer mates had arrived at the bar without me noticing. I slowly looked to my right where Miller was leaning against the bar a few feet away, his back to me.

"And what are *you* going to tell Elsie to do?" asked one of the officers.

"I'm going to tell her to make me breakfast in the morning." There was a wicked grin in his voice.

My fingers flexed against my palms.

"No way you're getting into her panties tonight," one of his friends said. "Not a chance."

"Why don't we make it interesting?" Miller pulled a bill from his pocket. "Five pounds, gentlemen?"

"I'll take that bet," said one friend.

"I can't even remember how much that is in real money," another said with a loud laugh.

I considered grabbing the back of his head and smashing his face against the gleaming bar top as hard as I possibly could. He wouldn't even see it coming.

Despite being substantially bigger than them individually, I knew I couldn't take the four officers in a fight if it came to that.

They took their drinks back to their table and the barman turned to me. "What can I get for you?"

"A pint," I said. "Actually, no. Do you have whisky?"

I returned to my companions, cocktail in hand, a third of it already burning in my belly.

Vera winced. "What happened?"

"What?"

She hesitated. "You look…"

"Murderous," Sheila finished.

I took another sip and cleared my throat. "Lieutenant Tosser and his chums are taking bets on whether or not he can…well, um…" I cleared my throat again. "Bed Elsie tonight."

Sheila crossed her arms over her chest and shook her head. "I bloody hate that arse."

I raised my glass in a mock salute and took another taste.

Vera frowned. "What do we do?"

"What do you mean?"

"Should we tell her?" Sheila frowned. "It can't be me though. She's not speaking to me."

"It can't come from me," I quickly added.

"Why not?"

I opened my mouth and then shut it, stalling. "Well, I…I'm

her boss. I don't think it's appropriate for me to… get involved in something like that."

"You're going to make me tell her, aren't you?" Vera rolled her eyes and finished off her pint just as Elsie rejoined Miller and his friends at their table across the room. "Well, this will be uncomfortable for everyone involved."

thirteen

Elsie

Garrett twirled me around the dance floor, showing off his agility as the band played bouncy Glenn Miller tunes. Spinning me back into his chest, he held me tight before smoothly turning me around and swaying with me.

With his arms around my waist, Garrett dipped me as the song reached its dramatic, horn-heavy finale. He smiled broadly and gracefully pulled me back into him. We separated briefly to applaud the musicians before Garrett slipped his arm around my waist again, leading me back to our table with his friends.

"Can I get you another cocktail, gorgeous?" Garrett leaned in and rested a hand on my knee.

"Yes, that would be lovely," I said. "Thank you."

He continued gazing at me.

I giggled, suddenly feeling self-conscious. "What?"

"Sorry." He chuckled. "You're just so dazzling. It's hard to not look at you."

My cheeks warmed. "Oh, stop. You're such a charmer."

"Don't you move," he said, sliding from his chair. "I'll be right back."

Not thirty seconds after Garrett left for the bar, Vera appeared beside me, gripping a small clutch bag tightly. She was technically smiling but it didn't reach her eyes.

"Hi. That's a lovely frock," I said, nodding to her simple blue dress. I had never seen Vera with her hair and makeup done before. I would never have guessed there was a good-looking lady under that no-nonsense, severe exterior. "The band is great, aren't they?"

"Yes, they're quite good," she said, glancing nervously at the rest of the people at the table.

"Oh, these are Garrett's friends, Russ—"

"It's a little warm in here," Vera said, giving her face a quick fan with her hand. "Would you care to get some fresh air with me? Outside?" She widened her eyes slightly, highlighting the significance of her request.

"Yes, it is a little stuffy in here I suppose." I turned to the rest of the table. "Tell Garrett I'll be right back."

Vera gave a quick nod and I followed her brisk pace outside the elegant double doors and over to a cluster of perfectly groomed topiaries. A few years ago light from the inside of the well-lit room would have flooded out onto the grass. Now all those high manor windows were blacked out and we stood in relative darkness.

I rested a hand on my hip. "Is everything alright?"

She fished a cigarette case out of her clutch, lit it with a match, and tossed the match onto the gravel drive.

Vera inhaled deeply. "How much do you like your American boyfriend?"

"This is only our second date. He's not my—"

"He's a real bastard."

I laughed. "Pardon?"

"I was at the bar and Lieutenant Miller and a few of his friends were there too. They didn't notice me so they were talking freely. Too freely, to be quite frank."

I suddenly wished my eyes would adjust to the darkness a little faster so I could read her expression. "Oh?"

"Miller made a bet with his friends that he could take you to bed tonight. The bet was his idea." She took another puff and blew the smoke out of the corner of her mouth. "I'm sorry. I just thought you should know what kind of man Miller really is."

My chest tightened and heat rose in my neck. My fingers quivered but I quickly smothered their shakiness by crossing my arms over my chest.

"Oh, you know how men are. They're all talk." I let out what was meant to be a casual laugh but it came out forced and a little creaky. "You must have misunderstood or misread things."

"Why would I be telling you if I thought there was a chance of that?" Vera sighed audibly. "He bet five quid.""Five?" I swallowed, my throat suddenly going dry and constricting. "Is that all? I thought I would have been worth at least ten."

"I know you and I don't know one another very well," she said, "but the Elsie Foster-Quinn I *think* I know would never, ever put up with that bollocks for a second."

"Thank you, I suppose." I smiled weakly. "I just need to make it clear to him that I'm not that type of woman and that he needs to be a gentleman if he and I—"

"He's not a gentleman, Elsie," Vera said. "I thought that was clear."

"This is really not your concern," I said. "I'm grateful you told me what he said but I'm not going to disrupt a nice evening over this."

Vera dropped her cigarette butt on the ground and extinguished it with her scuffed heel. "Fine. Do what you like."

Vera and I returned to the gala, quickly parting ways to our separate tables. I hated being treated like a child who couldn't handle things her own way.

I took my seat beside Garrett and he draped his arm across the back of my chair. "Everything alright, doll?"

"Everything is perfect," I said, reaching for my drink and taking a hefty gulp.

"Hey, Garrett," Garrett's friend Russ whispered, nodding to the double doors. "Look who just showed up."

Everyone at the table—and many other gala attendees—turned to survey the newcomers, two Black American soldiers in their service uniforms.

Russ hopped up from his chair, nearly tipping it. The pair saluted him as he approached. Russ, noticeably, did not return the gesture.

"Y'all know you're not supposed to be here," Russ said loudly.

The words echoed throughout the room and low, concerned whispers rose.

The two men exchanged worried looks.

"Did you not hear me?" Russ stepped closer to them. "This event is for whites only."

I clamped a hand on Garrett's arm. "You need to do something."

Garrett rose and I followed a few paces behind him. Russ was being tremendously rude but Garrett and I would make sure everyone felt welcome at—

"Don't make trouble, you two," he said gently. "You know this event isn't for you. You're not welcome here. Just turn around and leave. Nobody needs to make a scene."

I stared at the back of Garrett's head, my mouth slightly open. Vera was right. He was a bastard.

Before I even knew what I was doing, I planted myself in the huddle of Americans as they stared each other down.

"They *are* welcome here," I said, my heart hammering in my chest, before turning to them. "Have a sherry on me, please."

They smiled weakly.

"Thank you, ma'am," said the man on the left with a polite nod.

"You're both very welcome to stay," Rosetta said, her heels clicking on the floor as she joined us, her face awash with worry. "This event is for everyone." She cast a warning look to Garrett and Russ as she spoke the last word.

"If they're allowed in here, we're not staying," Russ announced. "We've got laws in our country."

I narrowed my eyes at him. "You're not *in* your country."

Russ' nostrils flared as he stared down at me. "Garrett, maybe you should tell this little lady to shut her mouth before I shut it for her."

The volume of the shocked whispers increased considerably.

Backing up, Garrett's hand slipped around my arm. "Come on, we're leaving."

"I'm not leaving with you," I snapped, pulling away. "Let go of me."

"Get your hands off of her this instant and get out," Rosetta said.

"Ma'am, stay out of this," Garrett said, his fingers tightening around my arm, pulling me towards the double doors.

"I said let go of me," I said, this time through clenched teeth.

With my free hand, I grabbed his pinky finger and pulled it off my arm, pushing it away until it was bent backward and he howled with pain.

"Ow, Christ!" he yelped, letting go of my arm and cradling his palm in his other hand.

Rosetta grabbed my hand and drew me to her side, away from the officers. Garrett threw me a scowl before he and his friends stormed out.

A subdued and uncomfortable applause sounded from parts of the room. I put my hand to my chest, trying to calm my racing heart.

Rosetta dropped my hand and held me by the shoulders. "Dear girl, are you alright?"

I nodded. "I'm fine."

She let go of me and turned to the two Black servicemen. "My most sincere apologies for their behavior."

One of them smiled sheepishly. "We didn't mean to cause a fuss."

"You didn't. *They* did," I said, crossing my arms and glaring at the double doors as if Garrett's crew were just on the other side. "This won't cause a problem for you back on the base, will it?"

The two exchanged worried looks.

Rosetta straightened her shoulders. "Don't give it another thought, gentlemen. I'll make a call first thing tomorrow and speak to their superiors. I was a nurse during the Great War so I know how to deal with commanding officers."

A nurse? The thought of perfectly pristine Rosetta Watkins getting splashed with the blood of soldiers every day was puzzling to me.

"Thank you, ma'am," he said, glancing at his companion again.

It was possible that their commanding officer would take Garrett's side and somehow punish these two servicemen just for trying to attend an event. I fought the urge to wince.

The United Kingdom wasn't without its own issues of racial inequality and prejudice, but it certainly didn't have government-mandated segregation. Seeing Garrett and Russ act that way so openly was troubling. As if there weren't enough hate in the world already, they brought their style of intolerance across the Atlantic with them.

"Please," I said, putting a hand on Rosetta's arm, "excuse me for a moment."

A thin veil of tears blurred my vision as I made my way around the perimeter of the room, up the staircase, and down a hallway. Shoving aside the heavy blackout curtain across the French double doors, I burst out onto the balcony and gulped frantically at the cool night air. I gripped the wrought iron railing until my knuckles went white. Staring into the dark distance while taking deep breaths, my pulse gradually calmed.

"Elsie?"

I nearly jumped out of my skin. Whipping around and slapping my hand on my chest, I backed up against the railing.

"Ben, you scared me half to death."

He smiled sheepishly. "Sorry. I just wanted to make sure you were okay." He gestured back into the hallway. "Maybe you came up here to be alone. I can go."

Just enough light escaped onto the balcony that I could see the crease between his brows.

I shook my head. "No, it's fine. I'm fine." My shoulders sagged. "I'm mostly just mortified. Sheila read him perfectly." I frowned. "Now she'll be saying 'I told you so' for days."

"No, she won't."

"No, you're right," I said, avoiding his gaze. "She wouldn't do that." I shook my head. "I was such a fool."

Ben leaned against the doorway and crossed his arms, the tweed of his suit jacket snug against his biceps. "You misjudged him. It happens."

Releasing a long breath, I folded my hands together in front of me. "I suppose I should get back downstairs or else the whole village will worry I've run away. I would rather fling myself off this balcony than have that."

"Please don't do that," Ben said, rubbing the back of his neck. "People would think I pushed you."

"I'm sure there have been lots of times when you wished you could push me off a balcony," I laughed, "or simply sent me home on the train. Cleaner that way, I suppose."

He smiled, his eyes sparkling mischievously. "I rarely think about doing that these days."

The lively music, only dulled slightly by our distance from the band, transitioned smoothly into a slow melody punctuated by lazy bass plucks. Lowering his eyes, Ben unfolded his arms and slid his hands into the pockets of his trousers. His sudden shyness was oddly adorable.

It was so odd seeing Ben in a three-piece suit and tie, his dark curls combed neatly into place and his beard trimmed. He certainly looked handsome. Ben's obvious discomfort detracted from the look but his effort was endearing.

"My dance partner left so I'll need someone to take his place, of course," I said.

He swallowed, his brows popping up slightly. "Uh, I'm a little out of practice."

My eyes narrowed. "But you must be able to foxtrot." I tapped on my cheek as I considered. "I think Vera would have made you learn how to dance when you were younger."

"Well, yes, you're spot on there," he said with a chuckle. "But it's been about fifteen years."

"We can do a practice run before going downstairs." I moved to the wide hall inside the balcony since the landing was a little snug for a box step.

"You're not afraid I'll crush your tiny feet?"

"You're stalling," I said.

He let out a breath and joined me inside. I slid my left hand to his shoulder and rested my right hand in his. My stomach fluttered as I felt his broad, rough hand on my upper back. Following the tune of the song, he lead us smoothly and better than I expected. He didn't look down at our feet as we glided across the floor and he didn't let me bump into anything behind me. His scent, something between spring grass and a forest, made the hairs on the back of my neck stand at attention.

However, I hardly noticed any of that.

More than anything, I was far too focused on how his eyes looked. Tawny brown with streaks of gold and framed by midnight lashes, his gaze never strayed from mine as he swept me across the room. He didn't look into my eyes as much as he looked into me.

The song ended and he eased us to a halt but neither of us moved away. The space between us crackled like the air before a summer thunderstorm. Heat rose in my skin as we stood motionless, breathless, like neither of us wanted to be the one to break the spell.

A creak on one of the nearby stairs made us both take a step back. Suddenly we couldn't make eye contact at all.

"Elsie, darling, there are a few people downstairs I would like you to meet," Rosetta said cheerfully. "Oh, hello, Mr. Grainger. I hope you're having an enjoyable evening." She threw him a quick polite smile but she obviously didn't suspect she had just interrupted anything.

Had she?

Ben nodded. "Yes, thank you."

As I followed Rosetta down the staircase, I subtly looked back at Ben over my shoulder. He ran a hand through his hair, leaving it untidy, and staring hard at the floor—the spot where I had stood moments before.

As Rosetta introduced me to so-and-so and so-and-so's son, I caught Ben striding out of the front doors at speed. He didn't look back.

fourteen

BEN

I kept my head down and my eyes away from Elsie for most of May.

She and I never spoke about the moment that passed between us that night at the fundraiser earlier on in the month, but we hadn't managed to return to the comfortable friendship we'd formed over the past few months.

As far as I knew Elsie hadn't spoken to Lieutenant Tosser since that catastrophe of an evening.

The Nazi bombers never returned to Bath but that didn't stop some paranoid Bathtonians from making the nightly walk into the surrounding countryside in the hopes of a peaceful, bomb-free sleep. A farmer I knew even discovered a chap sleeping in his hayloft on a rainy night.

It was late in May when Vera served steamed vegetables for supper before sliding a small mincemeat pie in front of me. I closed my eyes and inhaled deeply, letting its sweet smell overtake me.

Vera gave me a quick kiss on the top of the head. "Happy birthday, little brother."

Elsie looked at me. "Why didn't you tell us it was your birthday?"

The sincerity in her eyes was nearly enough to undo me.

I shrugged. "It's just a birthday. It happens almost every year."

She let out a little laugh, biting the corner of her lip as she smirked. I had to look away for fear of staring at her heart-shaped mouth.

"As if he would tell *anyone* it was his birthday," Vera said. "He's thirty, by the way."

I threw her a look of warning before smiling at her. "Thank you."

Sheila gaped at the pie. "How did you manage that on ration?"

Vera buttoned up her cardigan, preparing to depart for the day. "Several months of planning, a bit of trading, and the calling in of a favor."

"You didn't have to do all that for me—"

"Oh, hush," she said. "Eat your supper before it gets cold, will you?"

"Do you have any birthday plans?" Elsie asked before taking a mouthful of carrots.

Vera held up a hand before I could respond. "He'll be going to the pub with Amos for a couple o' pints and reading a book before bed." She raised an eyebrow at me. "Did I miss anything?"

I chewed slowly. "No, that about covers it."

"So I says, 'I don't know about 'im but I certainly wouldn't try fishing with that rod!'" Amos slapped his hand on the tabletop and laughed aloud at his own story, causing a bit of foam to slosh over the side of my glass.

Chuckling, I sat back in the booth and brought my beer to my lips before Amos did any more damage to it. He already had a rosy tint to his entire face so I knew more table slapping would happen soon.

The pub was lively that Saturday night. Frank and Leonard kept things cheerful, playing spirited melodies on the fiddle and fife, and several couples spun around the crowded floor. There were no chandeliers, no stiff suits required, no guest list, and certainly no band from London playing on a stage. This was far better than anything Rosetta Watkins could offer up.

No Elsie on a balcony, gazing out into a sea of stars.

I took a gulp of my beer. Just as I put my glass back down, a woman's hand slid a half-pint glass of frothy beer in front of me. I followed the hand up to see Pauline.

"Happy birthday, Ben," she said, her red lips curling mischievously in the dim light. "How are you?"

Amos smirked at me from his side of the booth.

I nodded to the glass. "Thank you, kindly. I'm well. And you?"

Pauline sent a meaningful look at Amos and he received the message.

"I think I'll go say hello to Eldon at the bar," Amos said, sliding out of his booth seat and practically running away from our table.

I cast a quick glance around the pub as Pauline sat across from me.

She didn't say anything for a moment, instead letting her dark eyes roam over me, taking me in.

"I've missed you," she said finally.

I rubbed the back of my neck. "That's, uh, very flattering."

"I knew you'd be here tonight for your birthday. I thought I'd invite you over for a—" She lowered her voice. "—late night drink."

I finished my beer and nodded to the half-pint glass she'd brought to me. "Is that what this is? You're trying to woo me? You'll need at least a full pint for that, miss."

Pauline laughed and rested her cheek in her palm, propping an elbow up on the table.

The image of Elsie biting the corner of her lip as she laughed appeared in my mind.

"I'm leaving Fairbury next week," Pauline said. "I'm moving to London for a new job."

"Congratulations," I said, reaching for the half-pint and taking a sip. "What's the job?"

"Secretarial work. Similar to what I'm doing now. Same work, different office. I need a change," she said. "I just thought it would be such a shame if we didn't get to say a proper goodbye before I left." Serene, she made direct eye contact and pursed her lips slightly.

I shook my head and tried to keep my tone friendly. "I don't think that's a good idea."

Pauline gave a little shrug, entirely unruffled by my rejection. She slid out of the booth and folded her hands in front of her.

She said something else but the sight of Elsie coming into the pub with Sheila blocked out everything else—in the room, in England, in the world. Elsie looked around the room, her eyes landed on me, and she gave a friendly wave. I nodded back to her, smiling.

"Oh, good lord," Pauline said, breaking the spell. "So it *is* the little blonde who works for you?" She laughed. "I bloody knew it."

I swallowed hard. "What? No." I promptly checked to see if anyone was watching our exchange. Fairbury had more than its share of gossips. "We're friends."

She tipped her chin and arched an eyebrow. "You're still a terrible liar."

"Christ, I'm not lying," I snapped, trying to keep my voice low.

"The way you just looked at her? I know that look. You certainly never, ever looked at me that way," she said, her tone mocking. "Are you in love with the city girl?"

I glared up at her. "No." I slid the half-pint glass to her. "Perhaps you should finish this."

"You don't even remember that I don't drink beer," she scoffed, rolling her eyes. "Goodbye, Ben."

She turned on her heel and marched out of the pub, thankfully not pausing at the booth where Elsie and Sheila now sat. Elsie watched Pauline curiously as she stormed by before sending me a quizzical look from the other side of the pub. I shook my head and gave an exaggerated shrug.

Amos returned to the booth, bringing a new pint with him. I gulped down the remainder of the half-pint glass and slammed it back on the tabletop.

"Have a nice chat with Pauline, did ye?" He tilted his head slightly.

I sent him a warning look. "She doesn't like being told no."

Just then Eldon bumped into the edge of our table. His eyes were heavy-lidded and he likely had more beer down the front of his shirt than in his glass.

"'Scuse me, lads. Din't see you there," he said, his speech garbled.

"S'alright, Eldon. Carry on," Amos said to his glass in a deep, stern tone.

Eldon studied my face for a moment. "I've been meanin' to ask ye if yer still gettin' Amos here to do your work for ye."

"Eldon, why don't you go sit down before someone gives you a sound kick in the arse?" Amos slid out of his booth and tried to aim Eldon away from our table.

I glared up at the drunk man. This wasn't the first time a local farmer had given me a hard time about my avoidance of putting down male calves. It wasn't even the first time from Eldon specifically.

Eldon shoved Amos off of him, spilling even more beer out of his glass, sending it splashing on the wooden planks of the pub floor.

"You shouldn't waste beer like that, you old fool," I warned, standing up.

My height didn't have many advantages but it did help to get arseholes to be quiet on occasion.

"Why can't you do it yerself anyway—put the calves down?" Eldon continued.

"That's enough," Amos yelled.

"Ye look like you wanna hit me," Eldon said, grinning stupidly with one eye half-closed. "But you won't. Do you get Amos to do *every*thing fer ye?"

I snatched the glass out of his hand, downed the rest of the beer, and slid the empty glass onto the table behind me.

I lowered myself to look directly at Eldon, face to face. "You're a sad, old, drunken bastard." I shook my head at him.

Blustering out of the pub, I only remembered Elsie was there when I caught her staring at me right before I whipped the doors open and let myself out.

"Wait," I heard Elsie call after me as I started the walk back to the farm.

My shoulders tensed. I didn't want to talk to anybody just then, even her. More than that, I didn't want to risk taking my anger out on her and looking like a tosser.

I stopped and looked back at her. "Why were you even there? What, were you and Sheila spying on me?"

She halted in place, her brow pinched. "We occasionally go to the pub.

We were there tonight because I was going to treat you to a pint since it's your birthday," she snapped.

Oh.

"You shouldn't go there," I said. "It's full of drunk idiots."

"You shouldn't have let what that git said bother you."

"I didn't let him get to me," I said, my jaw tight.

"Oh? Is that why you're so calm and collected right now?"

"I am calm!" I shouted.

She lifted an eyebrow. "Yes, I can see that."

"Why do women keep doing that to me today?" I barked. "The thing with their eyebrow? Like they know everything and they damn well don't. He *wanted* me to hit him."

"Did you want to?"

"Of course!"

"Perhaps you should have." She crossed her arms over her chest and allowed a hint of a smile to creep across her lips.

I planted myself directly in front of her, my chest heaving and blood boiling. Part of me wanted to kiss her roughly and thoroughly and part of me wanted to throw her over my shoulder.

"Would you have liked that?" My voice was husky and dark. The beer made me say it.

Elsie was the first to break eye contact, suddenly studying the road under us.

"I don't fight," I said, my voice low. "It's not worth it."

She looked back up at me and studied my face in the glow of her torchlight. "That's very grown up of you."

I shrugged.

"Come back to the pub and have a drink with us," she said. "If that chap gives you a hard time again and since it's your birthday and all, Sheila and I will rough him up on your behalf."

"I would pay good money to see that." I laughed. "No, I better not."

Elsie sighed. "Alright then. Good night." She turned on her heel and began the short walk back to the pub.

"You and Sheila better not be hungover in the morning!" I yelled to her as she walked away, leaving me alone in the road.

fifteen

Elsie

The scream that burst out of me upon seeing Percy in the farm yard at Honeyfield was so loud and such a high pitch that I alarmed even myself. I leaped off the milk delivery cart, ran to him, and threw my arms around his neck, squeezing him tight.

"I am *so* happy you're here!" I exclaimed, reluctant to let him go. I kissed him hard on the cheek before backing up so I could take in all of him. "It is strange to see you in uniform."

Percy laughed, gripping my hands in his. "It's strange seeing *you* in dungarees."

"My uniform just happens to be less flattering than yours, that's all," I said matter-of-factly. "It's quite comfortable, actually. Maybe I'll get myself some dungarees when we're back in London after the war. I'll set a trend." I grinned.

"Don't you dare," Percy said, bringing me in for another hug.

Strolling by us without a word, Ben began unhitching Sherlock.

"I can get that," I said to Ben.

He waved me off, not making eye contact. "I've got it."

I nodded, suddenly struck with a pang of guilt for abandoning one of my duties. Ben had already been kind enough to let me switch my afternoon off with one during the week as it was the only day Percy could visit.

"Thank you," I said quietly. "Did you two get introduced?" I was suddenly very aware of a level of awkwardness in the air between the two men.

Ben threw a glance at Percy over his shoulder. "No." He gave him a subtle nod of greeting. "Hello."

I rolled my eyes. "This is my best friend, Percy Montgomery. Percy, this is the farmer I work for, Mr. Grainger."

Percy stretched his hand out. "Very nice to meet you, Mr. Grainger."

Ben turned to face Percy and shook his hand. "Where are you serving?" He ended the handshake as soon as he could, turning back to Sherlock to continue working.

"I'm off to some middle-of-nowhere little hamlet in Scotland tomorrow." Percy frowned. "I was hoping to be stationed closer to London but *vita sic est*."

"Such is life," I translated.

Ben didn't turn around. "Mm-hm."

I turned back to Percy. "Want to come in for a cup of tea while I get changed and we can go to lunch?"

He followed me inside the cottage and Vera prepared him a brew while I made myself presentable. As I descended the stairs a few minutes later I overheard Vera and Percy chatting.

"I didn't know Elsie was…seeing anyone," Vera said, hesitating.

"Oh, no. We're not… She and I have been best friends since we were children. She's more of a sister to me," he clarified.

Percy and I were romantically involved only briefly one summer when he was home from school. To be fair, it was hard *not* to fall for Percy Montgomery—the wavy blond hair, the athletic frame, the chiseled jaw; he was a Grecian sculpture with boarding school manners. He was my first date, my first kiss, and my first (and only) foray into physical romance. We didn't sleep together, thankfully. I don't know if our friendship would have survived that. It was pretty uncertain for a while when he admitted that he was a homosexual. I didn't appreciate being used as his test subject and we didn't speak for months after that. During our separation, I realized I had always loved him but I wasn't *in* love with him. Eventually, I missed him too much and eventually forgave him.

"Tell me about Mr. Grainger," Percy said as we walked from the shuttle drop-off in Bath to a nice restaurant near Pulteney Bridge. "He's rather…tall."

"Yes," I said slowly, "I suppose he is quite tall."

"Quite nice shoulders too," he added, peering down at me, a smirk playing on his lips.

"I never noticed."

I'd obviously noticed. It was hard *not* to notice Ben's well-defined shoulders, arms, chest, thighs, calves, backside…well, everything really. He was a grumpy, sarcastic oak tree of a man.

"I suppose he's quite fit, yes," I admitted. "What exactly is your point?"

He opened the door for us as we reached the eatery. "You should have seen the look he gave me when you hugged me. I thought he was going to punch me."

I looked at Percy. "What do you mean?"

"I'm saying Farmer Grainger fancies you," he said in a hushed, playful tone.

"Fancies me," I repeated with a chuckle. "Certainly not. We can barely stand one another."

Percy continued grinning mischievously but remained quiet as we were seated at a table near a window. I sighed at the menu and frowned. I had hoped the options would have been better at a nicer restaurant like this one but even they could not escape the limitations of wartime rations altogether.

"I'm told the food is better for those serving in the war," I said from behind my menu. "At least you have that to look forward to."

When Percy didn't reply, I lowered my menu to look at him. Brow pinched, Percy stared blankly out the window, his hands gripping his menu with two trembling hands.

I moved the menus to the side and took his hand in mine. "You will be fine. You will be safe. Do you understand?"

Percy's parents were well-connected and they tried to keep him out of harm's way for as long as they could. Unfortunately, not even the Montgomery family could keep Percy's conscription at bay forever. His father managed to snag him a spot as an assistant to a general so he would be mostly doing paperwork and not at the front. I was so grateful for that.

Percy's gaze dropped to the tabletop. "But what if I'm not?"

"Then I will be furious with you."

He snickered and picked up his menu again. "Naturally."

"Elsie, darling!" Rosetta approached our table. "Lovely to see you."

"Good afternoon, Mrs. Watkins," I said. "Nice to see you as well."

"Montgomery," Rosetta repeated after I introduced the two of them. "Are Edward and Isabella your parents?"

Percy smiled wide, displaying his perfect teeth. "They are."

"I knew it," she said smugly. "You've got your mother's eyes but your father's bone structure."

"I believe my aunt bought a horse from you a few years ago," Percy said.

As they chatted, I couldn't help but think about how the two of them spoke the same language. It was like I was hearing my native tongue for the first time in months. However, instead of finding it comforting, I felt…ambivalent.

"I won't keep you any longer. I'm just meeting a friend for lunch," Rosetta said, waving to her companion at a nearby table. "Enjoy your lunch, you two." She gave me a playful wink before floating away.

I leaned in. "She absolutely thinks you're my beau."

Percy snatched my hand up from the table and kissed my knuckles gallantly. "Alas. It was not meant to be for Farmer Grain—ow!"

I pinched the meat of his middle finger before he could say another word.

Saying goodbye to Percy in Bath as I boarded the shuttle back to Fairbury was heartbreaking. Having the afternoon with him just reminded me of all the ways he was a wonderful man and friend, and it made bidding him farewell even harder than if I hadn't seen him at all before he shipped out.

Once the shuttle arrived back in the village, I dashed down the pavement to the post office. I managed to make it minutes before they closed for the evening.

"Good afternoon, Ms. Foster-Quinn," the postmaster said, smiling broadly. "I think I have a parcel for you."

"Brilliant, thank you," I said.

I didn't have to even tell him my name, I thought, suddenly feeling an unfamiliar warmth in my chest.

While the jolly postmaster rifled through some boxes to locate my package, Rosetta appeared at my side and nudged my arm gently.

"Lucky me. Twice in one day!" She laughed. "I'm not following you, I promise."

I smiled. "How was your lunch?"

She pressed her lips together firmly as she considered her reply. "Good," she finally said before lowering her voice slightly, "although rationing is affecting us all, I suppose."

I nodded solemnly. "I know what you mean."

"They're doing their best," she added. "Chefs aren't magicians, after all."

I knew of a few industrious chefs in London who dabbled in the flourishing black market in order to get access to the best cuts of meat, undermining the competition and risking harsh government fines.

Rosetta nudged my arm again. "And how was *your* lunch with Mr. Montgomery?"

"It was nice," I said, "but knowing he's going off to war worries me. He's not going to the front thankfully but I'm worried he will end up there somehow."

"Not to worry, my dear. He'll be back at your side in no time at all," she said. "He's very handsome. Very good family, too."

I opened my mouth to redirect her assumptions but closed my mouth again, knowing I needed to tread carefully. Percy's family obviously didn't know of his attraction to men but sometimes he and I hinted at a romantic relationship between us to keep them from getting suspicious.

"Yes, well, he is certainly a catch," I said. "A fine man."

She nodded in approval. "Hopefully we'll hear of an engagement before too long."

I hesitated. "Perhaps."

The postmaster slid the parcel onto the counter. Wrapped in brown paper and featuring a return address from London, I knew exactly what it was.

"Is that a book?" Rosetta peered at the package. "Apologies, I don't mean to pry. I just noticed the stamp on it was Hatchards."

"Yes, it's a gift for Mr. Grainger," I said.

She cocked an eyebrow.

"It was his birthday recently," I quickly added before realizing that I perhaps shouldn't have said anything about buying Ben a gift at all.

She tilted her head, considering. I swallowed and waited for her to tell me giving a gift to my boss was inappropriate.

"Mr. Grainger *reads*?" she finally asked, simpering. "Who knew?"

I forced a smile. "Yes. He reads quite a lot actually."

She chuckled. "He just doesn't seem the type." She waved a dismissive hand. "Well, wish him a happy birthday for me."

As I left the post office I had the sudden urge to throw a glare at her over my shoulder.

I returned to the farm just in time for the evening milking. After supper, helping with the washing up, and taking a quick bath, I wrapped my hair in a towel and put on my dressing gown. On my way back upstairs the light sound of gentle snoring caught my attention.

Stretched out across the couch that he was too tall for, Ben's long, sleeping form seemed right at home *and* ridiculous simultaneously. One of his legs rested on the coffee table and one of his long arms fell over the side of the couch. A gentle golden ray of evening sun filtered in through the small, round stained glass window on the back wall and landed in a colorful pool beside him.

I narrowed my eyes, peering at the book laying open on his gently rising and falling chest: it was my copy of *Mansfield Park*. I must have accidentally left it in the chair when I finished rereading it the week before.

I dashed upstairs, recovered the book I received in the mail that afternoon from my bag, and took it back downstairs. The bottom stair creaked as I stepped on it and Ben inhaled sharply as he woke, jerking his head upright and blinking. He looked at me and then looked at the book on his chest before putting his head back down.

I took a seat in the armchair across from the couch and smiled smugly at him, tucking the parcel under my arm. "Enjoying a bit of Jane Austen?"

"Obviously not. It put me to sleep," he scoffed. "Does anything actually *happen* in her books? It seems to be all mad family members and characters visiting other characters."

I snatched the book off his chest, noticed he was only two pages in, slapped it shut, and placed it on the nearby side table. "No one made you read it. Plus, people usually don't *start* with *Mansfield Park*. It's good but not her very best."

He sat up a little, propping himself up on his elbows. "How was your lunch with your fancy man?" His tight sideways frown hinted at his negative impression of him.

Was Ben…jealous?

"Percy isn't *my* fancy man. He's a chum." I considered my next words carefully, knowing they were risky. "He isn't particularly interested in…women, you see." I bit my lip.

His brow went from creased to popping up after a moment. "Oh."

"Obviously that's not something many people know so do keep mum about it." I slid the parcel out from beside me and tossed it onto his chest. "Here, for your trouble."

Ben surveyed the brown paper wrapping and return address. "What's this?"

"A belated birthday present." I smiled. "Open it."

Sitting up, he carefully unsealed the wrapping so it could be reused for something else. I couldn't help but find it endearing. I would have just ripped it open without a second thought.

Sliding the book out of the paper, he stared at the bold red, white, and black cover with his mouth slightly open.

"You got the new Agatha Christie for me," he said quietly. "You didn't need to do that." He finally looked up at me and his soft brown eyes sparkled with warmth and joy.

"I noticed you didn't have the new one on your shelf," I said with a shrug. "I hope it's good."

He flipped it over, his eyes glued to the back cover of *The Body in the Library* before he looked back at me. "Thank you, Elsie."

Something about the way he said my name in a deep and slightly raw near-whisper made my stomach hum.

He glanced at the Austen book nearby. "I wish I hadn't said anything about your book. Now I feel rotten."

"Well, just don't do it again."

He laughed and looked back down at his book, his smile spreading as his eyes scanned the text a second time.

Ben peered at *Mansfield Park* again and then at me. "Why do you like her books?"

I folded my hands in my lap. "Well, they're quite witty. She had a devastating, sharp sense of humor. Many of her stories and characters are satirical. She had a lot to say about family, society, and expectations of class and women."

He peered at the nearby novel again. "Really?"

"Oh, yes. Plus, the romantic relationships she wrote about are based in mutual trust and respect and not just instantly falling in love across a crowded ballroom." Speaking about romance—even the fictional kind—to Ben made my skin heat.

He rubbed the back of his neck. "I thought it was all swooning and fainting couches."

I let out a loud chuckle. "Not at all." I gestured to the book in his hand. "Perhaps you could give *Pride and Prejudice* a try instead. You might like it."

Hesitating, a playful, shy smile tugged at the corner of his lips. "If I read *Pride and Prejudice*, will you read an Agatha Christie?"

I nodded. "Sure. You'll have to pick out your favorite for me."

He beamed. "Okay."

We said good night as he stretched out on the couch again, opening *The Body in the Library* to the first chapter.

sixteen

Ben

Every smile she threw my way, every exchanged glance, every laugh—almost every little thing Elsie did had me wondering if there was something more to it. Did she smile at everyone like that or was that a smile just for me? Did her eyes always sparkle like that when she giggled?

Had something actually changed between us? Or was it just wishful thinking?

As we milked the cows that morning in early June I could hardly keep my eyes off Elsie. She caught me gazing at her, and I quickly looked back down at my milk pail. When I slowly raised my eyes again she was watching me, a playful sparkle in her eyes.

I wanted to kiss her. I wanted to bury my face in her neck and inhale her entire essence. I wanted to drag my lips across every inch of her. I wanted to taste her—

"I heard the War Office is sending five thousand Morrison shelters to Bath," Sheila said from behind us, carefully tipping the contents of her milk pail into the larger metal canister.

While the Anderson shelter was an oversized tin can families set up in their back gardens to use as a private shelter, the Morrison shelter was a reinforced bed-sized cage one could sleep in. The sturdy top would protect you from most debris from above and the chicken wire walls kept you safe from most debris that might attack from the sides. These could go in homes and saved people from having to dig up their gardens. Plus they could be built by those who didn't have back gardens *to* dig up.

"Sure, *now* they send them when it's too late," I scoffed.

It had been a little over a month since the Germans let loose the fires of Hell onto Bath.

"They could come back," Elsie said. "You never know."

I moved down to the next cow. "I suppose."

She was right. People in Bath and the surrounding villages still watched the skies for signs of danger every night, listening for the droning hum of Nazi planes. We continued to move the herd back inside the barn every evening instead of letting them gather together in the meadow on warm nights.

Elsie left to do the milk delivery after breakfast while Sheila and I headed up to the field to cut hay. I drove the tractor in tight, long ovals with the wide sickle attached and Sheila dealt with the grass sticking to the sickle spikes. Then Sheila took a turn on the tractor and I dealt with the snags.

It was during one of these turns that Mrs. Watkins, approaching on horseback, rode up the hill.

Shielding her eyes with her hand, Sheila turned the tractor off and it clunked aggressively in response.

"Good morning," she said with a wave as Mrs. Watkins dismounted her thoroughbred.

"Good morning, Sheila." She nodded to me. "Good morning, Mr. Grainger."

I nodded in greeting and wiped the sweat from my forehead with the back of my hand.

"I'm just doing my regular check-in with the girls," Mrs. Watkins added cheerfully, as if she did it all the time. "I see we're missing a land girl."

"Elsie is out on milk delivery," Sheila said, still wincing into the morning sun. "She usually gets back around lunchtime."

"Blast. I probably rode right past her on my way here." She planted a hand on her hip. "Not to worry, I'll track her down. Sheila, can you take a short break to have a chat?"

While she slid off the tractor and joined us, Mrs. Watkins said, "Mr. Grainger, did you get your birthday gift from Elsie? She's such a thoughtful girl."

I swallowed. "Yeah, I got it." My shoulders tightened slightly.

"What was the book?"

"The newest Agatha Christie," I said with a shrug. "I like mysteries."

I didn't like these questions—not from Mrs. Watkins.

"Did you ask her to buy you a gift?" She narrowed her eyes so subtly I almost missed it.

"No, of course not," I said sharply.

Mrs. Watkins smiled. "Very well. I'm glad to hear it. We've received reports from some of our girls who have been mistreated by the farmers they live with. Having them wash their car for them or they're not getting fed enough. Horrible things. I just need to make sure nothing," She hesitated, "untoward is happening."

Sheila looked between Mrs. Watkins and I. "Mr. Grainger has been a good boss to us."

I tossed her a grateful nod.

"Good. Excellent."

While they stepped off to the side to have their check-in chat, I started up the tractor and continued the grass cutting, all the while feeling my heart hammering in my chest.

Mrs. Watkins knew about the gift. Why would Elsie even tell her? What *else* did she tell Mrs. Watkins?

Glaring into the high grass ahead of me, I tried to focus on farm work and not think about Elsie. That was getting harder and harder every day.

Mrs. Watkins and her horse cantered away back down the hill and I stopped the tractor as Sheila approached.

I turned the tractor off. "Did she ask anything about me?"

"Not really. She just wanted to confirm everything was still going well with us," she said. "I told her I've been content here."

I nodded and shared a small smile. "Good." I let my eyes drift over the fields around us. "Did she say anything about the gift?"

"No," she said. "Even if she did, I didn't even know Elsie got you anything."

I nodded and started the tractor again.

"Good," I said beneath the loud rumble of the engine.

Despite Elsie's smiles and glances my way that afternoon and during the evening milking, I tried my best to keep my eyes down. I didn't need Mrs. Watkins' nose or anyone else's in my business and I didn't need some spoiled city girl spreading rumors about me to her society friends. I had no time or patience for that nonsense.

When we finished, Elsie cleaned and sterilized the milking machine in the sink in the back room of the barn. While Sheila was finishing up on the last cow, I stood in the doorway to the storage room.

Elsie continued scrubbing, a little smirk playing on her lips as I watched her. "May I help you?"

"I, um, thought I might ask you…"

Her hands froze in place and she looked up at me expectantly.

I cleared my throat. "Why did Mrs. Watkins know that you bought me a gift?"

Surprised, she chuckled. "Oh. She happened to be at the post office when I picked it up. She saw the return address was from a bookshop and asked what it was."

My lips tighten. "But…why did you tell her it was a gift for me?"

Elsie's back straightened. "Because it *was* a gift for you."

"Why didn't you just say it was a book for yourself?" I winced.

"Because Rosetta is my friend," she said firmly. "I didn't see a reason to lie."

I ran a hand through my hair. "Do you know how that might look to her?"

Furrowing her brow, she went back to cleansing the milking machine. "What do you mean?"

I fought the urge to groan out loud. "There are farmers all over taking advantage of their land girls: not giving them wages, not providing proper housing, having them do household chores instead of farm work. I don't want Mrs. Watkins to think I *asked* you to buy me a gift." I paused. "Because I certainly didn't ask for one."

She scowled up at me. "I already *told* her this morning that you didn't ask me to buy you something and that you would *never* ask a land girl to buy you a gift."

"Good," I said. "Thank you."

"I told her you have been a respectful boss." Her face softened. "Reluctant to accept our assistance at first but I believe we've grown on you." Her eyes gleamed.

"Yes," I said. "Like a fungus."

That night I got home late after a few drinks and a game of darts with Amos at the pub. The cottage was dark and quiet. I slipped my shoes off by the door in the kitchen and gave Sam a quick pat as his tail thumped against the floor.

As I passed through the living room, I heard something that made me stop—quiet inhales and exhales coming from the armchair. I silently turned on the tabletop lamp at the end of the couch and smiled at the sight of Elsie sleeping in the chair in her dressing gown, a blanket wrapped around her, and my well-worn copy of *Death on the Nile* by Agatha Christie in her lap. She was a few chapters into it already.

"Elsie," I murmured. "Elsie?"

Her eyes opened faintly before falling shut again.

Sighing, I relocated the book to the table and switched the light back off. Made bolder by beer, I carefully slid my arms beneath her small frame and peered down at her peaceful, slumbering face as her head fell limply against my shoulder. Avoiding the creaky spot on the bottom stair, I carried her upstairs, making sure to not bump her head as I maneuvered her down the hall and into her room. I thought she might be able to feel the frantic pounding of my heart but she didn't stir.

As I slowly lowered her down onto her bed and pulled my arms from under her, she opened her eyes again and gazed up at me from beneath heavy lids.

"Hi," she whispered.

"Hi. Go back to sleep."

Soon her eyes were closed again and her shallow sleepy breaths returned to their previous rhythm. Cautiously closing her door as I left, I went next door to my own bedroom. I sat on the edge of my bed and stared at the wall, a fervent realization shaking me of all the warmth and comfort of exhaustion and alcohol: if I didn't soon tell Elsie how I felt, I would go mad.

seventeen

Elsie

A light pink banner, faded from hanging in the sun too many summers in a row, rippled in the gentle breeze as it hung above the village square on that warm and sunny June day. In elaborate lettering it read *Fairbury Village Fair.* Union Jack bunting hung above doorways and windows while families from Fairbury and the surrounding villages crowded along cobblestone streets.

For a few hours we might actually forget there was a war on. For just one day some of us could possibly not wonder if the Nazis might bring their bombs back to us.

I peered down at little June in her new pretty sky-blue frock, her small hand clasping mine and her eyes as big as saucers, trying to take everything in. Stalls selling snacks and drinks were on one side while a few locals had set up carnival game stalls near the post office.

Vera entered at least three separate dishes into three separate cooking competitions that day.

"This is the last year I do one of these cooking contests," she'd exclaimed that morning as she rushed around the cottage kitchen like a mad woman. "At least while rationing is still on. It's too much stress."

Ben raised an eyebrow at her, teacup in hand. "That's exactly what you said last year. I told you not to enter so many—"

"And let Mary Sturgess take all the ribbons? No, no, no, no, no." She shoveled scrambled eggs onto our plates as she quickly spoke.

Ben tried again. "You could have just entered the pie contest this year and not—"

Vera whirled around and raised a finger at him. "Not a chance. Mary Sturgess will never best me. Not when we were in school and certainly not on Fair Day." She whipped back around and continued mixing something.

"Is Mum judging jams again this year?"

"She wouldn't dream of missing it," Vera said, combining more ingredients.

Sheila hesitated. "Is June going to the neighbor's during the fair then?"

Vera froze and slowly turned around. "Uh—"

"You forgot about June, didn't you?" Ben snickered.

"No, of course not. I just…didn't remember her." She winced and her shoulders slumped. "Yes, I forgot. The neighbors will be at the fair with their children so I can't ask them to watch her now." She looked back at Sheila. "You're coming to the fair, right?"

"Yes. I'd offer to watch her but I'll be busy helping Mr. Linden with judging the farm animal contest," she said before taking a bite of breakfast.

Ben shook his head. "I'm doing the sheepdog trials with Sam so I can't watch her either."

Hearing his name, Sam rose his head from the floor and tilted it quizzically.

Ben, Vera, and Sheila all looked at me simultaneously. I lowered my teacup.

"I can watch June," I said.

"Thank you," Vera said with a sigh, planting two flour-dusted hands on her apron. "She won't give you any trouble. Plus, there will be plenty of things to do at the fair."

And there were. Looking around at the bustling activity of the village square, it reminded me of the country fair I visited a few times during my summers in Suffolk growing up. Mum was always very specific about the activities a girl of my social standing could be seen doing; watching or participating in a showjumping event, yes; perusing the items at the bake sale, perhaps; playing games, absolutely not.

"Oh, look, June," I said, pointing to a wooden sign pointing slightly off the main road. "Would you like to go on a pony ride?"

She nodded and eagerly pulled me ahead.

Although a little timid at first, June faced her fears and clung to the reins of the small fluffy pony brought in for the kids as it slowly trod the perimeter of his pen. Slowly, her face brightened and turned into a joyful grin. I thought she might cry when she reached the end of her turn.

"Goodbye, pretty pony," she said, giving his mane a final brush before we left the pen, heading for the nearby petting zoo.

June giggled and shrieked with glee as a trio of young mischievous goats gobbled feed from her hand. She held an adorable piglet until he squealed and wriggled out of her arms, scurrying back to his brother and sister. We gave some very gentle pats to a pair of lambs and watched a brood of bright yellow chicks peeping with all their might.

When we came to the young calves at the petting zoo, Mrs. Osborne from the dairy farm next to Honeyfield smiled wide.

"Good afternoon, m'darlings," she said. "What a fine day for a fair!"

A young female calf poked her head out between the wooden posts of the pen and sniffed at June's arm before giving it a lick, sending June into hysterical giggles. The little calf pranced off to another—possibly tastier—child on the other side of the pen. A male calf lumbered over to us and gently fit his black head through the barrier.

I couldn't help but stare at the prominent white circle in the middle of his forehead.

Kneeling down to get a better look at the calf, our eyes met. He was much bigger than when I'd seen him last but I felt our connection in my bones.

I blinked hard. "Is this calf from Fairbury?"

"Aye, 'e is. I was wondering if you'd recognize the boy," Mrs. Osborne said. "He's growin' like a weed, that one."

As I stared at the calf, my mind was a confused jumble of thoughts. June gently brushed his neck, oblivious to the tear rolling down my cheek. I swiped it away with the back of my hand and rose.

"But I don't understand. How…"

He blinked up at me from behind long eyelashes.

"Ben brought him o'er soon after he were born and told Amos to keep him as a bull and Amos said yes." She heaved a shrug. "Don't ask me why—we already have a bull. But I suppose he's gettin' up in years now. This one will be a fine bull someday."

I cleared my aching throat and smiled down at June. "I helped this calf come into the world. His mum just needed a little help."

"Is that right?" Mrs. Osborne said.

I swiped at another tear, this time on my other cheek. "Thank you for taking him. Thank Amos for me as well, if you wouldn't mind." I knelt down again and scratched behind his ear. "I'm so glad he's...that you brought him today." I leaned in closer to him and whispered, "You be a good boy now."

Mrs. Osborne peered at her watch. "The sheepdog trials are starting soon. You ought not to miss that."

I took June's hand and followed Mrs. Osborne's directions to a nearby paddock where the trials were just starting. The event drew a crowd but Mr. Seaton from the village let us stand in front of him since he could easily see over June and me.

The first participant entered the ring with a gorgeous red merle border collie, its healthy coat gleaming. The collie flew around in a circle, quickly rounding up the five sheep as its master hollered commands and gave sharp whistles.

The other competitors leaned against the fence on the opposite side of the enclosure, their dogs sitting at attention at their feet, all of them closely watching the display before them. It wasn't hard to spot Ben in the group since he was easily the tallest. Sam's head darted back and forth as the sheep ran this way and that and the ginger border collie raced by.

Ben must have felt eyes on him because he scanned the crowd and gave a little wave from across the field before turning his attention back to the event.

When Ben and Sam finally hopped the fence to take their turn, my pulse quickened. While all eyes were on Sam and the sheep, I couldn't look away from Ben as he called out commands across the meadow, his deep voice traveling easily without the need to yell.

"Come by. Look back. Lie down. Away to me."

He saved that calf for me.

All chatter around me dulled to a low drone. June still clasped my left hand but my right trembled suddenly. I flexed my fingers and gripped the wooden fence in front of me.

Obviously I knew something had changed between Ben and I recently. I wasn't entirely oblivious. We were friendly with one another and we shared books. We spent most of our day together, so it was natural we would eventually develop a rapport upon getting to know one another.

Our newfound friendship didn't explain why I often found myself thinking about him when he wasn't around, especially at night when I knew he was just on the other side of the wall.

Had there always been something between us? Something I had been trying to ignore all this time?

I was jolted from my silent panic by June giving my hand a little shake. "Are you sick?"

"Hm? What do you mean, sweetheart?"

"Your face is all red."

"Oh." I put my palm to my cheek, feeling its heat in my hand. "I'm fine, dear."

Ben leaned over and gave Sam a rub along his neck while Sam's tongue lolled out the side of his mouth. The crowd around us clapped and cheered.

I looked over my shoulder at Mr. Seaton. "Did you catch their score? I missed it."

"Ninety-two."

"Is that good?"

He chuckled. "He's likely won the thing, love, so I should say so."

"Oh, good," I said before looking back down at June. "Did you hear that? Ben and Sam did well."

The two of them returned to their previous spectating area with the other competitors. My stomach fluttered as our eyes met across the field.

The calf. That night at the lake. The dance. The quiet smiles. The lingering gazes. The way he looked at me and said my name. The way he threw himself on me to shield me during the first raid.

The way I craved his mouth on mine.

The crowd was so tight around me I couldn't breathe.

I gave June's hand a gentle tug. "Why don't we go get you something sweet to eat?"

She nodded enthusiastically and we slowly made our way out of the crowd and back to the path. With sugar so hard to come by, I wasn't sure exactly what kind of sweet treat I might be able to find for her. I just knew that if I didn't get some air, I might faint.

Since it was Sunday, Vera, June, and Dora joined us for dinner. I was grateful. I didn't know how I would possibly make conversation or even look Ben in the eye. Since Dora judged the jam contest, she came home with a jar of the winning jam and we all enjoyed it on thick slices of bread acquired at the fair's bake sale. We had what was left of Vera's ribbon-winning pie after supper. I hadn't tasted so much sweet food in months.

"And you have yet another sheepdog ribbon," Vera said, turning to her brother. "Proper job."

Ben shrugged and tossed a bit of bread crust to Sam. "I didn't even really do anything. 'E did all the work."

"Sam went so fast!" June exclaimed, her chin smeared with bright red jam.

Ben smiled at June. "Did you like watching Sam round up the sheep?"

She nodded and Ben looked my way. "Did you?"

"I didn't even know Sam could do that," I said, suddenly feeling shy. "I've seen him herd the cows a few times but nothing like that."

"I was afraid he'd be out of practice since he only gets to deal with sheep at the trials these days." Ben looked at Sam, his eyes full of admiration. "But I guess he's still got it." He turned back to Vera. "And you won the baking contest. Again."

Vera straightened and grinned smugly. "Mary Sturgess didn't stand a chance."

June slid out of her chair and sat on the floor beside Sam, tenderly petting his back. "Good dog."

I couldn't sleep. I didn't even feel tired. Our work was so exhausting, even our half days on Sundays, so I rarely had trouble sleeping. But not that night.

When I heard Ben's bedroom door creak open, my eyes went to the dim light of a torch sliding in under my door as it moved along the hallway, disappearing as I heard his feet on the stairs. Minutes later the pickup's engine rumbled in the farmyard. Peering out of my window, I watched him turn left at the end of the drive. It was far too late at night for him to be going to see Amos and there was only one other place he ever went in that direction.

I didn't even think. I grabbed my torch, slipped my shoes on, and threw myself out the door, racing after him. I could hear my heart pounding in my ears as my feet hit the road, the smooth satin of my long coral-pink nightgown sliding against my legs with every step.

When I reached the bit of road just before the lake, I planted my hands on my hips and caught my breath. I didn't need to be gasping for breath for this. I wasn't sure what *this* even was, but I knew something had to happen.

The half-moon shimmered against the lake, sending sparkles across the gentle ripples of the water where Ben took lazy strokes.

My feet crunched on the road and Ben both froze in place, staring at me in the dark. I made my way down into the meadow, neither of us speaking until I reached the little wooden dock. I slid my shoes off, placing them neatly beside his heap of clothes.

"Are you sleepwalking?"

"No."

Ben's bare shoulders bobbed in the water as he floated in place. He watched as I sat on the edge of the dock and dipped my feet into the lake. Although considerably warmer than the last time I had gone for a swim, it was still a little chilly.

"You shouldn't be here, Elsie," he said quietly. "Someone might see."

Disregarding the absurdity of anyone seeing us out here, I said, "Why would that matter?"

"Well, you're in a nightie and I'm in my boxers."

"And?"

He paused before speaking in a low, husky tone. "Someone might think there is something between us."

"Isn't there?"

I had never been so bold in my entire life. I had no idea what was giving me the fortitude to speak so plainly. Hope, perhaps.

Ben let out a long breath. "You work for me, Elsie."

"Tell me to leave then."

He didn't. Instead he swam a little closer.

"You saved Brandon. I saw him at the fair today," I said. "You saved that calf for me, didn't you?"

He nodded hesitantly before looking away.

"Why didn't you tell me?"

He snickered. "I don't like goin' round boastin' about not being able to do what other farmers manage to do all the time." He looked back at me. "I shouldn't have done it—especially not for you."

"It was kind, Ben," I said. "Thank you."

He smiled weakly and gave a little shrug.

"Do you really want me to leave?"

If he said yes, I told himself, that was that. I would leave Fairbury. The humiliation would be too much to bear.

"I know I should say yes," he said, drifting nearer still, "but I can't."

He swam close enough for me to see the droplets of water gleaming in his hair and trickling down the lines of his powerful arms. I leaned forward and braced my hands on his shoulders. Ben's hands went to my waist as I slowly slid off the edge of the dock and into the water.

Ben let go of me and I treaded water in front of him. The lake was probably still quite cold but I didn't feel a thing.

"How would it look if I fell for a land girl who works for me? The people in the village would gossip for years and Mrs. Watkins would have my head—"

"That's it?" I said. "You're bothered by a little gossip? And that Mrs. Watkins might shout at you?"

Ben flinched at this and I thought maybe I had gone too far. I just didn't understand what he was afraid of.

He ran his cool hand up my arm and over my shoulder before finally letting it rest on my flushed cheek.

He tipped his forehead against mine and closed his eyes. "What if she sends you to another farm? What if she takes you away from me?"

His whispered words sent fire through me, warming my skin, fueling and inciting the glowing embers burning low in my belly.

"I won't go," I breathed.

Ben slid his hand to the nape of my neck, dripping cool water down my back, and brought our lips together for the most gentle, soft, and tender kiss. He nuzzled his nose against mine and smiled.

"I've wanted to kiss you for so long," he murmured, his lips brushing my cheek as he spoke.

My hands skated his muscled chest and I wrapped my arms around his neck. His eyes glowed with mischief as he put an arm around my waist. Pressed together, we floated backward as one.

My mouth found his again and I caressed his still, hesitating lips, first the bottom and then the top. His chest heaved against mine as I dragged the tip of my nose up along his bearded cheek to look him in the eye. I needed him to know this was okay. This was what I wanted and it was okay that he wanted it too.

His hand went to the back of my head and brought me back to him, our lips fitting together perfectly, like two puzzle pieces that had been separated for far too long. He was gentle and sweet and delicious. I could tell he was a man who knew exactly how to kiss a woman and the thought of him with someone else sent a surge of hot jealousy through me. I deepened the kiss with furious fervour and he breathed hard against my lips, making them hum under the pressure.

I wondered what else he could do for a woman.

Ben took long and lingering tastes of my neck as I clung to him, breathing hard into his shoulder, hooking my calves around the back of his thighs while the hem of my nightgown floated further up my legs. Suddenly we stopped floating and Ben let out a little laugh, his whiskers tickling my shoulder.

"What?" I murmured. "What happened?"

My vision focused. We'd bumped into the edge of the lake and were now surrounded by reeds. Before I could say anything, he circled his hands around my waist and placed me on the edge of the bank, like I was a weightless doll on a shelf.

Ben lifted himself out of the lake, and I tried not to look at the outline of his arousal straining against the drenched fabric of his boxers. Every single inch of my skin burned, even as I sat on the cool grass. He sat beside me, intertwining our fingers and laying a gentle kiss on each of my knuckles. I pressed lazy kisses to his shoulder and then touched my nose to his neck, inhaling deep the scent of him, the lake, and the night.

"Do you want to go back to the cottage?" he said, his voice raspy and quiet.

"No. Do you?" I pressed a slow kiss to his neck and then another along his jawline.

"No, I don't," he whispered.

My pulse raced and the oxygen ran away from my lungs. I laid a third kiss on his collarbone.

"Goddamn it, Elsie," he said, taking my face in his hands and kissing me even harder and deeper than before.

I slid onto Ben's lap as he devoured my mouth, his fingers clawing at my back. I felt weak with overwhelm. His lips traced a love letter onto mine, his arms enveloping me tightly.

I pulled away to catch my breath and my hands, as if working on their own, untied the bit of ribbon from the front of my heavy, sodden nightgown. Ben's eyebrows went north, as did his hands to caress my flesh.

Under me, his hardened bulge pressed into a rather sensitive part of me and a tiny, breathy whimper escaped my lips. Ben watched my face contentedly as he rolled his hips to press into me again and I bit down on my lower lip. He broke into a giant grin at this.

"What are you—*oomph*—smiling about?" I asked as he did it again.

"I ought to remind you that you are in a soaking wet nightie, in a field, in the middle of the night, and on top of me." He laid back in the grass and chuckled, his shoulders shaking.

"And?"

His eyes were bright and playful. "It's just…unexpected, I s'pose." His smile faded. "We can stop if you want. It's alright. I don't want you to feel like you…"

He trailed off as I peeled the soaked-through nightgown away from my skin, lifted it over my head, and tossed it aside. For a moment I just watched him take me in, his eyes grazing every bare inch of flesh on display before him.

"For my entire life, I've been told how to act, how to walk, how to speak, when to speak, whom to speak to. How to be a refined young lady." I sighed. "Being here with you makes me feel…free."

"Free?"

"Free." I nodded. "I'm going to use that freedom to tell you…" I lowered myself onto his chest and slowly kissed from his clavicle and up to his earlobe. "...that I don't want you to stop."

eighteen

BEN

I squinted hard as the rays of the early morning sun crested over the edge of a cloud, waking me from my deep sleep in the meadow.

I know it was a deep sleep because I *should* have been woken up by the tiny blonde freight train snoring away beside me. I'd heard her snoring from her bedroom many times before, but with Elsie tucked under my arm the volume of her snores was startlingly impressive.

The sweet smell of her disheveled hair filled my nostrils, and I smiled to myself as I thought about the night before.

I had taken my time, caressing and tasting, exploring her while her fingers raked my hair and her thigh muscles spasmed. It was her first time so I was as gentle as I could be. I made sure she was not just comfortable but enjoying herself too.

I'd never made love under the stars before. I don't think I glanced up to admire them even once—I couldn't look away from Elsie as she bit her full bottom lip, whimpered, and writhed.

I felt myself hardening as I recalled the sublime sensation of being inside her, watching her ease herself up and down and listening to her quiet moans and little gasps.

As perfect as the night before was, it was nothing compared to watching the waking sun break through a scattering of blue and grey clouds while Elsie slept tight up against me. I could have stayed like that forever.

Elsie's snoring suddenly stopped and she slowly sat up with a yawn. I eagerly gave my cramped arm a stretch as she smiled sweetly at me.

"Good morning," she said, her eyelids heavy.

She was even beautiful drowning in my plaid shirt. Her nightie was probably still soaked from our swim the night before.

"Good morning," I said, propping myself up on my elbows.

I reached for her to kiss her but she shied away.

"What's wrong?" I dropped my hand, my stomach going cold.

She hesitated. "I have morning breath."

I grimaced. "Oh. Well. In that case." I grabbed her around the waist and pinned her into the grass under me, kissing her on both cheeks, her neck, and then on her lips as she giggled and shrieked playfully.

"You have morning breath, too," she exclaimed, trying to dodge my pecks.

Elsie put her palm on my cheek, running the pad of her thumb over my bearded jaw. A small smile appeared on her lips as she looked up at me.

I was very close to telling her I loved her. I had never told a woman that before.

"Is there a chance your alarm clock is going off in your bedroom?"

I winced and rolled off of her. "Yes."

Elsie sat up. "Apologies but I'm not giving you your shirt back straight away."

I looked at her bare knees poking out from under my shirt. "Do you even have knickers on?"

"Yes, but they're wet."

I smirked wickedly.

"From swimming in the lake," she clarified loudly. She hastily turned to me. "It's Monday."

"'Tis."

"Isn't that chap from the War Ag coming first thing?"

"Oh, bloody bollocks."

We collected our things in a mad rush and got into the pickup, Elsie sitting low in her seat to avoid detection—from who or what, I wasn't sure. One of the cows? Maybe she thought Sheila might happen to look out her bedroom window. Once parked, Elsie scampered inside and I waited a few minutes before getting out.

"Are you just getting home? At this hour?"

I whipped around to see Vera frowning at me from atop her bicycle.

"Christ, woman," I said, hand on my chest. "You scared me half to death."

"I thought you stopped seeing Pauline," she said, swinging her leg over her bike and walking it to the toolshed where she kept it during the day.

"I did," I said. "I was just over at Amos' for an early morning chat."

"You've got a stick in your hair, a grass stain on your arm, and you're missing your shirt. What, did you get into a fight with him?"

I grunted. "Why are you here so early anyway?"

"Thought I might get an early start since it's inspection day. You didn't forget, did you?"

"No."

"Sure you didn't." She nodded at the cottage. "Get inside. I'll make y'a brew."

If I found Elsie distracting before, it was nothing compared to that morning as we milked the cows. To make matters worse, we were trying to be quick about it so we'd be good and ready for Glenn Watkins' arrival.

As Elsie bid me good morning and pretended she hadn't woken up beside me earlier, a small grin tugged at the corner of her mouth and she let her pinky finger graze against my palm on her way to get her milk pail and stool. Even that tiny touch was enough to transport me back to the night before.

I perched on my stool and tried to focus on milking. Elsie placed her stool beside me and went to work. I wondered if she'd noticed her arms had filled out a bit from months of working on the farm.

My eyes traveled down her forearms to her hands. I wanted to grab one of those hands and pull her into the storage room, push her up against the wall, hoist her legs up around me and—

"Oy, your pail is close to overflowing," Sheila warned, breaking my trance like a pin popping a balloon.

Elsie smothered a giggle by puckering her lips tight together. God, I wanted to kiss those lips again.

Clearing my throat I smiled weakly up at Sheila. "Thanks." I looked up at Dottie. Even she was judging me and knew my mind was still elsewhere—back in a lakeside meadow specifically.

Carefully pouring my full pail into the canister, I tried desperately to think of an errand I could send Sheila on to get her out of the barn for ten minutes. Five minutes. Two minutes even!

Stop it. You're obsessed. Concentrate. You have a job to do.

The job was always important—a lot of people depended on me. But it was more important than ever to focus on getting things right that day. I'd had a few War Ag inspections before, but the first one had caused a rift between me and Mum. Glenn had told me to dig up Mum's beloved lily garden, the namesake for the road I'd lived on my whole life, and I never said a word in protest. She wouldn't speak to me for a month after I dug up her flower beds and Vera and I turned them into a vegetable garden. But I couldn't exactly go against the War Ag's orders. That's how farmers across Britain got in trouble. It was my patriotic duty to grow vegetables and do as I was told, no questions asked.

Then why did I feel so guilty about that bloody garden?

Glenn Watkins arrived right on time, driving his spotless Lagonda into the farmyard, crawling along slowly so as not to kick up too much dust onto the tires I imagine. He gave Vera a wave as he spotted her working in the very vegetable patch he'd ordered me to create. Vera gave him a polite nod and then scowled when he looked away.

"Good morning, old chap," Glenn said, throwing his open hand into mine and gripping it firmly like we were chums. "Good to see you. How's the place holding up?"

Startled by his friendly demeanor, I stumbled. "Fine. Good. Fine and good."

"That's great to hear. Let's have a look around, shall we?" He fetched a clipboard and pen from his car. "I see you've kept up the veg patch by the front wall there. Very good. Much more useful than flowers in a time of war."

My jaw clenched. "Right."

As I followed him and his stupid little clipboard around the farm as he checked boxes and made notes, I thought about the rumor I'd heard; Glenn was fit as a fiddle until it came time to enlist and then he suddenly had a rare heart condition that nobody in the village knew anything about. He had since been known as a slimy coward, using his familial connections to get out of serving in the Army.

But I suppose checking boxes on a form was one way of helping with the war effort.

I followed him into the barn. The herd had already been relocated to the pasture for the day so Sheila was cleaning the stalls.

"Ah, you must be one of Mr. Grainger's land girls," Glenn said, nodding jovially at Sheila.

"Yes," I said. "This is Sheila. She's a very hard worker."

"Nice to meet you, Mr. Watkins," she said, wiping the perspiration from her forehead with the back of her wrist.

"How are you enjoying life at Honeyfield?"

"It's tough but I really like it," she said. "I especially like caring for the cattle."

"When the Germans flew over, they shot at the cows in the pasture," I explained to Glenn. "None of them were hit, thankfully, but one of our calves was injured. She saved its life."

She smiled proudly.

"And what about life outside London?" Glenn asked. "Do you like it here?"

"I could definitely see myself staying in Somerset after the war. Maybe in Bath."

I raised my eyebrows at her but didn't question her reply. I suppose I'd assumed she'd be anxious to get back to London as soon as possible.

If Sheila felt that way, was it possible Elsie did too?

"Where is your other land girl?" Glenn asked. "Miss Foster-Quinn?"

"She's out doing the milk delivery," Sheila said before I could. "She'll be back around lunchtime."

"Oh, that's right. I've seen her out and about in the mornings." He tapped his pen on his clipboard and continued on to his next stop.

We strolled around the field where the herd grazed and Glenn gave each cow and calf a quick once over and asked a few questions. Had I found it a challenge to keep them fed with healthy food? Was I meeting my milk quotas every day? Had I received any complaints about the milk from my cows from customers? Had any of the cows suffered any illnesses?

He seemed satisfied with all my answers, nodding and making a few notes on his clipboard as I spoke. I forced myself not to snicker at him—what did he know about cows or farming? Nothing.

"There was some concern about your transition from sheep farmer to dairy farmer when the war began," he said, lowering his clipboard and setting his shoulders back. "But you've done quite well here and the War Ag appreciates your hard work. We may revisit turning your pastures into crops in the future but it's hard to say for certain right now since there is likely to be a shortage of animal feed soon. But we'll deal with that a little later on, shall we?"

He offered his hand again and I shook it.

"Thank you, Mr. Watkins. I appreciate that."

He scribbled something on his clipboard and we began the walk back to the farmyard. "I'll put in a good word for you and you can put in a good word for me. How does that sound?"

I tilted my head slightly. "Hm?"

Glenn tapped his pen against his clipboard again. "My aunt speaks very highly of Miss Foster-Quinn and I thought I might get to know her a little better. She is certainly pretty as a picture."

My whole body clenched. "I suppose she is."

"So, will you?"

"Will I what?"

"Put in a good word for me with her?" He smiled sincerely.

"Well, I don't..." I cleared my throat. "I don't like to get involved with the personal lives of my, um, workers."

He frowned. "I suppose that's only appropriate. Very well." He took one last look around us before clipping his pen to the clipboard. "Good day, Mr. Grainger."

"Good day." I nodded and he headed back to his car.

His car slowed on the road as he met Elsie and Sherlock returning from the milk delivery. I puttered around the farmyard so I could watch the two of them. He got out of his car to speak to her and she hopped down from the cart. Of course Sherlock liked his routine and kept trotting along, leaving Elsie on the road. The two of them spoke for a few minutes before he got into his car and Elsie returned to the farm on foot.

I was unhitching Sherlock from the cart when Elsie sneaked up behind me and planted a kiss on my cheek. I quickly glanced around to make sure we were alone. Not even Sherlock was paying attention to us.

"Hi," I said.

"Hi." She hooked her thumbs into the pockets of her trousers, leaning closer to me. God, she was so cute.

"What did Mr. Watkins want to discuss with you?" I nodded in the direction of the road.

"He just asked me about working here and how you treated us, that sort of thing. He seemed in good spirits so I take it the inspection went well." She brushed Sherlock's mane.

"It did," I said. "He didn't ask you anything else?"

"Well, yes, he did but it doesn't matter."

I raised an eyebrow at her.

"He asked me if I would like to have dinner and go horseback riding with him." She rolled her eyes and broke eye contact with me.

"And what did you say?"

She laughed. "I said no, thank you, obviously. I said I fancy someone else." She smiled coyly.

Palming her cheek, I pressed my lips to hers. My stomach warmed as she nuzzled her nose against mine.

I gestured to Sherlock. "You can take 'im riding if that's something you enjoy."

The aged workhorse snorted and whipped me in the shoulder with his tail.

I looked at him. "That's rude."

Sheila emerged from the barn, wiping her dusty hands on her trousers, and I swiftly took a step away from Elsie. Elsie narrowed her eyes.

"Do you want me and Elsie to work on hay bailing?" Sheila asked, her cheeks already red from working in the heat.

"Aye," I said. "Go get yourself a drink of something cold first. Can't have you two getting heatstroke."

Sheila nodded and disappeared into the cottage and Elsie crossed her arms over her chest and waited for me to explain.

"I think we need to keep this quiet for now," I said in a hushed tone.

"Why? We're both adults."

"Rosetta could have you transferred to another farm—"

"Why would she do that? This doesn't affect my work—"

"Because she doesn't like me and would not want you to have anything to do with me."

Elsie scowled. "You make her sound like a meddlesome witch."

"Not meddlesome, just self-important," I corrected.

"What about Vera and Sheila?" She put her hands on her hips. "They're going to find out soon enough—"

"Fairbury is terrible when it comes to gossip. If someone knows something, it always gets out. And I'm not ready for…" I stumbled, "…*this* to get out yet."

She exhaled loudly and stormed off towards the cottage. "Fine."

I leaned the back of my head against the cart. This was already exhausting. "Damn it."

That evening the three of us finished milking the cows and were just sterilizing the pails and milking machine for the following morning.

Elsie hadn't spoken to me all afternoon, specifically avoiding my longing gazes and turning her nose up whenever I smiled at her. It was childish, I suppose, but maybe I deserved it.

Sheila squeezed the bridge of her nose and winced.

"Are you alright?" Elsie asked.

"Just a headache," she said. "It's nothing. Probably just the heat."

Elsie threw me a meaningful look.

"Why don't you call it a night? Elsie and I can finish up here," I said.

"Are you sure?" Sheila asked, a tinge of hope in her tone.

Elsie nodded. "We're just about done anyway."

As soon as Sheila left the barn Elsie turned to me, her eyes full of fury. She was ready for a fight while I was just happy to have two minutes of alone time with her.

"Rosetta is *not* self-important and neither am I," she spat.

I blinked at her. "I never said you were."

"You probably thought I was self-important when I first came here. Right?"

I hesitated *just* long enough to make her angrier.

She groaned and scrubbed harder at her milk pail. I thought she might put her hand through it.

"And you hated me," I reminded her. "You probably thought I was simple. Just a dumb country peasant."

Elsie peered at me, the intensity of her scrubbing easing. "You're not having regrets, are you?"

"No, of course not."

We were both quiet for a while.

"I won't tell Sheila," she said quietly. "And I'm not anxious to tell Vera. I don't know what I would tell her anyway." She put the milk pail upside down on a towel to dry overnight, putting on a faux-casual voice. "Good morning, Vera. Did you know I fancy your brother quite a lot? We got to know each other exceptionally well in a meadow recently and I think I'd like to do it again." She glanced at me and then looked away.

I lifted my brows. "Oh?"

Elsie crossed her arms again and tilted her chin up, adopting her snooty expression and avoiding my gaze. "Well, yes. Not in a meadow, specifically. I suppose I wouldn't mind if you're amenable to it."

I grinned as I dried my hands on a towel. "Amenable to it?" I moved closer to her until she was forced to look me in the eyes. "Yes,

I suppose I'd be amenable to that."

The irritation still lingered in the stiffness of her jaw but the heaving of her chest and the intensity of her stare hinted at something else. Elsie grabbed a fistful of my shirt, yanked my face down to her level, and pressed her lips to mine. She slung her arms around my neck, and I kissed her back with just as much ardor, wrapping one arm around her waist and pinning her against the wall of the cramped storage room as our yearning mouths fought to claim just one more taste. I dropped gentle kisses along her jaw before slowing down to savor the softness of her neck against my lips. I slipped my free hand up under her shirt, squeezing one of her perfect round breasts and running my thumb over her nipple. She let out a soft, low breath in response.

"Oh, yes." She bit the corner of her lip and closed her eyes. "I think I'd be extremely amenable to that."

nineteen

Elsie

"Would you consider coming to London with me this weekend?"

Ben's lips froze in place on my bare shoulder. In the dim, flickering candlelight of his bedroom I couldn't fully see his expression, but I could certainly feel the sudden tension between us.

He slowly turned to me, his nose bumping into my cheek. "Uh…I can't."

"Why not?"

It had been a month since Ben and I began our covert relationship. I spent most nights in his bedroom now, becoming an expert at stifling my moans by pressing my mouth against Ben's skin or into a blanket. I was confident Sheila still had no idea Ben and I were sleeping together, and we planned to keep it that way, at least for the time being.

It wasn't just making love though. Sometimes we just talked, whispering late into the night. I told him about my brother's capture by the Italians in North Africa the year before, and he shared his worries about his younger brother serving in the Army. He told me about his late father and the responsibilities that came with taking over the farm. I explained the many expectations my parents had of my brother

Jack and how he was considered peculiar for becoming a teacher and marrying someone outside our social circle.

Sometimes we just read our books together in bed, occasionally stopping to read especially inventive lines to one another.

We'd even told each other embarrassing facts about ourselves.

"So, you've *never* cooked a meal on your own?" Ben sat up, his eyes wide.

I shook my head. "I haven't. I didn't even consider it an issue until I came here. I realize now how ridiculous that is, but I've just always had somehow to cook for me. Thank goodness for your sister or I'd starve to death."

He stared at me. "It's like you're from another planet." Then he slapped a hand over his mouth and tried to push his laughter down.

Then I hit him in the head with a pillow.

I loved waking up beside Ben. If I woke up before him, sometimes I just watched him sleep as dawn's earliest rays crept in around the blackout curtain. I found myself watching his chest rise and fall, and I wondered how I could ever care for another person as much as I did for him.

To be honest, it terrified me.

"We've been together for a month and I want to show you off to my parents at their anniversary party," I said. "I can show you my favorite places in London."

"You don't think Vera and Sheila will become suspicious if we *both* go somewhere for two days?"

"So what if they figure it out? It wouldn't be so terrible if they found out, would it?" I slid out of his lap. "They wouldn't tell Rosetta. It's not like they're friends."

"It would get out, trust me." Ben frowned. "We both know your parents would not approve of me."

I couldn't argue with that. I had already told him about the various men my parents had introduced me to over the years, hoping I would become a baroness or a viscountess, or the wife of an MP, or the wife of the oldest son in line to a great inheritance. That last one was especially risky, in my opinion, given how Diana Mitford's marriage to

Bryan Guinness turned out.

The gentlemen my parents introduced me to were all frightfully dull. None of them enjoyed novels and they were strangers to concepts like charm and wit.

"But if they had a chance to get to know you, they would adore you." I snuggled into him and rested my chin on his shoulder.

He leaned his cheek on my forehead. "I can't leave the farm at a moment's notice. You being away for two days is going to be hard enough."

"But you hired those schoolboys for the summer."

"Another reason I can't leave right now," he said with a chuckle. "I'd come back and find the whole farm up in flames."

I nodded and scooted off the end of the bed.

Ben sat up. "Wait, where are you going?"

"I'm going back to my room," I announced. "Good night."

"Elsie, don't—"

I shut the door behind me and grumpily flopped into my own bed. The little room felt like a stranger to me now, unfamiliar and uninviting. I was simply too annoyed with Ben's desire for secrecy to spend another moment in the same bed with him.

The outside world changed from green to grey as the crowded train left Somerset and entered London, pulling into the station shortly after eleven. The uniformed chap I sat with got my suitcase down for me.

"Thank you," I said. "Are you on leave?"

"Only for the weekend," he said in a cockney accent, rolling his eyes. "And half that time's been spent on the bleedin' train tryin' to get here."

I smiled apologetically as if *I* was personally responsible for train delays and cancellations.

"That's dreadful," I said. "Well, you're here now. I hope you have a lovely time."

He beamed. "I'm surprisin' my girl for her birthday. At least I made it in time for that."

"Jolly good," I exclaimed. "I'm sure she'll be so happy."

His pleased-as-punch expression stung through no fault of his own. I pictured him popping out from behind a door and his girlfriend crying tears of happiness, all their friends and family applauding their joyous reunion. I wanted to show *my* boyfriend off to *my* family too. I wanted Ben to be able to put his arm around me in public. I wanted to be able to talk to Sheila about the giddiness and glow that comes with a new relationship. I wanted that. I hated being Ben's dirty little secret.

His certainty that sharing the news of our romance would cause trouble was ridiculous.

I hadn't spoken to him in private for two days, ever since he had declined my invitation to join me in London to attend my parents' anniversary party. I wasn't angry with him, exactly, just conflicted about a lot of things.

The life of a farmer's secret lover was surprisingly stressful.

Gripping the handle of my suitcase tight, I wove between the crowds in the station, making a beeline for the taxi queue. As I slid into the black hackney and gave the driver my address, I waited for the feeling of contentment to wash over me. I was home. I was home in *my* city.

But the feeling never came.

I of course knew every building and every street between the train station and North London, although many remained pockmarked by bombs and shrapnel. Monuments were still wrapped in protective coverings. Sandbags still lined the sidewalks, braced against street corners, and ready for the next aerial bombardment. Even as we reached the St John's Wood street where I was born and raised, my surroundings felt strangely unwelcoming. Every topiary was impeccably shaped—not a leaf out of place. Every home on that street included a wrought iron gate in front of a high Georgian-style façade, perfect for keeping the riffraff out and the superiors in.

The driver pulled up to my parents' home and told me what I owed him.

I just stared out the window as I considered asking him to take me back to the train station.

The driver quietly cleared his throat. "We're here, love."

"Sorry," I said, fetching a few quid from my bag. "I must have fallen asleep."

We both knew I was lying but he thankfully didn't call me out on it.

I swallowed and got out of the cab, gripping the handle of my suitcase even tighter than before, as my mouth went dry and tacky. I heard the hackney pull away, leaving me alone on the pavement in front of the chalk-white fortress I grew up in.

I swallowed. Taking a deep breath and exhaling slowly, I tried to calm the tumult in my stomach and the quivering of my hands.

I can have a bath without having to boil water, I reminded myself. The food will be more varied and prepared by our cook. I won't have to use an outdoor privy.

My feet dragged me through the gate and up to the front door. George, our family's butler, let me in and offered to take my suitcase up to my bedroom.

"Thank you, George," I said. "I hope you're well."

I almost missed it but his eyes widened in alarm for a millisecond. "I'm well, Miss Foster-Quinn. Thank you."

Mother appeared and wrapped her arms around me. "Oh, my darling girl, you're here!"

"Hello, Mum!" I kissed her cheek and squeezed her back.

She backed up from me to take in all of me, her smile fading slightly. "My goodness, you're so tanned. And your arms are…different."

I self-consciously brushed my right upper arm with my left palm. I knew my arms had become fuller and more muscled but I didn't expect it would be noticeable.

"Farm work will do that," I muttered.

"Are you sure you can't stay for longer than the weekend?" Mother clasped my hands. "Even just a week?"

"I'm lucky I got the weekend off as it is," I said. "There is a lot of work—"

"This is the first time you've been home in six months. I have half a mind to call Rosetta and put in a complaint about that farmer you work for," Mother scoffed, dropping my hands so she could gesticulate. "He's making you work far too hard. He probably lazes about while you do all the work—"

"Absolutely not," I retorted quickly.

Her eyebrows went up.

"What I mean is Mr. Grainger has been a good boss. He treats us very well."

It felt strange to call him "Mr. Grainger" again but I knew Mother would need to sit down if I suddenly called him by his Christian name.

"Alright, alright." She waved a dismissive hand. "Well, we don't have to say another word about the farm this weekend. You're here and that's what matters."

I nodded, suddenly feeling even more unsure about this visit. "Of course."

What would be so wrong with talking about the farm?

My mother and I shared a love of event planning; Mother knew exactly how much sparkle to bring to an event, no matter the time of year or if there was a war on or not. That evening's anniversary party was no exception. I floated around the floor, champagne flute in hand, as guests filtered in, saying my hellos as necessary.

"You smell like a barn."

I whipped around to see Jack, my older half brother, grinning.

His pretty wife Nora playfully pinched his arm.

"Ow!" Jack laughed, leaning away.

Nora rolled her eyes. "He's teasing, love. You smell like Chanel No. 5."

I hadn't always adored my sister-in-law. I was certain someone from outside our social circle and who owned her own sewing business wouldn't be a good fit for my beloved older brother.

The warmth in their eyes as they gazed at one another told me everything I needed to know. They were a perfect match.

"This is very chic. Well done, you," I said, gesturing to Nora's soft brown cocktail dress with fashionable square shoulders and knee-length hem. It was dotted with round gold circles and the waist was nipped in with the use of a gold belt. She sparkled under the chandeliers. With her strawberry blonde hair in a French chignon, she was easily the most glamorous person in the room.

Nora had an exceptional gift for turning unloved, frumpy frocks into stylish creations, and she had quickly become sought-after for her abilities, especially when ladies wanted to update a dress they already owned and didn't want to spend their precious clothing ration coupons on something new.

In the span of a year I had gone from thinking we were too good for her to thinking perhaps she was too good and *far* too talented for all of us combined.

I had chosen a simple black frock with frills around the neckline. I had worn it the year before to a friend's party—I still wasn't used to wearing the same dress to more than one social engagement. However, as we were all reminded over and over again: there was a war on. As if anyone of us could ever escape it.

"I thought you might wear your WLA uniform tonight," Jack said. "The idea of you wearing wellies is hilarious."

"Mock me all you want." I narrowed my eyes at him. "You wouldn't last one week on the farm."

He laughed aloud. "You're right about that."

Nora gave him a soft elbow in the ribs. "Stop picking on your sister. Elsie is doing important work and we owe her the same level of respect we owe everyone else sacrificing to help Britain win the war."

I put a hand to my heart. "Thank you, Nora."

"You're right. I'm being a git. I apologize," he said. "I can't imagine how difficult this year has been for you. You'll have to tell us all about it at dinner."

I caught them up over a delicious meal as the champagne and cocktails continued to freely flow.

"Apologies. I must not have heard you correctly," Jack said, interrupting and lowering his voice to a whisper. "Did you just say you had your arm *inside* of a cow?"

"So the lot of you had just been shot at by a Nazi plane," Nora clarified a few minutes later, "and the first thing you do is jump in the pickup and race *towards* Bath while it's on fire?"

Jack's eyes widened. "And then you went back the following night as well?"

"That is correct, yes," I said.

Nora and Jack exchanged astounded looks before staring back at me.

"You would have done the same thing in my place," I insisted. "We helped a lot of people that night. The attack was so unexpected. Everyone was so unprepared."

"We saw photos in the paper," Nora said. "It looked bloody awful."

Nora was no stranger to the devastation of Nazi aerial attacks, having previously lost both her workplace and her flat in two separate bombing raids.

Jack smiled wide, his eyes glassy. He stood up suddenly, champagne flute in hand.

"What are you doing?" I whispered.

Nora sighed up at him. "Those drinks must be stronger than I thought."

"We are here tonight to celebrate the anniversary of my beloved parents," Jack announced glass in hand. "Frankly, I don't know how many years they've been married—eighty-seven or so, I believe."

The guests laughed graciously. I winced, embarrassed *for* him.

"But I think we ought to honor the achievements of someone else who is here tonight." He winked at me before continuing. "My sister Elsie is home from Somerset this weekend where she has been serving in the Women's Land Army."

I forced a polite smile and fought the urge to slide down in my seat.

"I just learned," he continued, "that Elsie rushed into Bath right after both bombing raids to help survivors get to safety." He raised his flute of champagne. "For her courage and her hard work helping with the war effort. To Elsie."

"To Elsie," many repeated.

"Here, here!" others replied.

After their applause faded, I said loudly, "I did not put him up to that, just so you all know."

Jack took his seat again, still smirking like a fool.

I tilted my head at him. "Do you feel less guilty for teasing me about wearing wellies now, darling brother?"

He considered only briefly. "Slightly, yes."

Once dinner was over, the band played and couples danced and friends mingled. While Jack spun Nora on the dance floor, I missed Percy. He was usually my date for these events. He was a terrific dancer and always made me laugh. The two letters I had received from Percy recently were intentionally vague, mostly saying nothing of substance in a full page of elegant handwriting.

Father approached me, tumbler in hand, and stood beside me at the wall.

"Having a nice time at your anniversary party?"

He sent me a meaningful look before lifting his whisky to his lips. He hated social events but knew they made my mother happy. Father also knew it was important for his business to socialize with anyone and everyone of means.

"I didn't know about your Bath rescue missions," he said. "You could have been killed."

Despite his usual monotone speaking style, he managed to sound half admonishment, half amazement.

"We were very careful, I promise."

He cast his eyes out to the floor where couples swayed along to the upbeat jazz music.

"Your mother and I discussed it before dinner and we think it would be best if you didn't go back to that farm."

My gaze shot up to him. "What?"

"You should be closer to home," he said, "and that type of work isn't for a girl like you."

"What do you mean a 'girl like me'?"

"Don't be coy."

"But I have been doing the work and doing it well," I reminded him. "So, I suppose that must mean I *am* suited for that type of work."

"I thought you would be pleased you had our blessing to quit." He glowered down at me. "You enjoy working in the muck in the hot sun all day? You enjoy the smell of manure, do you?"

"There is more to it than that," I said.

"Oh? What could possibly be enjoyable for you on a farm?" The deep crease that lived between his brows deepened further.

Ben's shy smile flashed in my mind, followed by the memory of my fingers gripping his sinewed shoulders as he hovered over me.

"I like the fresh air," I said nonchalantly as heat rose in my neck. "I like working with the cows. The village is lovely." I straightened my shoulders. "I like knowing that what I do matters. People depend on us."

He narrowed his eyes slightly, thinking. Finally he waved a dismissive hand and shook his head at me. "Very well. You get to tell your mother you're not staying though."

After he wandered away to talk to someone else, Nora appeared at my side, handing me a glass of white wine. Her cheeks had begun to have the same pink shine as Jack's but I wasn't sure if hers was from dancing or drink. Perhaps both.

I lifted the glass to my lips.

"So, tell me about Ben."

I almost sprayed my mouthful of wine back in her face.

I managed to swallow the gulp and stared at her. "Pardon?"

Nora erupted with laughter. I impatiently waited for her to finish laughing so she could explain the question.

"Well, you see, while you were describing all the things you have done in the last six months, you told us about living with Mr. Grainger and Shirley—"

"Sheila."

"—and spending time with Viola—"

"Vera."

"—and little Judith—"

"June."

"—and then you suddenly began calling Mr. Grainger 'Ben' and every time you mentioned him, your face glowed." She arched an eyebrow and grinned smugly.

I took another large gulp of wine as my cheeks burned.

"I have no idea what you're talking about," I said. "Ben and I are just friends."

"Jolly good," she replied swiftly. "When did the two of you first kiss?"

"Last month." I cringed hard after the words escaped my lips.

"Right," she said, unsurprised. "If it makes you feel any better, I don't think your brother noticed the lovesick look on your face when you mentioned Ben. Men never notice these things." She still looked far too amused about this situation.

"It isn't funny," I whined in a whisper, my speech speeding up. "I don't know what to do. He's worried that the local WLA rep will punish him for having a relationship with a land girl and I'm worried because he's a farmer. I'm Elsie Foster-Quinn. I'm supposed to marry a rich American or a noble or something, not a farmer."

Nora's eyes softened as she looked across the room to Jack who was chatting with our dreadfully dull uncle. "You can't help who you fall in love with."

I smiled weakly.

Her expression turned playful again. "Jack would kill me for suggesting such a thing to you, but would a casual little summer fling with a handsome farmer be so bad?"

"I think I love him," I blurted before biting my lip, my eyes widening at the realization. "Oh, God. Oh, God, what is happening to me? I thought this was supposed to be a good feeling. I just feel like I'm going to be sick."

I handed her my wine glass so I could put both palms on my middle and take deep breaths. Had the floor always been a little wobbly? And why was it so hot in here?

Nora caressed my back as she watched me panicking. "Oh, darling. You're in trouble."

twenty

BEN

It had been less than twenty-four hours since Elsie left for London and I already missed her so much. Her voice, her smile, her wit, her dimples, her laugh, her mischievous green eyes, her lips—

"Hello? Are you alright, mate?" Amos, bringing me back to reality, frowned at me from across the table at our usual booth at the pub.

I gave my head a shake. "Sorry. I must be tired. What were you saying?"

He rolled his eyes and sat back in his seat. "My cousin, John?"

I nodded.

"'Ere, he was tellin' me one of his neighbors just—" he lowered his voice "— lost his herd to foot and mouth."

I sat up straight. Half the other pub patrons were farm owners, laborers, or had someone in their family who depended on farming for their livelihood. Spreading the word around Fairbury that foot and mouth was in Somerset could cause panic.

"Foot and mouth?" I whispered. "Is he sure?"

Amos nodded solemnly. "Aye. Damn nasty, catching stuff." He gestured to me. "I haven't heard of any other cases but you best make sure everyone who goes near your cows is careful."

"Right. I will." I sat back, thinking frantically. "How's 'e gonna manage?"

"He'll get some kind of insurance for the herd but it's a loss." Amos reached for his glass, shaking his head. "Damn shame. First war, then the raids, now this."

I'd never dealt with foot and mouth before—not with cows and not when we raised sheep. I certainly knew farmers who had though. Twelve Wedmore farmers lost their herds to the blight four years before. All a farmer could do was start over and hope for the best. We were in the middle of a war—no one could afford to start over now.

"Thank you for the warning," I said. "Hopefully it's only that one farm."

We both knew that was rarely the case but neither of us dared utter the cursed words.

When my alarm went off the next morning, I instinctively reached for Elsie beside me. All I found was the empty spot where she usually slept and a pillow that still smelled like her posh shampoo.

To make up for Elsie's visit to London, one of the schoolboys I hired on for the summer came in early to help with the milking. The kid, Morris, had only milked a cow for the first time that morning so he was a little slower than Elsie would have been.

When I finished pouring my last milk pail into the canister I cleared my throat and crossed my arms over my chest. "Have either of you visited any other farms in the past two weeks or walked through any farmland?"

Sheila and Morris exchanged curious glances. Sheila shook her head.

Morris hesitated. "I don't think so."

"If you're walking anywhere, make sure you absolutely do not take any shortcuts through farmland," I said. "I'm serious. This is important."

Sheila frowned at me. "Did something happen?"

"Everything is fine," I insisted. "Just…don't cut through any pastures." I paused. "And don't visit any other farms."

Sheila narrowed her eyes at me, then at Morris, and then looked back at me.

I sighed. "Morris, why don't you go inside and get Vera to make you some tea?"

"Oh, no, thank you. I'm fine." He beamed.

I threw him a glare and he practically ran out of the barn.

Sheila stood up and planted her hands on her hips, waiting for me to speak.

"Did you and Elsie learn about foot and mouth disease during your training?"

She shook her head again.

"Well, basically it's one of the worst ways a farmer can lose an entire herd of animals—cows, sheep, pigs, goats," I said. "It's contagious as anything—spreads between animals in a herd and then spreads between farms. To keep it from spreading, a farmer's whole herd is destroyed."

Sheila's eyes grew wide. "What does it do to the animals?"

"They get painful sores in their mouths, on their teats, and around their feet. Sometimes they'll be tired like they don't want to move. If the animal manages to survive, they're sometimes useless after." I shook my head. "It's terrible."

"Is it in Fairbury?"

"Not that we know of," I said. "A few villages away. We need to start checking the cows every time we milk them—check their udders, check their mouths, everything."

"What did you mean about cutting through pastures?"

I nodded at her feet. "It can spread between farms on your shoes."

She peered at her feet and then back up at me. "Does anyone else in Fairbury know? Should we warn the other farmers?" Sheila looked ready to run out and spread the news that very second.

"I don't want to be the cause of a panic, especially if it was stopped by that one herd," I said. "Amos is the one who told me. I'll talk to him. If he thinks more people need to know about it, we'll deal with it then."

Sheila nodded, avoiding my gaze, her jaw stiff. "Alright."

I hoped I hadn't made a mistake by telling her.

We were both quiet as we ate breakfast. When Sheila left to deliver the milk, I sent Morris back out to the barn to scrub the milk pails and milking machines and clean the stalls. I looked up at Vera as she stared into the middle distance over the table, her eyes glazed over and rimmed by dark shadows.

"You alright?"

"Yes, I'm fine. Why?" Vera dusted some flour from her sleeve cuff.

"You look…tired."

She glowered. "Yes, well, I *am* tired. I'm here all day *and* I have a young child *and* an elderly parent at home. Of *course* I'm tired." She lifted her tea to her lips. "Good grief."

"Sorry," I mumbled before quickly changing the subject. "Have you heard anything about a case of foot and mouth disease?"

Vera's eyes snapped open. "In Fairbury?"

I filled her in on what I knew.

She closed her eyes and massaged her forehead with her thumb and index finger. "Just what we need right now."

On Monday, just after lunch, Sheila returned to Honeyfield after the milk delivery. I'd been in the barn, checking the feet, mouths, and udders of every cow for the hundredth time when I heard Sherlock's heavy hooves in the farmyard. I was surprised to see Elsie climbing down from the cart, suitcase in hand, her frame hugged by a navy blue dress with a red sash and a matching red felt hat.

"Look who I found walking down Lily Road," Sheila said, unhitching Sherlock.

"Welcome back," I said.

Inside my heart was racing.

"Thank you." She smiled shyly at me. "It's good to be back."

I smiled wide. I couldn't help it. I didn't even care if Sheila saw.

Part of me feared Elsie might just not come back at all, but here she was. I desperately wanted to hold her and kiss her until she couldn't breathe.

Instead she took her suitcase inside, fetched a quick bite to eat, and the three of us went to work in the upper pasture for the afternoon. Elsie likely caught me gazing at her every five minutes.

She was back after only a couple days and suddenly I was a lovelorn, pathetic sap of a man.

It was around four o'clock and my shirt was drenched in sweat as the July heat pounded down on us.

"Alright, that's enough for today," I announced. "Not worth any of us getting sick from working in this heat." I lowered my voice so only Elsie nearby could hear. "Plus, I'm taking my girl to the cinema tonight and I want good seats."

The elated little squeak that came out of Elsie made me laugh and I bit down on my lower lip to stifle it.

We got the cows back in the barn for the evening milking and I, once again, explained the threat of foot and mouth disease and what we needed to look out for.

"That's terrible," she said. "Can we not warn other farmers in the area so they know to be careful?"

Sheila threw me a knowing look since she had suggested the same thing.

"Not yet," I said. "I don't want me or Amos to be seen as gossiping troublemakers just spreading rumors. That farmer might not want everyone in Somerset knowing he lost all his cows."

"But we could potentially save the lives of cattle and the livelihoods of families in the area," Elsie added. "Isn't that worth it?"

I frowned. When she put it like that, it made my excuse sound pretty weak.

"I'll talk to Amos about it." I nodded stiffly. "Hopefully it turns out to be just that one case and doesn't get any closer."

Although Bath still wore the scars of April's two raids, the city's movie lovers flooded into the Odeon for that evening's showing of *Mrs. Miniver*, a wartime romance starring Greer Garson and Walter Pidgeon. Elsie chose the film—I was hoping she would choose *One of Our Aircraft is Missing,* but if she said she wanted to watch grass grow, I would have agreed to it.

We joined the queue at the cinema and I laced our fingers together. She looked at me, her eyebrows perked up.

"What, not embarrassed to be seen with me now?" She grinned playfully.

"Never." I lifted her knuckles to my lips and kissed them. "I just assumed you would be embarrassed if people knew you were my girl."

She gazed at me thoughtfully. "No." Her eyes twinkled impishly. "Is that what I am now—your girl?"

I gave her hand a squeeze. "Yes. You're mine."

Elsie leaned into me and nuzzled her nose against my chest. "Good."

I kissed the top of her head. Just that one word alone made me feel invincible—as if nothing or nobody could bring me down.

And then we watched the pre-film newsreel.

It started off jolly, beginning with America's defeat of the Japanese during the Battle of Midway. A few other theatre spectators whooped and cheered as footage of burning Japanese ships played on the screen. Many people saw that battle as America giving the Japanese no less than what they deserved after the cowardly attack on Pearl Harbor six months before.

The next stories were upbeat features on fashion on the ration and a reminder to use kitchen waste for compost in your vegetable garden.

Finally there was a brief story about a Czechoslovakian town called Lidice that was completely destroyed by the Nazis. All of its residents, including children, were either shot or taken prisoner. The theater patrons went silent.

Elsie gripped my arm. "Oh, my God," she whispered.

As usual the newsreel ended on an encouraging note—that the Allies were courageously fighting the evil enemy and they would not rest until the battle was won.

Elsie and I exchanged worried looks in the dim, smoky theater as the film began. We both had loved ones serving on the front, facing these monsters so we could be safe.

Suddenly watching a film and eating popcorn in a cinema seemed a selfish thing to do.

Elsie was quiet as we drove back to the farm from Bath.

"Did you like the movie?"

"Oh, yes," she said. "I'm just tired, that's all."

After a few minutes of neither of us saying anything, she turned to me. "Do you and Walter exchange letters?"

"Rarely," I said. "I feel like I'm bothering him when I write to him. I don't have anything interesting to say anyway." I glanced at her in the darkness of the pickup cab. "What about you and your brother?"

"Only occasionally," she said quietly. "I never know what to say to Archie. Surely he wouldn't care about anything *I* do when he's off fighting a war." She sighed. "He and I were never close anyway. If Jack were ever sent off to fight, I don't know what I would do."

Elsie told me about Jack signing up to serve as Archie had done but was given a teaching job instead.

"Have you heard from your friend Percy?"

"Yes," she said, her tone lightening a bit. "He seems to be getting on well, or at least he's pretending to for my sake."

Once we got back, neither of us bothered with our usual "you go in first and then I'll sneak in later" act. It was late, we were both tired, and hiding our relationship from Sheila seemed such a low priority compared to the heaviness of the film and the newsreel and so neither of us bothered.

Elsie changed in her room and then slid into bed beside me, resting her head on my chest as I draped my arm around her.

"What if all of this is for nothing?" Her brow pinched in the middle. "What if we're all working so hard just so some Nazi bastards can come and take everything from us?"

I was silent for a moment. "I can't believe you just cursed."

"I save it for very special occasions," she mumbled into my skin.

I let out a long exhale. "I don't know what is going to happen. No one does. Not Hitler, not Churchill, not Stalin, not Roosevelt, not you, and certainly not me. But we do our best, fight on for another day, and know that we're on the side of good. That has to be enough."

She closed her eyes. I thought perhaps she dozed off. She eventually opened her eyes again but I could tell sleep wasn't far off. "I was thinking about Paris. Have you ever been?"

"No." I twirled a bit of her silky golden hair around my finger.

"It's beautiful. I was thinking I would love for us to see it together. On the train I was considering what would need to happen for you for us to be able to go and the list was a bit overwhelming." She smiled weakly. "But then I realized that I might not get to see Paris ever again, because Paris could be destroyed tomorrow."

We were both quiet for a while.

I shrugged. "I could take you Bristol. They call it the Paris of the West Country."

twenty-one

Elsie

I had been so close to telling Ben I loved him. I wanted to stay with him and be with him and I wanted to tell him so much. I had been remarkably close. But one thing had stopped me.

I wasn't sure I had the fortitude of a farmer's wife.

What Vera could do in the kitchen was basically some sort of witchcraft—how she created nutritious, appetizing, and filling dishes was beyond me, never mind how she managed to do it with just wartime rations. She did all the cooking and cleaning *and* took care of June and Dora. I simply didn't know how she managed it.

I wasn't oblivious. I knew if Ben and I married, *I* would be the one to inherit Vera's cooking and cleaning. *I'd* be the one caring for our children.

Jack, Archie, and I had nannies, cooks, and staff when we were little. I had a feeling no nanny would work in the Grainger household.

Vera looked drained, peaked, and annoyed *all* the time. Was that my destiny—to look cross and exhausted every single day as I puttered around the kitchen and scrubbed floors? The idea of it was too abysmal to consider.

Perhaps wives were less miserable when cooking and cleaning for their actual husbands and children and not their brother and his farm hands. Perhaps that was just Vera. I simply didn't know.

These were the thoughts winding around my mind as Sherlock turned into the long drive to Honeyfield Farm after I'd finished the milk delivery on that warm morning in August. I tilted my head when I noticed Ben's pickup was gone. He hadn't mentioned needing to go fetch something.

As I unhitched the cart Sheila came rushing out of the cottage, her eyes wide with fear.

"Elsie," she exclaimed, rushing to my side, "there's been an accident."

I froze. The time between that sentence and her next words seemed to stretch on for an agonizing eternity. In that single second I counted and imagined all the horrible ways Ben could have been hurt or killed.

"Vera fainted and hit her head," she added quickly. "She bled quite a lot and poor June saw it and started screaming. Ben took Vera to see the doctor in Bath."

I put my hand to my mouth. "Oh, my God. Was she conscious when they left?"

"Yes," Sheila said. "Of course Vera tried to play it off as nothing at all—"

"Of course."

"—but Ben looked awful worried when they left," she added. "I think I got all the blood off the floor but poor June might be having nightmares for a bit."

As if on cue, June peered out of the open doorway to the cottage kitchen, tear streaks visible on her plump cheeks.

"Poor thing," I said before looking back at Sheila. "Today of all days."

The timing was truly unfortunate. June rarely came to the farm with Vera but had that day because Dora was visiting her cousin in Chippenham and their neighbors who sometimes watched June were away.

"There is even a bit of blood on the sleeve of June's dress," Sheila said, wincing. "I'm not going to mention it in case she starts screaming again."

"Oh, God, that's horrible." I smiled weakly at June, watching as she wiped at her runny nose. "Why did Vera faint?"

Sheila shrugged. "I have no idea."

We were both quiet for a moment.

"What are *we* going to do?" I bit my lip.

"One of us needs to watch June and the other one needs to keep working up in the field. Ben said we're already a bit behind on silage. I'm better at driving the tractor so I should—"

"I'm a good driver," I insisted.

"You've never been able to get the tractor started by yourself once," she reminded me.

"But you have much more experience with children than I do—"

"June has adored you ever since you found her in the forest." Sheila patted my shoulder. "You'll be fine."

"But what about the evening milking?"

"Morris and Howard will have to do it. They're capable lads," she said. "You will be fine."

"Right." I laughed nervously. "Of course. Of course I'll be fine. What could possibly go wrong?"

I chuckled uneasily again and Sheila arched a brow at me.

"What if she accidentally…" I struggled to find the right words. "…dies?"

"It's a few hours, Elsie. Have you never looked after a…" She barely paused. "No, no, you haven't. Of course you haven't."

I studied the ground, embarrassed.

"She's already had lunch so that's taken care of. Just try to keep her entertained for a few hours and then you should…" Sheila detoured. "Right, I'll come back to help make supper for everyone. I'm sure Vera and Ben will be back by then anyway."

I waved a dismissive hand. "Obviously. We'll be fine." I tried not to whimper as she headed for the upper hill.

When I returned to the cottage I discovered June at the table in the kitchen, coloring a page of an activity book. I subtly checked the floor for any remaining blood Sheila may have missed.

Sitting across from June I folded my hands together on the table in front of me. She went back to coloring.

"Are you alright, darling? Seeing Vera get hurt must have been quite a shock."

She didn't respond.

"She'll be fine. Ben is taking her to the doctor and he will make sure she's right as rain."

June kept her eyes down as she switched crayons.

"You and I are going to spend the afternoon together. Doesn't that sound lovely?"

She finally looked up at me and shrugged.

Sighing, I sat back in the wooden chair. Yes, her adoration for me was positively palpable.

"What are you coloring there, sweetheart? Is that a pony?"

"It's Sherlock."

I almost pointed out that Sherlock was not a glamorous show pony *or* bright purple but that seemed a bit rude.

"This one reminds me of the pony you rode at the fair," I said, pointing at the following page. "Do you like horses?"

June nodded, her focus still on her coloring.

"Have you ever been up in the cart that Sherlock pulls?"

She flicked her eyes up to mine. That got her attention.

"He and I have spent a lot of time together since I do the milk deliveries," I explained. "I bet he wouldn't mind taking us into the village for a bit. What do you think?"

She nodded enthusiastically, her pigtails flying.

So I hitched Sherlock up to the cart once again while he eyed me, snorting with derision.

"Oh, hush, you," I whispered to him as I adjusted the bridle. "We won't be long. Be a good boy for June please."

I lifted June into the cart and she took a seat at the front, picking up the reins. Sherlock began trodding down the lane, leaving me to chase after them. Thankfully his leisurely pace was about my walking speed.

I grabbed the rein on his bridle and said, "Whoa." Shading my eyes from the harsh sunlight with my hand, I frowned up at June. "Young lady."

She burst into a fit of giggles. I gave an exaggerated huff and brushed the horse's mane. "Did you see that? June just tried to steal you away."

June kicked her legs as she laughed. Sherlock huffed and flicked his tail.

Pleased with myself, I climbed up into the cart and joined June at the front. She gripped the reins and stared up at me with giant, hopeful dark blue eyes. As she held them, Sherlock began plodding again, causing June and I to lurch back slightly.

I was confident June could yank or snap the reins and Sherlock wouldn't change his pace one bit. Leaving me behind in the farmyard was certainly his idea, not hers.

"You can hold the reins," I said. "But just *hold* them, okay? I'll take them when we get to the village."

Smiling wide she nodded again.

It was warm that day but not unpleasantly so. A refreshing cool breeze flowed down into the valley between Bath and the hills surrounding Honeyfield and Fairbury, making the green pastures surrounding us shimmer in the afternoon sun as the blades of grass waved hello.

If not for the unevenness and bumpiness of Lily Road, I might have fallen asleep right there on the cart.

"Do you miss your mummy?" June suddenly asked when we had almost reached the village.

"Yes, of course," I said. "You must miss your mummy, too."

She twisted her little mouth, uncertain, and then shrugged.

"She never comes to see me," she said quietly.

"Oh, sweetheart," I said. "She would if she could. I'm sure she misses you very, very much."

Little June turned six early in the spring, making her only three years old when children were evacuated from Britain's cities to live with strangers. It was quite possible she didn't actually clearly remember her mum, especially if her mother wasn't able to visit her regularly.

"Does she write to you?" I asked.

"Sometimes," she said. "She sent me a dolly on my birthday."

I smiled. "That's topping."

"My daddy is away," she said.

I recalled Vera telling me June's father was a member of the Royal Tank Regiment. I hoped with every fiber of my being that June's parents survived the war so she could go back home to them. Vera likely dreaded the day when June would leave Fairbury. I knew how much the girl meant to her.

Just as agreed, June gave me the reins as we reached the village. It occurred to me that I had only ever taken Sherlock out on the milk delivery and rarely needed to direct him this way or that. Thankfully he responded to the tug of the reins fine and we stopped outside the little village shop. I likely didn't need to but I tied him to a sign to stop him from wandering off, just in case, and I helped June off the cart.

I didn't remember much from when I was June's age. However, I *did* remember adults buying me things in exchange for my good behavior. I hoped that was still the way of things.

"Alright, little miss," I said, looking around the little shop, nearly stripped bare for the day and it wasn't even half-two. "What would you like?"

June gasped as her gaze landed on the shelf carrying a few sweets and she looked back up at me, her eyes like saucers.

I immediately regretted taking her there.

"I can't buy you sweets, I'm sorry," I said. "I don't have your ration book."

And Vera would kill me if I used any coupons without her permission.

Shoulders drooping from disappointment, she wandered over to the corner where a few toys and books lined a shelf. She slid a book off the shelf and studied the title and the line drawings on the cover.

"*Milly-Molly-Mandy Stories*," I read over her shoulder. "I know that one. I think you would like it. Would you like me to get that for you and I'll read you some this afternoon?"

The way her eyes brightened and her smile spread filled my heart near to bursting. If I could make June into a reader, I could feel like I had accomplished something great.

Sheila found June and I reading together on the couch when she finished up in the field.

"Well," she said, wiping the perspiration from her forehead with the back of her arm and grinning, "don't you two look proper cozy?" She flopped down in the armchair across from us, her skin glossy and pink.

"Elsie got a book for me." June beamed.

"*And* June held Sherlock's reins all the way to the village," I added. "We've had a nice time together, haven't we?"

She nodded, somehow with her entire body, and wiggled her toes. "Yeah!"

"I'm so glad." Sheila smiled. "We should probably start preparing supper—"

"We're not done this story though," June said, poking at the page.

I frowned down at her. "Sheila is right. We want to have supper cooked and ready for when Vera and Ben get back—"

"But we're not done," she said, suddenly erupting with tears. "We're not done."

Then she released an ear-splitting howl and sobbed. Snapping the book closed, she buried her face in her hands and wept, shoulders heaving.

Slowly turning to Sheila I widened my eyes, horrified. Sheila didn't look the least bit bothered by this reaction. Did *all* children do this? Was *this* normal?

"I think somebody is tired," Sheila said under her breath, putting the book aside and leaning forward in her chair. "What if you help us make supper and Elsie reads you the rest of the story after? Would you like that?"

June wiped the tears from her cheeks and slowly nodded. Just like that, her little chaotic spell was over. Sheila barely blinked at the rapid change in mood.

"That was amazing," I whispered as we went to the kitchen. "You're like a magician."

Sheila snorted. "Hardly." She planted her hands on her hips and began accounting for what we had to work with. "Now. I haven't a clue what we should make. I think we've got plenty of veg downstairs."

"We should make a cake," June announced, climbing into one of the chairs at the kitchen table and flipping her coloring book open.

Sheila and I exchanged pitying smiles. I'm sure Sheila was also thinking back to when Vera was racked with guilt for not being able to gather enough ingredients to make June a birthday cake. Chocolate, sugar, and anything sweet was so hard to come by. Even eggs were precious commodities unless you had an exceptionally generous friend who kept chickens.

I checked the clock on the kitchen wall and winced.

"They'll be back soon," Sheila whispered, squeezing my shoulder. "I'm sure everything is fine." She gave another survey of the pantry.

I peered around the various kitchen shelves. "Shouldn't there be a cookbook somewhere?"

"Vera is too good a cook for that," she explained. "But yes, many people use cookbooks."

I made a mental note to order myself a stack of them from London.

"Right," Sheila said with a determined nod of her chin. "I think we should do potato and cheese bake with carrots."

I was disappointed we weren't tackling something a little more gourmet, but considering I had never peeled a potato in my life I may have been getting ahead of myself just slightly.

The cooking process went…reasonably well. Sheila gave me a few useful tips in between her directions.

"You're supposed to cut the skin from the potato, not take half the potato with it."

"If you don't peel those carrots faster, we will be here all night."

"Oh, Elsie, you were supposed to grate *some* of the cheese, not the whole wedge."

"Add a bit more salt. A bit more. A bit more. More. Oh, my goodness, not that much!"

When the dish was almost complete, I exhaled loudly. "I cannot believe I was intimidated by cooking before. It's actually quite simple."

Sheila frowned at me. "Mm."

"Thank you for showing me the ropes," I said. "Obviously I need a bit more practice but then I'll be right at home in the kitchen."

She probably didn't understand the feeling at all but the sudden knowledge that I could make my *own* meals was rather invigorating. Hopeful even.

"Could we do this again tomorrow with a different dish? Ooh, maybe something French!" I clapped my hands together and bounced slightly.

She hesitated. "Maybe Vera could give you a cooking lesson next. I'm sure she's got lots of tips for you."

"Jolly good." I nodded eagerly. "This is so exciting. I was starting to worry I would…" I trailed off, suddenly realizing I was stepping into dangerous territory. "Um, that-that I would just, um, never know how to cook anything myself."

Sheila raised a brow at me. "Is that all?"

"Yes, of course. What do you mean?" I inspected my nails thoroughly.

"I always assumed you would just go back to London and marry a rich man so you would never have to do something so—" Sheila adopted a posh accent and lifted her nose slightly. "—common."

"Is that what I *sound* like? Please tell me I don't sound like that!"

"Not as much as you used to," she said.

"Going back to London *was* my plan but now I'm not sure." I glanced at June and lowered my voice. "You see, Ben and I are…together."

Sheila's expression remained neutral. "I am entirely shocked by this news."

I laughed. "How long have you known?"

"Probably before the two of you even knew," she said, a glint in her eye. "Vera knows too, by the way."

Pressing a palm to my flushing cheek, I leaned back against the counter. "Unbelievable."

"You think Ben won't want you if you can't make a meat pie, is that it?"

"I don't know," I said. "Vera can't keep house for him forever so if he and I are meant to be, it's got to be me."

Sheila gripped both my shoulders and looked me straight in the eye. June looked up from her coloring book to watch the exchange.

"Listen to me. I've seen the way he looks at you. You could feed that man a plate of twigs and leaves as long as you were at the table beside him, he probably wouldn't even notice."

A smile spread across my face. "Thank you for saying that."

She let go of my shoulders to check on dinner. "I bet you never expected to be thinking about settling down in the country when you signed up to be a land girl, did you?"

"No," I said. "Not in a hundred years."

twenty-two

BEN

"You need to be a good girl for me, okay?" Vera handed me a cup of tea while June sat coloring quietly at the kitchen table. "I won't have time to play with you today."

I smirked. "I'll do my best."

Vera threw me an unamused look as June giggled and Sheila rolled her eyes.

My sister turned around to continue the washing up from lunch and I sat beside June with my tea. Towel in hand, Sheila dried the dishes and slid them into the cupboard as Vera took them out of the sink. The first few times she tried to help with the dishes Vera nearly got defensive, like she thought Sheila was intruding or thought she wasn't doing a good job. Vera eventually realized Sheila hated sitting still when she could be helping.

Elsie, still out on her milk delivery at that time of day, was used to having people clean up after her so almost never offered a hand. To be fair, I didn't either.

"Are you alright?" Sheila said quietly as Vera's hands suddenly went still in the sink.

She shook her head slightly. "Yes, of course. Why do people keep…keep…"

Vera took her dripping hand from the sink, reached for the edge of the counter but it slipped off. She crumpled to the floor, like her legs turned to damp paper underneath her, and her head hit the counter with an awful thud. Sheila gasped, dropped her towel and knelt down beside Vera before I could even slide my chair back from the table.

"Christ!" I exclaimed, whipping around the table and dropping to my knees beside Vera.

Blood quickly pooled around Vera's head. A loud, sobbing screech burst from June and she ran from the room.

Sheila and I gently rolled Vera onto her back and Vera's eyelids slowly opened.

"Oh, thank God," I said.

She looked at us, confused. "Why am I on the floor?" She tapped at the wound on her forehead and she blinked a few times. "Oh."

"You fainted and hit your head," Sheila said, quickly grabbing the dish towel she'd dropped a moment before and pressing it hard to Vera's head. She looked at me, suddenly in full medical professional mode. "Hold that on her head, hold it tight. I'm going to try to clean her head so we can actually see where she's bleeding from." She hopped up, grabbed a flannel and ran outside to run it under the pump.

Vera winced as I held the towel in place. "I can hold it myself."

She didn't reach for it though. Instead she caught sight of the gooey mess of blood on the floor beside her and the sodden, burgundy of her shirt.

Sheila ran back in, knelt beside Vera—entirely disregarding the puddle of blood one knee rested in—and carefully wiped at the blood on Vera's forehead and face.

"It's right along the hairline here," Sheila said, pointing at a one-inch line still bleeding freely. She held the wet cloth to it before looking down at Vera. "You haven't been feeling well for a while, have you?"

She flick a dismissive hand. "I'm just tired."

"Tired people don't usually faint," I snapped. "I *knew* you looked bloody unwell."

This was my fault. I knew Vera didn't look right and I was too wrapped up in myself that I didn't even notice just *how* unwell she really was. What if she'd fallen and cracked her head and it was worse? What if she'd been alone and bled to death on the floor?

"I'm taking you to the emergency clinic in Bath," I announced.

"You bloody well are not," Vera said as I pulled her into a sitting position, leaning against the cabinets.

"Go," Sheila said, already looking for more towels for us to take with us.

"I can't leave June here alone," Vera said, resignation in her voice.

"Hush," I said. "Sheila and Elsie will take care of the farm for the afternoon."

I carried her out to the pickup, all the while Vera scowling, a dish towel held against her forehead.

"You can stop glaring at me now," I said once she was settled in the passenger seat and I was driving us down the lane toward Lily Road. "I should have taken you to see a doctor weeks ago."

"This is ridiculous," she said. "I'm fine."

"Yes, obviously. Healthy people faint and crack their head open all the bloody time."

Vera lifted the towel away from her head for a moment and I caught her wincing at the sight of it. She touched it lightly and hissed, recoiling. "I wish Sheila had gone to the cellar to get flannels from the scraps box instead of using my good dish towels."

I rolled my eyes and pressed harder on the accelerator.

The waiting room at the hospital in Bath was crowded. I made Sheila take the one single empty chair but she soon gave it to a heavily pregnant woman who came in after us.

"Here, let me look," I said, slowly peeling the sticky towel off Vera's head.

Her forehead was a mess of smeared, dried brown blood and her hairline was crusty with red gunk. A thin stream of blood began winding its way down to the side of her nose. I winced and wiped the fresh blood away.

"Bollocks, that looks painful," I said quietly, putting the towel back. An older woman glared at me and my filthy mouth.

"Sorry," I mumbled.

Vera snickered and leaned against the wall beside me. I peered around for a hospital employee.

"You shouldn't be standing," I said. "I'm going to go see if they can bring in another chair for you—"

"Don't you dare. I'm *fine*."

"Will you stop saying that?" My voice was a bit louder and a few people glanced our way, probably worried they might see a row while waiting for the doctor.

"You fainted," I reminded her, lowering my voice. "There's something obviously wrong besides that." I nodded to the blood-soaked towel pressed to her forehead. "You look different—"

"Tired," she said. "Yes, I know—"

"No, it's more than that." I looked at her raised arm as she held the towel in place. "Maybe thinner."

"Everyone is thinner," Vera said. "I can hardly remember what sugar tastes like."

After two and a half years of rationing, a lot of people had lost weight. Sugar and butter were two of the first things to go and meat was tricky to come by. Chocolate, sweets, and biscuits were added to the rationed foods list the month before.

Vera took the flannel off her head again and grimaced. "Perhaps you could see if the nurses could give me a clean towel that's not drenched in blood? I'm scaring the children."

Sure enough a nearby child sat with his mother, glancing over at Vera, horrified but unable to look away completely. He noticed me glowering at him and immediately looked down at his lap.

"Hello, sir," said the nurse at the front desk without looking up at me, shoving a clipboard my way. "Fill this out and we'll get to you as soon as we can."

"We already filled that out—"

"Please have a seat then, sir."

"Do you happen to have a clean towel my sister can put on her head?

She's still bleeding but the towel we have is more blood than fabric now."

She finally looked up, peering around me to check on my sister in the waiting area. She wrinkled her nose. "One moment please."

When she returned with the soon-to-be-ruined towel, I thanked her.

"You don't happen to have a spare chair back there, do you?" I smiled weakly. "I'm afraid my sister is going to faint again."

The nurse looked at me like I had just asked for the moon. "No. There's a few chairs down the hall that might be empty. Just come back when you're closer to the front of the line, alright?"

"Thank you." I hesitated. "And how long might that be?"

She sighed at me.

I thanked her again and waved to Vera to follow me. Thankfully the chairs happened to be empty.

Vera held the bloody towel in her free hand.

"You can throw that away, you know."

"It's a perfectly good towel still. Just needs a little bleach and it'll be fine."

I gave up.

After a while I cleared my throat. "I'm glad we have this time to talk."

"We talk every single day."

"But not about, um, personal things."

Vera's mouth formed into a tight frown. "Oh, God. What is it?"

I let out a long breath. "I should have taken you to see the doctor ages ago. I feel terrible."

"What would you have told the doctor? That I look wretched?"

"Yes, exactly."

She rolled her eyes.

"We've barely talked about Herb or Walt since they left," I added.

Squaring her shoulders, Vera averted her gaze from mine. "What about them?"

"I worry about them and think about them every single day," I admitted. "I keep trying to write to Walt but everything I want to tell him sounds daft. He's at war. How could he possibly care about anything happening back here?"

Vera was quiet for a while.

"Herb was never much of a letter writer," she said finally. "But every day I don't hear from him, I think, 'That's it. I'm a widow. It's happened, I just know it.'"

Her voice wavered as she spoke the last few words and I wanted to put my arm around her to comfort her but I knew she wouldn't like it. Getting her to open up about her husband was already a big step.

"He's going to be fine," I said. "He and Walt are going to come home."

"You don't know that."

"I do. A fortune teller told me."

"Oh, shut it." She elbowed me playfully in the ribs and sniffed.

"I want you to know you're doing a good job with June. She was very lucky that you were the one to pick her up from the station that day. No child could ask for better."

"I probably traumatized the poor thing today," she said with a weak laugh. "But thank you for saying that."

I felt like I owed my sister some honesty. I took a deep breath.

"I've been seeing someone," I blurted.

Inspecting the new towel for blood, she didn't even blink. "Oh, you mean Elsie?"

I stared at her.

"The pair of you aren't exactly subtle." She shrugged. "And Sheila knows too."

Rubbing the back of my neck, I chuckled. "Ah."

I waited for Vera to tell me her opinion of Elsie but when she didn't right away, I got nervous.

"You don't like her," I finally said.

"I never said that," she said quickly.

I swallowed. "I want to ask her to marry me."

Vera turned sideways in her chair and stared at me, the bloody cloth falling limply from her lap and landing with a sickening splat on the hallway floor. "You can't be serious."

"I am. Why is that so hard to believe?" I picked up the bloody flannel so she wouldn't need to bend over and send any additional blood to her head.

Snatching the towel from me she cautiously shook her head and sat back in her chair. "It's just impractical. She grew up with servants and a cook. You can't marry someone like that. Why can't you ask Sheila instead? At least she knows how to wash a dish—"

"Because I don't love Sheila," I snapped.

Vera pursed her lips. "You love Elsie though?"

"I wouldn't ask her to marry me if I didn't."

She studied me for a moment. "A marriage is more than finding someone pretty. It's a partnership for the rest of your life. You barely know this girl."

"A lot of couples get married without knowing one another since Sunday school," I said, referencing her marriage to her childhood sweetheart. "But I *do* know Elsie and I *know* I can't imagine my life without her."

"Do you think she'll say yes?"

"I…" The question had plagued me for a month. I probably would have asked her by now if I knew the answer would definitely be yes. "I think so."

A pair of nurses walked passed.

Vera stood up. "Let's go see if there are some empty seats now."

I knew this was her way of avoiding the conversation but I followed her out to the waiting room anyway. Neither of us wanted to talk about that topic in front of others so we just sat in silence.

She was finally taken in to see the doctor and I reluctantly held the gruesome bloody towel.

Vera was quiet once we were back in the pickup and heading towards Fairbury. Stitched up and given painkillers, she dozed on and off during our drive back to the farm.

"So," I said when she was awake and we were nearly home, "what made you faint?"

She glanced at me, her mouth twisted as she considered her words carefully. "He said he's confident I fainted because of…" She sighed loudly "…malnutrition."

"What, like scurvy?"

"No, *not* like scurvy!"

I laughed. "Are your teeth going to fall out next? Now *that* might scare June a bit—"

"It's not scurvy," she repeated firmly. "It's the damn rationing."

Thinking, I remained silent for a moment. Then it hit me.

"You've been giving some of your rations to Mum and June, haven't you?"

Vera redirected her gaze out the window, probably to avoid looking at me.

I turned towards the road that would lead us home. "I guess we all do crazy things for the people we love, even if they don't make sense to anyone else."

When we arrived back at Honeyfield, June ran straight to Vera and wrapped her arms around Vera's leg.

"You're all better!" June exclaimed.

Vera patted her hair. "That's right. I'm all better now."

Sheila appeared around the corner and headed for the oven. "Welcome back! You're right on time."

Elsie smiled shyly at me as she came out from the living room before heading for the cabinets. Maybe not having to hide our relationship from Vera and Sheila wouldn't be so bad.

"Did you require stitches?" Elsie asked, fetching some plates down for dinner.

"A few," Vera said, her eyes looking upward towards the fresh bandage on her upper forehead.

"Please, have a seat," Elsie said as she divided steamed carrots onto the plates while Sheila scooped something out from a baking dish.

"That smells good," Vera said.

"It's potato and cheese bake," Elsie announced proudly, beaming. "Sheila taught me how to cook this afternoon."

I could feel Vera looking at me but I didn't meet her eyes.

"We're getting there," Sheila added, warning in her voice.

"Hopefully it's alright we used potatoes, margarine, and cheese. We weren't sure what you had planned for future meals," Elsie said, grabbing silverware from the drawer and setting them on the table.

I winked at her as I reached for a knife and fork and she bit her bottom lip to stop from grinning.

"That's alright," Vera said with a laugh. "Gosh, it's been ages since I've eaten a meal at this table that I didn't cook." She looked at June. "I hope you were a good girl for Elsie and Sheila."

She nodded. "Elsie let me ride Sherlock all by myself."

Elsie's eyes widened as she set our steaming plates on the table. "That's not exactly what happened."

"And she bought me a book and read to me."

Vera smiled weakly and lowered her eyes. If I didn't know any better, I would say she looked almost guilty. "That was very kind. I hope you thanked Elsie for the gift."

"She did," Elsie said. "We had a lovely time."

After we ate a delicious meal and the two land girls and the child evacuee filled us in on their afternoon, I drove Vera and June home. At first Vera insisted that she do the washing up but I think her drowsiness won out in the end.

When I returned to the cottage Elsie was drying dishes while Sheila washed.

"You're relieved of your duties for the day, Buckley," I declared.

Sheila shrugged as her hands left the sudsy water. "I'm not going to ask questions. I'm meeting a friend at the pub anyway."

After she left I wrapped my arms around Elsie's middle from behind and rested my chin on top of her head. "What a day." It was the first time I'd ever held her in the kitchen like that but it just felt so natural, like we'd embraced in the kitchen a thousand times before. It felt like home.

Elsie leaned back into me. "Is your sister alright?"

"Yeah," I said. "She will be."

I slid my arms away and into the soapy sink, picking up where Sheila left off.

"I told Vera about us today."

"I told Sheila."

We both laughed.

"She already knew," we said in unison before laughing again, this time louder.

"So much for trying to keep it between us," I said, shaking my head.

"Did you really like the food tonight or did you just say that to be kind?" Elsie asked very suddenly, her tone accusatory.

I laughed. "It was really good, I swear!" I glanced at her. "I hope you didn't take my comment about you not knowing how to cook to heart—"

"Of course I did," she snapped.

My shoulders fell. "I was teasing. I shouldn't have said it."

"It's fine." She shook her head. "I should probably know how to cook *something*."

"I can cook a few things," I added. "I like to do a bit of baking during the winter months when I'm less busy, but I haven't done any since rationing began."

"Baking? Really?" She arched an eyebrow.

"Yes." I chuckled. "Is that so hard to believe?"

Her face relaxed. "Perhaps not."

"I really didn't mean anything—"

"I know you didn't mean anything. I just..." She closed her eyes and released a long exhale. "I want you to know that I take this seriously. I take...*us* seriously. If you're just with me for a jolly time, I need to know."

My hands froze mid-scrub and I turned to look at her.

I could have asked her to marry me then. My mind and my heart screamed at me to propose. But I didn't.

"I take us seriously too," I said.

Elsie studied my face for a moment before her mouth spread into a sweet smile, her eyes gleaming.

We both knew this wasn't just a casual wartime romance. We weren't like all those hasty flings that lasted a week before a trip down the aisle. It was something real.

I whipped my hands out of the sink and thrust them into Elsie's hair, bringing our lips together. I kissed her firmly and deeply as she moaned into my mouth, her fingers clawing at my shirt, fumbling to untuck it from my trousers. Clamping my hands on her ass I lifted her, and she wrapped her legs tight around my waist as I carried her out of the kitchen and upstairs, our mouths entwined and frantic.

As I tossed her roughly onto my bed—no, *our* bed—I grinned mischievously as her chest heaved, her eager eyes telling me all I needed to know.

"You worked so hard on dinner," I said, my voice husky. I climbed up the length of her body before dragging my teeth against the side of her neck. "But I'm still hungry."

twenty-three

Elsie

The rest of the month sped by in an exhausting blur. It was about to get even busier since the sugar beets would be harvested in a few weeks. There was also a chance Sheila and I would be loaned to another Fairbury farmer who had an apple orchard and was desperate for help.

When the alarm clock sounded on that particular morning at the end of August, I wondered if I could actually get out of bed. I rolled over and held the pillow over the side of my head, trying to smother the sounds of a day's new dawn.

The alarm halted and Ben slid an arm over my middle, pulling me closer.

"It's time to get up," he whispered in my ear.

"That can't possibly be true," I said from under the pillow. "I don't believe it."

He slid out of bed and pulled a shirt on. "I need you and Sheila to get started on the milking while I run over to see Amos."

I moved the pillow aside and propped myself on my elbows. "Exchanging gossip so early in the morning?"

He laughed. "Not quite. I heard a rumour about another possible case of foot and mouth disease. I need to see if he knows anything about it."

"Ah yes," I said, scooting out from under the sheets. "Farm gossip."

Ben grinned. "Plus I want to tell him about this charming maid I woke up next to this morning."

Milking the cows had become so second nature to me since coming to Honeyfield Farm that I barely had to be conscious to do it. I just couldn't seem to wake up that day.

That is until my neck and forehead began sweating. My shaking hand went from an udder to the seat of my milking stool as I tried to steady myself, fighting off a wave of dizziness. Knocking over my stool and nearly my full milk pail, I dashed out of the barn and around the corner, promptly emptying my stomach of all its contents. I winced at the bitter taste on my tongue as I stood back up, wiping my mouth on the back of my arm.

When I returned to the barn Sheila was staring at me with wide eyes.

"Are you alright?" She rose from her stool. "Did you just vomit?"

Nodding I stared at the ground, fighting off the frenzy of thoughts in my head while trying to do mental math. Hands trembling and heart pounding, I looked back up at Sheila.

"I think I might be…" I pointed at my stomach.

"About to have an upset stomach?"

"No!"

"Hungry?"

"No! Well, yes," I said quickly. "But I mean I might be…"

Sheila's eyes became large. "Up the spout?"

I grimaced and looked around to make sure nobody was around to overhear that. "Possibly." I shook my head. "It's probably the flu—"

She rose quickly. "When was your last monthly?"

"It's been a while but sometimes I skip a month when I'm really busy or tired or—"

"What about your bosoms?"

I placed a protective hand on my chest. "I beg your pardon!"

Sheila rolled her eyes. "Your tits," she clarified, loudly and clearly, "do they hurt?"

"Oh." I frowned. "Quite sore actually."

She nodded hesitantly. "My cousin's were quite sore before..."

"Before what?"

She cringed. "Before she had twins."

Seeing my reaction Sheila grabbed her milking stool and placed it at my feet. "Sit down with your head between your knees. Deep breaths."

I did as she directed, gulping air as my pulse continued to race.

"How could this happen?" I peered up at her. "Don't answer that." I put my head down by my knees again. "We were careful."

"Not careful enough apparently," Sheila said, patting my back.

"Ben can't know. Not yet. Not until I know for certain." I raised my head slightly again. "How do I do that?"

"Well, there's that one test you can do where you put an onion in your, um..." She gestured vaguely to her own lower abdomen area.

"I'm *not* doing that one. Your cousin didn't do that, did she?"

"No. She pissed into a cup and then put a metal bolt into the cup."

I put my head back down as dizziness threatened again. "And how does that work exactly?"

"You leave the bolt in the cup for a few hours and if the bolt leaves a mark on the cup, that means you're—" She sighed "—pregnant."

"That is the most ridiculous thing I've ever heard." I propped an elbow on my thigh and cradled my forehead in my palm. "This cannot be happening."

"What about going to see a doctor?"

I slowly sat up. "I'm afraid he'll ask to speak with my husband and then when I say, 'Oh, I don't have one of those for I am a ruined woman of low morals,' he'll tell me to leave his clinic straight away."

"Could you maybe just say your husband is away fighting or something?"

I lifted my left hand and wiggled my empty ring finger.

Sheila knelt down in front of me and took my hand. "You *know* Ben would marry you in a heartbeat if he knew, right? I think you should tell him, even if you don't know for sure."

I shook my head. "I don't want him to ask me because he has to. I want him to ask me because he wants to."

"I'm going to go gulp as much water from the pump as I can," I announced, slowly standing. "Then back to milking. Then I need to find a cup or a jar I can throw in the bin when I'm done with it."

Ben didn't return to the farm before we finished the milking and the post-milking cleanup. It worried me. His absence did make it considerably easier to poke around in the tool shed for a jar and a bolt though. I scrubbed the dust from the jar with some water from the pump while Sheila chatted with Vera inside.

I had never made water in a jar before.

Sheila wrinkled her nose. "Are you going to do that in the privy?"

"Of course!" I whispered. "I'm not going to do it in front of you!"

"What if you miss the jar and piss on the floor?"

I let my expression go blank. "Yes, it would be such a shame if the privy suddenly reeked of urine."

Thanks to my very full bladder, *some* urine made it into the jar but about half of it landed on the wooden floor of the privy or splashed up onto my legs and shoes. I cringed at the disgusting wet warmth and let out a long, horrified howl.

This is just a sample of what motherhood will be like, I thought as I dropped the bolt into the jar and screwed the lid on. I hid the jar in the tool shed where it wouldn't be disturbed and went to change my stinking trousers.

I wasn't sure if Sherlock was just going extra slow but the milk delivery felt like it took ages. I was late already because of Ben's absence and the whole jar fiasco. Plus Sheila insisted on loading the heavy milk onto the cart by herself.

"Just in case," she said.

The slow trudge to and from the village gave me time to think about what it might be like to be a mother—to care for a tiny person that came from my body. I saw how Ben was with June so I knew he would be a wonderful father, probably better than my cold and distant father ever was.

Thinking of my father, I winced. Mother and Father would certainly be disappointed in me for becoming pregnant before marriage, especially when the father wasn't of our social standing. I wondered how long I could possibly wait to tell them. Maybe until after the baby was born? Or, perhaps, the child's fifth birthday?

The idea that the love between Ben and I had perhaps created a whole new person made me smile softly to myself. I slowly slid my hesitant hand down to my belly and touched it lightly.

"Are you in there?" I whispered down to my stomach. "If you are in there, I just want to say…hello."

Glancing over his shoulder, Sherlock snorted at my strangeness. He was the only one around for miles as I delicately caressed my upper abdomen.

"Oh, hush, you," I told him. "I'm having a very strange day."

When we returned to the farm I was relieved to see the pickup in the yard. After unhitching the cart and telling Sherlock to keep mum about what he saw me do today, I let myself into the cottage.

I had definitely interrupted something.

Vera and Sheila sat at the table, both gripping cups of tea, while Ben paced, running his hand through his dark hair. Vera pulled deeply on a cigarette and blew the stream of smoke from her nose.

"What is happening?" I dropped the stilted words slowly and hesitantly.

I briefly considered asking if someone had fainted again but thought better of it.

"There are cases of foot and mouth all over the bloomin' place," Ben said, his brow deeply furrowed. "There's going to be a few stories in the newspaper on Saturday."

I swallowed. "How many cases?"

"At least a hundred," he said, shaking his head.

My mouth fell open.

"A few people have already been fined for not keeping their dog on a lead because it can spread the disease," Sheila added.

Worried, Ben glanced at Sam. "A couple o' farmers I know are saying they'll shoot any trespassing dogs."

Sam, laying in usual spot by the fireplace, tilted his head at Sheila and let out a small whimper. I was grateful Sam never wandered from home.

"Amos' farm is okay?"

Ben nodded. "For now, yeah. But I won't be going over there for a while. You all know to be careful, yeah?"

We all nodded.

As the afternoon crawled on I was too distracted to even worry about the foot and mouth disease crisis. I was too busy thinking about that jar of urine in the tool shed. Sheila had warned me not to look at it until after supper. When it was finally time to check the test, Sheila and I exchanged looks of uncertainty.

Sheila lowered her face to get a closer look. "Is that a mark or just some dirt?"

"I think it's dirt."

"It could be a mark," she said. "Or it could be dirt."

We stared at it for another silent minute.

"You should drink more water."

"What?"

"Your piss is *very* yellow. That means you're not drinking enough water."

I glared at her.

"What are you going to do?"

"I don't know."

I lied.

Ben was away that evening, attending a meeting in Bath with other cattle farmers in the area. They were petitioning the local governments to do more about people trespassing on their land for dog walks and berry picking which assisted in the spread of foot and mouth from farm to farm. Sheila was out with a friend too so I could slip out unnoticed.

While hiding my pregnancy test jar in the tool shed that afternoon, I'd found a bicycle tucked away behind some boxes. Besides a bit of rust on the frame, it was fortunately in good condition. Good enough to get me to Rosetta Watkins' estate anyway.

As I pedalled down the country road that skirted around the village and lead to Rosetta's home, I whispered to myself, "Please be at home. Please be at home."

When I stopped the bicycle in front of her drive, I touched the tips of my toes to the cobblestones and looked around. Going any further onto the Watkins property was technically going against Ben's orders of visiting other farms. I decided to take the chance since I wouldn't be going anywhere near their cattle and into their fields. The Watkins would be careful about their cattle herd so I doubted they were at risk.

Besides all of that, this was of utmost importance.

I waved as I spotted Rosetta bringing her thoroughbred closer.

"Good evening, Elsie. What a lovely surprise!" She swung her leg over and dismounted gracefully.

"Good evening. I'm sorry to interrupt your ride," I said. "He really is a magnificent animal."

I caught myself using a slightly different voice. Had I always done that?

"The finest horse in the county," she agreed.

"I'm afraid I'm here on a matter of some urgency."

Rosetta turned her gaze from the steed to me. "Is everything alright, my dear?"

I swallowed and bit my lip. "You said you were a nurse during the Great War. That's correct?"

She narrowed her eyes slightly. "Yes."

"I think I may have a rather delicate health issue to deal with," I finally said. "I need help."

"Well, I can tell you from my experience as a woman and a mother that you certainly *sound* like you're with child," Rosetta said with a disappointed sigh as we talked privately in her parlour over tea. "Goodness. When you mentioned my nursing background, I thought you were going to ask me about gangrene or something."

I let out a surprised laugh. "No, nothing that terrible."

She gave me a stern look. "I needn't remind you you're unmarried. That's still quite bad."

I lowered my eyes. I expected that response but it still didn't feel good.

"I know," I said. "I made a mistake."

As soon as the words left my lips, I knew I didn't mean any of them. I hadn't an ounce of regret. The realization caused a bloom of warmth in my chest.

"No matter. Either way, you need a proper examination with a doctor," Rosetta said. "I have a doctor friend who lives in the village. I'll call him and make sure he is discreet."

I smiled wide. "Thank you so much. I knew you would understand."

"Of course, my darling." Her brow pinched. "May I ask who the father is?"

Swallowing, I hesitated. As far as I knew my relationship with Ben was still only between us, Vera, and Sheila. If Ben thought Rosetta would be miffed about Ben and I before, she would certainly be furious now.

"It must be that lovely Montgomery chap you introduced me to," she said, her eyes lighting up a bit. "He has a very good family. Do you know if he is still stationed in Britain?"

"I-I...believe so," I stammered. "Scotland, I think."

I am so sorry, Percy. If this gets back to your parents, I will never forgive myself.

"Given the circumstances, he should be able to pop down here or you can travel north and the two of you can get married right away," she said. "As long as it's not that horrid American brute who nearly ruined our fundraiser."

"No," I said quietly. "Not Garrett."

"Very good. I'll go telephone that doctor and then we can take a quick drive over there." She whisked off to make the call, leaving me alone with my thoughts.

Rosetta only considered two young men as romantic options for me: Garrett the horrid American and Percy, a homosexual. Both were well educated and from families of wealth and status. To Rosetta Watkins, the idea of me becoming romantically involved with Ben, a farmer, was so beyond the realm of possibilities that she didn't even consider him a contender. I had lived with that kind, intelligent, funny, beautiful man since February and yet she still considered it more likely that I would sleep with Garrett Miller—that arrogant, vile rat—after knowing him for only a couple weeks, simply because of his social standing.

I let out a long, unsteady breath as my mind cleared.

Rosetta simply considered Ben unworthy of my affection.

My fingers curled together in my palms as my shoulders tightened. I wanted to scream. I wanted to run out of that manor with its ridiculous chandeliers and its truly irrational number of paintings of horses—honestly, how many horse paintings does one person need?

For the second time that day I placed a gentle hand on my stomach. If there was a baby in there, I owed it to them to still see a doctor. I just couldn't stand to be with Rosetta Watkins for another minute.

I stood as soon as Rosetta returned to the parlour. "He said he can see you. Ready to go?"

I plastered on a fake smile, something I had perfected with years of intense practice. "I am. I think I'd better do this on my own though. Perhaps you can write down his address for me?"

She pursed her lips. "Are you sure? I don't mind—"

"I'll likely feel extremely uncomfortable," I said bluntly, "but given that I'm most likely pregnant with an illegitimate baby, meeting a doctor is far from the most uncomfortable thing in my future. Now. His address?"

I took pleasure at her shocked expression, her eyebrows disappearing into her perfectly styled hairline.

As I rode my bicycle into the village, I wondered if her eyebrows would simply cease to exist entirely if I told her Ben was the father and that we made love by a lake.

twenty-four

BEN

Dear Walt,

Three years ago today, you, me, Vera, and Mum all sat around the wireless, listening to Mr. Chamberlain announce we were at war. I don't think I'll forget that night for as long as I live. This has been the longest three years

Dear Walt,

Vera probably wrote it in one of her letters but I thought I should tell you myself: I'm going to ask a land girl to marry me. Her name is Elsie and she's wonderful. I think you'll get on well. I'm not sure what the rules are when it comes to farmers marrying their land girls but

Dear Walt,

There are cases of foot and mouth disease all around Bath. I don't know what we'll do if we

Dear Walt,

I hope you're safe and well. Sending your Christmas gifts with this so hopefully you get it before Christmas, unlike last year. (Sorry, again.) Vera made you those cookies you like. (If they happen to be hard as rocks by the time they reach you, do not tell her. I'm still not sure how she managed to get enough butter to make them.) I hope you enjoy the comics. I was going to send you a book but we didn't want to go over the weight limit.

I groaned and shoved the letter aside. Tossing the pen on the table, I watched it roll into the crumpled balls that were the last attempts at a cheerful letter from home, brother to brother. The best thing I could think of to say was listing what was in his care package and nonsense about the weight? Ugh. It was useless. Faking holiday cheer was not on my mind that morning.

It was early still—too early to milk the cows. I couldn't sleep. I kept thinking about the herd and all the ways the disease could possibly reach our farm.

Since I had some free time as I drank an early morning brew I decided to write my younger brother a letter. Instead of thinking about the dangers of disease I began thinking about the dangers of war.

It was like one of those nightmares where you think you're awake but you're actually still dreaming and the monster is still after you.

Later that day and after the evening milking and the washing up of the equipment, Sheila went inside ahead of us and I took the opportunity to grab Elsie around the middle and squeeze her tightly. I buried my face in her hair and breathed in deep the smell of her skin.

"Hello there," she said in a low voice, leaning back into my chest.

I kissed the top of her head. "Hello."

How is that I could spend all day with a person and it still didn't seem like enough?

She turned around and smiled up at me, laying a hand on my chest. "We will make it through this. This will not be what takes down Honeyfield Farm. We've survived three years of war. We've survived Nazis shooting at us. This will not be what gets us."

I was quiet for a moment.

"I love you," I said. "You know that, right?"

She glowed. "I love you too."

I pulled her closer to me and kissed her. The way her lips felt warm and soft as they pressed to mine and the way her fingertips grazed lightly against my neck sent jolts of joy through my body.

"We should—"

"I have—" she said at the same time.

"Sorry," I said, chuckling. "Were you saying something?"

Elsie shook her head. "Nothing. I'll tell you later. We best get inside before our supper gets cold."

Before we reached the cottage Vera and Sheila came outside. They exchanged wary looks with one another and Vera took a long drag on her cigarette.

"Bloody hell, what *now*?" I crossed my arms over my chest to help protect myself from more bad news.

Vera swallowed. "I was just telling Sheila that when I was at the bakery today someone told me several of Watkins' cows have foot and mouth and their herd had to be destroyed today."

Sheila immediately threw a worried glance at Elsie.

"That's the fourth case in Fairbury," I said, rubbing the back of my neck.

Nobody said anything.

"It's sad but at least they won't be ruined by the loss of their herd," I continued. "None of us have been there recently…" I looked down at Elsie. "Right?"

Avoiding my gaze she opened her mouth but nothing came out.

I felt my jaw clench. "You were? When you were there last?"

"Late last week," she said quietly. "Thursday, I think."

"I told you not to visit any other farms and the first thing you do is go straight *to* one? What were you thinking? What could have been so bloody important that you *had* to see Mrs. Watkins—"

"We were just visiting," Elsie snapped. "I didn't go into any fields. I was on her front drive and in her house. That's *all.* I didn't *see* any of her cows, let alone get near them—"

"You don't have to see them, Elsie," I corrected sternly. "You could have carried the disease back here on your shoes—"

"From her parlour?" she shouted, her fists clamped at her sides.

"Why *were* you there?"

"I told you," she said. "We were visiting. Rosetta is my friend."

I ran my palm over my face. "Un-bloody-believable. You have no idea what you could have done because you just needed to see her for a chat." I shook my head. "You couldn't possibly understand the damage—"

"Ben, that's enough," Vera said sharply.

Elsie's chest heaved as she glared at me, fire in her eyes.

I charged back to the barn. "Sheila, we have to check the cows."

"We've checked the cows over twice today already," Sheila said.

"We're checking them again," I shouted back over my shoulder.

When Elsie began to follow I turned on my heel to face her. "Don't. It could still be on your boots. I don't want to see you near this barn or the pastures or near any of the cows until Mr. Linden gives us the all clear."

I stormed into the barn. "Sheila, you start on that side," I barked, gesturing vaguely to the stalls further down. "Check around and between the hooves. Check their gums, tongue, udders, around their nose and look for drooling or soreness. If you see *any*thing that looks unusual, even if you're nearly certain it's nothing, let me know anyway and I'll come check."

"Yes, sir," she mumbled as she passed me.

Vera crossed her arms and watched me as I checked the first heifer over, lifting the cow's feet up and checking all around her mouth.

"Was that necessary?" Vera asked quietly.

"What?" I focused on my search for signs of disease.

When she didn't reply I looked up at her. She pursed her lips at me and arched a brow.

"She should know better," I said quietly, moving along to the next cow. "But she obviously doesn't."

"Did you have to scold her like she was a misbehaving child?"

I shot Vera a glare. "Why are you still here? You should be on your way home by now."

"Do you think it's easy for her to be here? This is the life you have always known. Just because you don't like Mrs. Watkins doesn't mean she's not allowed to be her friend—"

"That's not why I'm mad," I shot back. "She put the herd at risk—"

"You've been checking these cows for signs twice a day for weeks," she reminded me. "Milk production has not gone down a bit. The herd is fine and you know it."

"We could easily have missed something. Lots of other farmers missed signs and now their herds are gone." I gently pried a reluctant cow's jaw open and peered inside its mouth. Satisfied, I moved onto the next one. "Besides, you don't even like her."

Vera glanced at Sheila. "I never said that. I wasn't sure you two were…a proper fit before. You're both argumentative, stubborn arses so maybe you deserve one another."

I sighed. "I slept like shite last night and I took it out on her. Assuming we don't find anything, I'll go apologize to her—"

"And if you *do* find something? What then?" Vera rubbed at her forehead. "She made a mistake. Maybe she had a reason for being there."

"She would have told me about going over there if it was a good reason," I said. "No, it was something she wanted to hide from me."

I even wondered if Elsie was seeing if she could get reassigned to the Watkins farm since it would be an easier situation. That's what Elsie was originally looking for in a job assignment, wasn't it—an easy, cushy job with a bedroom in a big fancy house?

I didn't mention this to Vera though. She already looked like she wanted to give me a swift kick.

"Sheila," I yelled across the barn, "do you know why Elsie went over to the Watkins' place last week?"

She stood up straight and crossed her arms as she faced me. "Yes." Her tone was flat and her jaw was set.

"And?"

"I'm not telling you a bloody thing." She turned back around and kept checking the cows.

I threw my hands in the air and turned to the next cow.

My blood running cold, I spotted the brown sores right away. Dottie had two round, raised spots on her lower lip.

"Oh, God," Vera breathed.

"Sheila, I need your help over here." I pointed to the cow in the stall next to Dottie. "Check that one over everywhere. Check 'er twice." I looked back at Dottie. "Damn it."

I grabbed a rope from the back room and looped it around Dottie's neck to lead her outside and away from the rest of the herd as quickly as possible. She tried to go out the back door towards the pasture and mooed at me, confused, when I pulled her toward the front doors. I didn't even want to risk spreading it to the grass in the pastures where the cows would sleep soon or graze the following day.

"Did he find something on Dottie?" Sheila asked Vera.

Vera nodded.

"Oh, no."

Once outside I inspected every inch of Dottie. Her udders and feet were free of the disease but her gums were swollen and her tongue had another one of those sores, same as on her lips. I rubbed her neck and released a long exhale. Every part of me just wanted to take an evening swim in the lake, eat my cold supper, and go to bed.

I looked around the farmyard. "I'm sorry about this, old girl."

"Does she have it?"

I turned around to see Elsie standing just outside the cottage, hesitant to come any closer.

Nodding, I looked away from her.

"I'm so sorry, Ben," she said. "I just really needed to—"

"I can't talk about this right now," I said, tying Dottie's rope to the door of the toolshed. "I have to build a bloody fence for 'er so she doesn't try to get into the pasture through the night."

"Ben, I need to tell you—"

I shot her a look. "Not now." I didn't want to scold her again or get angry with her like Vera said and I didn't trust myself not to say something I'd regret.

Elsie's lips tightened and she nodded, her brow pinched and her gaze hitting the ground. I wanted to forget about everything and hold her—but I couldn't. I just couldn't.

To avoid seeing the devastation on her face I went into the toolshed to look for some boards I could use for a fence.

Elsie knowingly made the choice to risk my herd and my family's farm for a chat with a friend. And now my cattle were infected and would have to be destroyed. I didn't see how I could forgive her for that. She'd been at Honeyfield for less than a year. She never saw how hard my father worked to make sure the farm prospered. She didn't know what it meant to owe your life to the soil you worked—how could she possibly know that when she was from a different world?

And how could I have ever thought she could be a permanent part of mine?

Later that evening Sheila and I ate our cold suppers in silence. Vera had gone home and Elsie hid upstairs. None of the other cows were showing signs of foot and mouth yet. It was only a matter of time. I knew how fast the disease spread. It was only a matter of time.

I'd tried to call Mr. Linden but his housekeeper said he and just about every other vet in Bath were run off their feet with calls from cattle farmers so he wouldn't be able to come see Dottie for a day or two.

Sheila stared at the third plate of food on the table and then peered at the ceiling. She snatched a piece of bread from the plate in the middle of the table and added it to the third plate before picking it up and carrying it out.

"She can come downstairs if she's hungry," I mumbled.

Her glare was a dagger. I actually sat up straighter in my chair, it startled me so much.

"She needs to eat," Sheila said slowly. "Stop being such an arse," she continued, her feet heavy on the staircase.

I cursed under my breath and looked at Sam as he laid in front of the fireplace. "I'm not being an arse, am I?"

He let out a huff and adjusted his position so he looked away from me. Hell, even my dog was mad at me.

A few minutes later Sheila returned to the kitchen, plate still in hand. She stared at me. "She's gone. She took her suitcase."

twenty-five

Elsie

It was nearly nine o'clock when I reached a bed and breakfast in Fairbury, my chest heaving from the long walk while lugging my suitcase.

The older woman who opened the door scowled at me and pulled her dressing gown tighter around herself. "Can I help you, miss?" She eyed my suitcase.

"Can I have a room for the night?" I tried to smile sweetly but it was not my best effort.

She narrowed her eyes at me. "Aren't you the young lady who delivers the milk from Honeyfield Farm?"

Bloody hell.

"Yes, that's me," I replied quickly. "Do you have a room available? I have money."

Pursing her lips and crossing her arms over her chest, she looked me up and down. "It's a bit late for checking in."

"Well, I'm glad I caught you before you went to bed."

Let me in, you miserable old hag.

She huffed. "Alright." She stepped aside and closed the door after me. "I'll need payment first. Breakfast is at seven o'clock. I'll need your ration book."

I nodded, grateful I'd remembered to grab it on the way out of the cottage earlier that evening.

After my room was paid for she showed me to my room on the second floor and, once the door was closed, I flopped onto the bed and didn't move for fifteen minutes. I packed in haste but made sure to only pack necessities so the suitcase wasn't too heavy for the long walk through our upper fields, over the stone wall to the next farm, and through acres of apple orchards. I knew I wasn't supposed to carry anything heavy, but if I arrived back in London without my suitcase my parents would know something was very wrong straight away.

As tears began streaming down my cheeks and onto the quilt under me, I slid my hand down to my belly and caressed it.

"It's okay," I whispered to the baby and to myself. "Everything will be alright."

Ben hated me.

He hated me, he distrusted me, he blamed me. It was all in his eyes as he said, "Not now," like I was a bother and not the woman carrying his child.

He didn't know that, of course. But I had seen all I needed to see.

I wanted to tell him about the baby before that horrible moment, but he was so worried about the herd and the farm that there was never a good time to bring it up. I wanted the moment to be perfect. When I was ready to settle for imperfect, it was too late. He didn't want to hear a word of anything I had to say.

Rolling over onto my side I brought my knees up and sobbed into one of the frilly pillows to help stifle the agony in my heart.

"These eggs are simply divine," exclaimed the overly enthusiastic woman from the other side of the breakfast table. "Are they the powdered ones or are they real eggs?"

"Powdered ones from America," Mrs. Sutton, the B&B owner, said. "I'm glad you like them. I learned a few tricks to making them taste like the real thing from *The Kitchen Front*."

They did not taste like real eggs at all but I didn't point that out.

Overly Enthusiastic Woman kept glancing at me. Finally after the tenth look my way, she whispered, "Are you feeling any better?"

Mrs. Sutton's suspicious eyes darted between us.

"I'm fine, thank you," I said, reaching for my teacup.

Earlier that morning Overly Enthusiastic Woman, another B&B guest, was on her way to our shared loo and I had galloped out of my room, gave her a slight shove, slammed the door shut and vomited rather loudly. I had apologized profusely to the woman after.

"No, no," she said, "that's quite alright. I had the same thing when I was…" She glanced at my empty ring finger. "…when I was, uh, younger."

"I think I ate something off last night," I said at the breakfast table, hopefully putting their nosy minds at ease. "I feel better now."

Mrs. Sutton stared at my naked ring finger and pursed her lips as I put my teacup down.

I realized those disapproving looks were just a preview of the next several months of my life. It would become so much worse and constant once my pregnancy began to show.

Part of me believed Ben would be waiting at the shuttle stop when I arrived the next morning. He was not.

I thought perhaps he would look for me when he learned I had disappeared the night before. He would have to assume I'd gone to a B&B—where else would I go? But no. He simply accepted I'd left and was fine with that. He didn't even love me enough to look for me.

He never loved me at all.

Once in Bath I made my way to the train station. I hated myself for searching the platform for Ben, thinking he might rush in and beg forgiveness. Every time a new passenger came from the ticket office and onto the platform, I looked to see if it was him. With a wall of tears blurring my vision I boarded the train, found the first empty seat, and dropped into it. I had never been more miserable in my entire life.

"Miss, would you like me to put that suitcase up in the overhead for you or…?"

I stared blankly at the passenger. "What?" I sniffed.

Patiently, she gestured to the suitcase I held tight in my arms.

"Oh. Yes, thank you."

She tucked it into the shelf above us, slid her case next to it, and took the empty seat beside me. Without a word, she fetched a handkerchief from her bag and handed it to me.

That tiny gesture of kindness caused me to go from watering eyes and sniffling to fully crying again.

She patted my shoulder. "We're all going through it these days, aren't we?"

All I could do was nod.

As the train rolled through the lush farmland of Somerset and into London, I considered what might happen next. If I told my parents I certainly knew what they would demand of me: I would be sent to Scotland for the remainder of my pregnancy, deliver the baby in secret and in shame, and give the baby away to another family. A similar solution was chosen for one of my friends growing up. Her boyfriend left her for another woman while she was expecting so off to Scotland she went. She came back completely broken, as if her soul had all the color drained from it.

Mother and Father would certainly disown me if I didn't agree. No daughter of theirs would live as an unmarried mother. Giving it up for adoption or offering it to a couple who couldn't have children of their own was the most logical answer to my problem.

And yet.

I put my hand to my abdomen again, palming it protectively. I couldn't. I couldn't do it. I could not and would not give up my child, no matter what my parents insisted.

Perhaps Jack and Nora would take me in once my parents evicted me from their home. Surely Jack would make sure I was alright, just as he had when we were growing up.

My eyes had dried and my sniffles had subsided by the time the train pulled into the station in London thirty minutes late because of the delay in Reading. Train delays were such a common occurrence during the war that they were just a regular part of the trip.

My taller seatmate got my suitcase down for me. Smiling weakly I offered her the handkerchief back.

She wrinkled her nose, looking at the damp wad of cotton, marred by mucus. "No, that's alright, dear. You keep it."

While sitting silently in the back of the hackney, once again heading north, I considered the legal practicalities of becoming an unwed mother. Would I be obligated to tell Ben about the baby? Perhaps I would be forced to give it to him if I did. I suppose that would be better than giving it to a stranger. But then where would I live? Perhaps the child would live with me in London and then travel to Fairbury to see Ben on weekends?

My thoughts drifted to less complicated matters; what the child might look like. Would it have my blonde curls and slightly upturned nose? Would the child have Ben's tawny eyes or his shy smile?

The thought of his smile—and how I would probably never see it again—was a hot iron to my heart.

George met me at the door with raised brows. "Miss Foster-Quinn! We were not expecting you." He took my suitcase and closed the door after me.

"Yes, well…" I swallowed, realizing I had not planned what I was going to say to anyone. "Plans changed rather quickly, I'm afraid. Are Mother and Father at home?"

"Your father is at one of the factories but he will return tomorrow. I believe your mother is taking tea in the garden with Mr. Parker," he said. "I will have more tea brought out for you."

"Thank you, George." I smiled at him, studying the faint lines of his aging face for a moment. I realized then that I had known the man my entire life and yet I had no idea if George was married or if he had children. I had never, ever before thought to ask.

"Is everything alright, Miss Foster-Quinn?"

I nodded. "Apologies, George. I'm just tired from the journey."

Crossing the elegant foyer I let myself out into the back garden. My mother was speaking animatedly about some charity event to my brother Jack while he sipped his tea. She glanced over her shoulder when she heard my footsteps and then turned all the way around in her chair.

"Elsie! What on earth are you doing here?" She jumped up and embraced me.

I didn't think a hug could feel so nourishing to a soul. I squeezed her tight and didn't want to let her go.

Jack smiled with his entire face, eyes gleaming. "You sneaky devil, what are you doing home?"

Mother backed up from me and waited for an explanation.

I did my best everything-is-fine face. "I…I got fired from the farm."

She put a hand on her chest. "Oh, darling. That's too bad." I had never heard someone put less effort into a lie. "Well, your father will be relieved, that's certain."

Jack hugged me next and then stepped back, his eyes narrowing slightly. "What did you do?"

"Have you read anything in the newspapers about a foot and mouth disease outbreak in Bath?"

My mother and brother exchanged blank looks and shook their heads.

How could something so dire in one part of the country not even make the London papers? Did a single Londoner not know there was a world outside of the capital city? Or perhaps they just didn't care.

"It's quite bad," I explained. "Godfrey and Rosetta Watkins just lost their entire cattle herd to the disease the other day. I went there to visit Rosetta and I…brought the disease back to Honeyfield Farm and now…" The words caught in my throat as I recalled the many hours I had spent with those cows and also the look in Ben's eyes as he said, "Not now."

Clearing my throat I lowered my eyes to the decorative stone pathways of the garden, abundant with colorful flowers and shrubs.

"I'm sure you didn't mean to cause any harm," Mother said, rubbing my arm. "Come sit and have tea with us. You'll feel right as rain in no time."

Jack picked up his tea again, his brows knit together. "You're not in legal trouble, are you?"

"Oh," I said. "I…I don't think so."

I hadn't even considered that. I certainly had not heard of anyone getting sued for spreading the disease between farms, just fined for trespassing. Surely Ben wouldn't consider legal action against me.

Right?

"I'm thrilled you're back but sorry to hear things didn't end well for you at the farm," Jack added. "What will you do now?"

Again, I had not a single word of a response prepared.

"Get a job at an office, I suppose," I said as one of the staff brought out fresh tea for us and an additional teacup for me. "I really don't know, to be honest."

Bees floated from flower to flower nearby, happily spreading pollen about the garden. Tilting my head slightly, I quickly surveyed the plants around us.

"Mother, why haven't you added a vegetable patch to the garden?"

Jack squeezed his mouth together to hide a mischievous smirk. Meanwhile, Mother pursed her lips and put her tea down, clasping her hands in her lap.

"Darling, you know we get plenty of vegetables from the gardens at Channel House."

"Yes, but you could get more if you used this land too," I said. "*Everyone* has given up at least some of their back gardens to grow vegetables. If there was too much, perhaps some of the vegetables from Channel House could be donated to the people in the village or maybe given to the soldiers staying there now."

She blinked hard at me. "We have already been forced to give up Channel House because of the war. I'm not about to give up my flowers as well. Besides, who would do all of that? I've lost several members of the staff to factory jobs already—"

"You could do it," I said. "Perhaps in the spring we could make a project of it together and put in a vegetable patch. I could teach you."

I said it before remembering I would be about eight months pregnant by the time March came round again.

Jack's eyes flicked to our mother and then back to me. Mother picked up her tea again and studied me.

"Dearest, don't be silly." She rolled her eyes. "You know I don't have time to tend to *vegetables*." She said the last word like the very idea was repulsive to her.

I was asking her to grow a few carrots and tomatoes like everyone else but she acted like I had suggested she don a uniform and get ready to face Hitler personally.

Sipping my tea, I kept silent. I would soon be telling Mum of her illegitimate grandchild so I needed her on my side.

George appeared in the doorway leading to the garden. "Mrs. Foster-Quinn, you have a telephone call."

Mother looked relieved to have an excuse to leave. "I'll be right back, darlings."

As soon as she shut the door behind her, Jack grinned at me. "What really happened?"

I shook my head. "I think killing an entire herd of cattle is a good reason—"

"There's something more to it than that," he said. "Did you and the farmer have a falling out?"

I sighed, closing my eyes. "Nora told you."

"Of course she did."

"Everything is a terrible mess," I said, returning my teacup and saucer to the small table between us. "I," Tears pricked my eyes as I met his gaze. "I can't say I'm terribly fond of this feeling."

Jack's shoulders sagged. "You really do love him, don't you?"

"I think I always will," I whispered. "That's what hurts the most."

twenty-six

BEN

"Your tea is getting cold."

I blinked hard and whipped my head up. "What?"

"You've been staring at that newspaper for ten minutes," Vera chided. "I don't think you're even reading it, just staring."

Cattle Disease: "Worst for 25 Years." 177 Cases Up to Date

The newspaper article included the names of all the farms where cases of foot and mouth had been found, the Watkins farm included. I had yet to get Mr. Linden over to Honeyfield so our case wasn't yet confirmed. Dottie's condition had worsened slightly but no other cows were showing symptoms of the highly contagious illness just yet. The not knowing was miserable. I just wanted the whole thing to be done and over with.

I kept having terrible dreams where I walked into the barn to do the morning milking and the entire herd was mooing in agony. Sometimes the nightmares sent me back to a few years ago when our sheep were sent to slaughter and I would wake up in a cold sweat.

If those dreams weren't bad enough, the dreams with Elsie in them—good or bad—felt ten times worse. Sometimes I would wake up and swear I heard her sleeping beside me or felt her snuggle up to me. Then my eyes would open and it would be just me, alone in bed. And I'd remember all over again. It was a punch to the gut every single time.

Each time thoughts of Elsie crept into my mind as I went about my work, I reminded myself how careless she was with the safety of the farm. With each passing hour since she'd left, I'd become increasingly angrier with myself for reacting the way I did and scaring her off.

Elsie Foster-Quinn was a stubborn, spoiled brat and by far the best thing that had ever happened to me.

Sheila poked her head into the kitchen door. "Why doesn't your horse like me?"

"Pardon?"

"He won't move," she exclaimed. "I got the cart loaded up to go deliver the milk and he won't budge. Elsie said he just *goes* when she would get up on the cart but he won't *go* for me."

"The stubborn arse misses her," Vera said as I rose from the table.

"He must be in a mood," I said, throwing back the rest of my cooled tea. "I'll do the delivery."

Once out in the farmyard I brushed Sherlock's neck and he snorted at me, watching me curiously.

"I miss her, too," I whispered. "But she's gone."

His ear twitched in response and I climbed up into the cart. Picking up the reins I waited for him to go, but he just snorted at me again.

"You old bastard, please don't do this today," I grumbled.

He turned his head enough to look at me.

"I'm sorry," I said. "I didn't mean that. I'm just having a bad time of it right now."

He turned back to face front again and slowly began trotting towards the road. At least the long journey gave me plenty of time to wallow in my misery.

At the second house I retrieved the empty bottles when the door opened and Mrs. Moore appeared, a baby on her hip.

"Oh! Hi Ben. You're not Elsie."

"Uh, no. No, I'm not." I smiled weakly. "Have a good day—"

"Is Elsie not feeling well? I noticed she didn't do the delivery yesterday either."

I swallowed. "She's gone back to London, actually." I climbed back up on the cart.

"Oh, what a shame," Mrs. Moore said to her baby. "We liked Elsie, didn't we?"

Something similar happened at one of the next cottages further down.

"Is Elsie not doing delivering anymore?" Mr. Seaton said as I handed him his fresh milk.

Again, I explained that she'd returned to London.

"That's too bad. She was a lovely girl," he said. "She always complimented my flower boxes."

By the tenth time, I was taking it personally.

"Is Elsie—"

"She's gone back to London," I snapped. "Have a good day!"

When we finally reached the last stop of the delivery route, I knocked on the door. "Milk delivery, ma'am," I called.

Mum opened the door, studied me and let out a long sigh. I frowned.

"You don't answer the door that way for everyone, right? Sigh at them while looking annoyed?"

"I'm not annoyed," she clarified. "Just disappointed."

"Oh, well, that is *so* much better, truly."

"You're delivering milk meaning Elsie isn't back. Shame. I miss having tea with her." Mum left the door open for me to come in.

Ah. That's why Elsie was later getting back from the delivery run on some days.

"I should probably get back," I said, gesturing to the cart. "I have a lot—"

"Oh, hush," she said, already pouring tea for the both of us. "Sit down, will you?"

I did as I was told and resignedly drank my tea in silence.

She slid her spectacles off, folded them up and pointed at me with them. "What are you going to do?"

I shrugged. "I can't really do anything until Mr. Linden confirms that the herd has—"

"Not that," she snapped. "What are you going to do about your girl?"

"My girl?"

"Yes. Elsie. What are you going to do to get her to come back to Fairbury?"

I huffed. "Vera told you about that, too. Perfect."

"She didn't have to," she said. "I come for dinner every Sunday. I saw how the two of you looked at one another. I know what love looks like."

I immediately studied the flower pattern of the table cloth. "Did Vera tell you why Elsie went back to London?"

"Something about how she went to see Mrs. Watkins and you blame her for your cow getting sick. Yes, I heard." She shook her head. "For such a smart boy, you can act like such a fool sometimes."

I looked back up at her. "What?"

"Vera told me you were considering asking Elsie to marry you. She made a mistake and suddenly you are treating her so poorly that she leaves." She shook her head and took a long sip of her tea. "No matter what happens with the herd, you will regret it if you don't at least try to get her back."

"I might have to have a chat with my sister about keeping secrets," I mumbled.

"I know you don't like to take chances," Mum said, setting her cup down and looking directly at me, "but it's the things we take the leap for that end up meaning the most. If this war has taught us anything, it's that we shouldn't wait to tell people how much we love them."

"What if I try and she just…doesn't want to be with me?"

"Be honest with me, Benjamin." Mum folded her hands in her lap. "If you could go back to the day when that toad from the War Ag told you to dig up my lilies and put in a vegetable patch, would you say the same thing again?"

I snickered. "I'd tell him where to stuff his official recommendations." I shrugged again. "What does that have to do with trying to get Elsie back?"

She leaned forward in her chair. "Because this is *so* much more important than a flower garden."

Early the following morning I finished the milking with Sheila and we were doing the cleanup when we heard a car coming up the drive. Sheila grinned and I raised an eyebrow at her as Mr. Linden got out of the car. I rushed to the open barn doors.

"Mr. Linden!" I called across the yard. "I thought you said you couldn't come to check my herd for another two days."

He beamed. "Miss Sheila here said you have a train to catch in a few hours so I shuffled some clients around to come here first."

Sheila appeared at my side, still looking quite smug indeed.

"Thank you," I whispered to Sheila as I led Mr. Linden to the ramshackle fenced-in pen I'd built for Dottie. "This is the one. I think the sores on her lips are worse but she doesn't have any blisters on her udders or around her hooves that I could see."

Mr. Linden put on a pair of gloves, let himself into the small pen, and began his thorough inspection of the cow.

He looked back at me as he ran a thumb over the inside of the cow's ears. "None of the other cows are showing any symptoms?"

"No, not yet."

"We've been checking them at least twice a day," Sheila added, her arms folded over her chest, watching as Mr. Linden worked. "None of them look sick and we're getting the same amount of milk as usual."

He checked her udders and feet. "And someone in your household visited a farm with an infected herd last week?"

"Yes, it's been a week. Maybe a bit over a week now."

The vet nodded. Finally he gently pried the cow's mouth open to look at the sores and swollen gums inside. "Right." He looked back at me. "She doesn't have foot and mouth, Ben."

I stared at him. "Say that again?"

"It's bovine papular stomatitis," he said, removing his gloves. "It's not foot and mouth at all. Actually, it's not uncommon for papular stomatitis to be misidentified with foot and mouth. I'll give her some mild antibiotics and that should clear up the issue with the gums and she'll be right as rain."

My eyes darted between Sheila, Mr. Linden, and Dottie. "I-are-I… are you having me on?"

How could a vet's diagnosis make everything so much better *and* so much worse at the exact same time?

Sheila put her palm over her mouth, her whole face alight with joy. Mr. Linden joined us on the outside of the pen and Sheila wrapped her arms around his neck and kissed him on the lips.

"Thank you!" she exclaimed. "Thank you, thank you!"

"Goodness, Sheila," I mumbled.

Mr. Linden chuckled and gestured to his car. "I'll go get that medicine."

Sheila rolled her eyes at me as he left us alone for a moment. "Me and Abel have been seeing one another for months. We're just a lot more subtle than you and Elsie ever were."

I opened my mouth to speak but nothing came out. Closing it again I just nodded at her. "Well done."

"Now," she said, "you'd better go put on your Sunday best, grab that suitcase from the kitchen, and have Vera drive you to Bath. If you miss that train I will never let you forget it."

I grabbed her shoulders. "You're a saint, Sheila!"

"I know!" she yelled as I dashed for the cottage. "Good luck today and don't muck it up!"

twenty-seven

Elsie

One good thing about living with my parents again: being able to have morning sickness in an indoor, flushing loo instead of having to run outside.

One bad thing about living with my parents again: Mother saw me dash into the loo to vomit before breakfast.

She was still in the hall when I opened the door.

Mother stared at me, horrified. "Are you poorly?"

Please, please, please don't just magically know I'm pregnant.

I wasn't ready to tell her yet. Perhaps I would summon the courage in six or seven years time.

"I woke up with a dreadful headache," I lied, rubbing the side of my temple for added effect.

She frowned, her lips tight. "Should I have a tray brought up to your room?"

Smiling weakly I nodded. "Thank you, Mother. I think that would be best."

Back in my room, I grabbed *Wuthering Heights* from the side table and wriggled back under my sheets in my four poster bed. As much as I missed Ben, Sheila, and the farm, it had been lovely to sleep in for the first time in ages. And getting to have breakfast in bed? Absolutely divine.

Or so I expected it would be.

A member of our staff knocked before setting my breakfast, arranged prettily on the tray, on my side table. The young woman gave a quick curtsy and turned to leave.

"Thank you," I said.

She turned around again, her brow slightly pinched in the middle. "You're welcome, Miss Foster-Quinn." Her cockney accent reminded me I was back in London.

I hesitated.

She folded her hands in front of herself. "Is there anything else I can get for you, miss?"

"Please, call me Elsie," I said. "What's your name?"

The maid's eyes widened slightly. "My name is Victoria, miss."

"How long have you worked for my parents?"

She smiled politely. "A year and a half."

Oh. She worked here before I left. I likely treated her like furniture.

"Of course," I said, faking a little laugh. "How do you like working here?"

"Um, it's fine, miss. It's a good job and I'm treated well." She rubbed her thumb over the thumbnail on the opposite hand. "Why, did Mrs. Foster-Quinn say something about me? Did I do something wrong?"

"No," I blurted. "No, no, nothing like that. I was just…chatting." I shook my head at myself. "My apologies. You're probably busy. I'll let you get back to your work."

Victoria gave another quick curtsy and basically ran from the room before I could ask her any more questions. I slumped back into my bountiful heap of pillows, plucking a piece of toast from the tray and taking a big bite.

I would have to get one of the ration books for pregnant women, I realized woefully, or risk having a malnourished baby.

Perhaps it was for the best I was soon to be evicted from this house. Soon the staff would all think I was mad and there was a chance

I would go back to being how I was before. I didn't want to be Miss Foster-Quinn, the prim and perfect daughter of Robert and Caroline Foster-Quinn. I wanted to be Elsie. Just Elsie.

I didn't want to be like that again, and I certainly didn't want my child to see me like that.

When I finished my breakfast I had a bath, did my hair and makeup, and pulled out an outfit I hadn't seen in ages from my wardrobe—a forest green knee-length skirt with brassy buttons up the front and a simple pale yellow blouse. As I rolled my stockings up I caught sight of my reflection and was nearly startled.

I hadn't seen that woman in so long. I almost hated to admit it but I missed her.

I *liked* wearing pretty, stylish things. I *liked* wearing makeup and doing my hair. I had tried to keep up with it when I was in Fairbury but exhaustion usually won out in the end. Plus, there wasn't much point to wasting precious, scarce makeup when you might just sweat it all off in the fields. I missed wearing my own clothes.

Of course I would have to get Nora to help me keep up with the latest fashions since my clothes would need to be altered soon. I kept forgetting.

Standing in front of my mirror I ran a hand over my abdomen. I didn't even know when I might begin to show. If my morning sickness continued to strike every day, I wouldn't have to have a bulging belly for my mother to figure it out.

Later I joined Mother and Father for lunch.

"Are you feeling better now, darling?" Mum smiled, her eyes caring.

"Yes, thank you," I said.

"I must say, it is so lovely to see you in your usual clothes. You really look like your old self again," she added.

I certainly didn't feel like my old self. Not at all.

Father gave a stiff nod. "No more dungarees for you, I hear?"

"That's correct," I said, reaching for my tea. "I was fired. Rightfully so. I wasn't cut out for it, like you said."

Inside I recoiled at my own self-deprecation. Why did I do that?

"Yes, I told your father about your silly little mistake." Mother waved a dismissive hand.

"It wasn't really a silly little mistake," I said timidly.

"You don't need to be concerned about the farm anymore," Father said. "I'm sure it was quite the adventure though. Have you given any thought to what you might do for war work—"

"It wasn't a silly little mistake," I exclaimed.

Mother and Father both gawped at me.

"Darling," she said. "There is no need to shout."

"My carelessness risked the lives of an entire herd of dairy cows," I said, speaking slowly and clearly in the hopes that they might understand. "A person I care about could lose his farm—a farm that has been in his family for generations—all because of me."

I studied my plate. It seemed the better option than to look at either of them.

Everybody in this house thinks I'm mad as a hatter, I thought.

"Is there a chance this farmer might take legal action against you?" Father's face was entirely relaxed as he spoke.

"He wouldn't do that," I said before reconsidering. "At least, I do not think he would."

Father sniffed. "He would be a fool to try it."

I feared the full meaning of his statement. Half the chaps Father played cricket with at uni became barristers.

Finally I looked up at them again. "I have to go back."

My mother's eyes bulged. "You cannot be serious. You only got back a few days ago!"

Father sputtered. "What? Surely you can just call them—"

"They don't have a phone—"

"Then send them a telegram, Elsie," Mother ordered. "Stop being ridiculous."

"It's not just that. I need to be there." Gradually my eyes widened at my own epiphany. "I *want* to be there."

Beaming I slid my chair back from the table as that wonderful realization flowed through my veins and lit up my spirit. "Excuse me. I have to go pack."

Ignoring their calls for me to come back, I started up the stairs for my bedroom.

"Miss Foster-Quinn?" George said from behind me. "There is a man here to see you—a Mr. Grainger?"

Was I dreaming? Had he really just said that?

Turning around slowly I looked past George to see Ben—*my* Ben!—standing just outside the front door, gazing up at me. Time seemed to slow as I descended the stairs, never taking my eyes from his. My heart pounded so hard I thought I might faint.

"Thank you, George," I said, nodding to excuse him.

Time stood still as Ben and I stared at one another.

"Hello," I said finally.

"Hello." Ben whipped off his flat cap, revealing a forehead glistening with perspiration. After a beat he foisted a hardcover book at me. "You forgot your copy of *Pride and Prejudice* at the cottage." His gaze hit the floor.

I smiled and took the book from him. "Thank you for bringing it to me." I held it to my chest as I considered which of the thousand things I wanted to say to choose first.

Mother floated in from the dining room. "Good afternoon. Can we help you?" She eyed Ben's old, weathered suitcase next to his feet and his faded cream-colored shirt sleeves rolled up just past his elbows. "Are you…selling something?"

Embarrassed, I winced. "This is Mr. Grainger. He's a friend of mine from Fairbury. Mr. Grainger, this is my mother." I gestured for Ben to follow me before she could say anything more. "We'll be in the garden." Whisking by I put the book on the table beside the staircase.

Picking up his suitcase and following me as directed, he nodded to Mum as he strode by. "How do you do, ma'am?"

If Mother told me to stop and explain myself I didn't hear her. The thoughts in my head buzzed so loudly I couldn't focus on anything except my urge to throw myself into Ben's arms and never let him go ever again.

But I wanted him to say what he came to say first.

I led Ben to the bench near the fountain. He carefully set down his suitcase and perched on the bench's edge beside me, glancing at me anxiously every ten seconds or so.

He watched the fountain in silence. Finally I couldn't take it.

"I can't believe you're here," I blurted with a nearly hysterical laugh. "You actually came!"

"I guess it was rude of me to just show up unannounced. Sheila gave me the address." The deep line between Ben's brows eased as he smiled softly. "I needed to see you. I needed to talk to you."

My fingers instinctively reached for his hand but I pulled them back, curling them into my palm, just in case.

"I was scared," he said quietly, his eyes finding the fountain again. "I was scared and I took it out on you. I've never regretted anything more in my entire life than the way I talked to you that day—"

"No, *I'm* sorry. I risked the herd—"

"It's not about the herd." He closed his eyes. "I was terrified I didn't deserve you and that you'd eventually figure that out. I'm so, *so* sorry." He finally met my gaze. "I want to be with you. I want to wake up with you beside me every morning. I want to hear your snoring beside me every night." He paused. "I want to marry you. I want to have a family with you."

My heart leapt in my chest as he spoke those last words. My eyes brimmed with tears as he continued.

"I want to grow old with you. I want to lay in bed reading with you. I want to…" He searched for the right words. "I want to burn food with you."

I laughed. He placed a palm on my cheek and wiped at my stray tears with the pad of his thumb. I leaned into his hand. Just to be touching him again was pure bliss.

"I hope those are happy tears," he said, leaning his forehead to mine.

"Yes, they are." I sniffed. "Very, very happy."

He peered behind him at the house. "I can't give you the same life." He looked back at me. "We'll never have a butler or a chandelier hanging from the ceiling."

"I don't need those things. I just need you." I kissed him lightly on the lips. "Besides, you shouldn't hang butlers from the ceiling. They don't like it." I smirked.

"Christ, I love you so much," he said, grinning, before pulling me closer and kissing me deeply.

I melted, struck pleasantly breathless by the intensity and warmth of his mouth on mine, the pressure of his lips and the tickle of his beard on my skin.

Nervous my parents might see, I broke off the kiss and nuzzled my nose against his. Suddenly Ben slid his hand into his trouser pocket and pulled out a walnut shell.

I laughed. "Of course you would have a walnut in your…"

I stared as he unwrapped a bit of twine from around the shell and carefully opened it at the hinge, revealing a ring. Tiny intricate flourishes embellished its gold band while the centrepiece featured a delicate gold flower, its petals curling inwards. In the center of the flower, tucked neatly between the petals, a small dome-shaped diamond sparkled.

I gasped into my palm. "Oh, my God." I wiped furiously at the fresh tears appearing in my eyes.

Ben knelt on the ground in front of me. "What do you say?"

"I say yes." I thrust my shaking hand at him so he could slide the lovely ring onto my finger.

We both stood and I threw my arms around his neck, clinging to him as he hugged me, lifting my feet off the ground.

"Do you like it? It was my grandmother's," Ben explained. "I got it from Mum last night."

"It's beautiful."

I pulled him down by his shirt collar and kissed him again.

When we parted, I cringed.

"What?"

"We have to tell my parents."

Ben glanced at the brick walls surrounding the garden. "I could probably climb that."

I giggled. "What about me? You'll just leave me here?"

"No, I'll carry you on my back." He shrugged. "Or I can just toss you over, that could work."

I sighed. "There will be no tossing me over a wall. We have to tell them."

For the second time that day, Mother and Father stared at me. Then they looked at the ring, then at Ben, and finally back at me.

My mother took a seat in the nearby armchair. "You're marrying a farmer?"

Father took out his cigarettes and lit one, inhaling deeply, exhaling smoke hard from his nostrils, and glaring at the pair of us. Mother usually didn't allow him to smoke in the house but this was apparently an exceptional circumstance.

"You can't be serious," Mother added, looking back at me. "This is ridiculous! What could you be possibly be thinking?"

"How will he support you?" Father demanded. "You already told us you killed all his cows for goodness sake."

My heart jolted and I looked up at Ben. I had forgotten to ask about them.

Ben looked unconcerned. "My herd is fine. We had a scare with one of our cows but it turned out to be an unrelated, minor illness. Nothing to worry about."

I squeezed his hand. "That's wonderful news!"

Father's eyes narrowed and his jaw set. "He can't afford to keep you in all the nice clothes you like so much!"

"Thankfully my sister-in-law is a wonderful designer. I'm sure we can work something out," I said. "She'll make me a wardrobe that is practical for working on the farm *and* stylish."

"This won't last, mark my words." Mother wrinkled her nose. "I should never have let you go to that farm."

"I don't think it was a coincidence that I ended up at Honeyfield instead of Channel House. Somehow, some way, I was always meant to be there," I smiled up at Ben, "and stay there."

Father glared at the suitcase at Ben's feet and scoffed. "If you think you're sleeping under this roof tonight—"

"I wouldn't dream of it, sir," Ben said.

"We're going out now. I want to show Ben some of my favorite places in London before he goes back to Fairbury tomorrow. Ben will sleep at Jack's tonight and I'll be back this evening," I said, "or am I also banned from sleeping here?"

"Yes," Father snapped.

"Of course not," Mother said at the same time.

They exchanged a quick glance. Father rolled his eyes and stormed out of the room, cursing under his breath.

Once we were holding hands on the pavement and on our way to the train, Ben asked, "Did that go better or worse than you expected?"

"Oh, much better," I said. "I knew there was a chance Father might try to punch you."

He laughed. "You didn't think to warn me?"

"You're twice his size." I shrugged. "You would have managed."

We took the tube to Piccadilly Circus. We didn't have a lot of time to sightsee in London but there was one place I *had* to show him.

Ben's eyes widened as we emerged from the underground. The throngs of people walking every which way, bicycles whipping by, the enormous Bovril and Wrigley's advertising signage, the Guinness clock, red double-decker buses twirling around the circus at a clip—he took it all in, his mouth hanging slightly open.

I pointed to the middle of the chaos. "You see that bit with the war posters on it? That's where the statue of Eros usually is." I frowned. "I'll bring you back here one day when London isn't in survival mode." I nodded towards Piccadilly. "This way."

As we made our way down Piccadilly I tried not to look at St. James, a beautiful 17th century Anglican church. During the early months of the Blitz a German bomb crashed through its red brick roof, blowing out its stunning stained glass windows and destroying much of the Christopher Wren-designed interior.

Ben winced at the great holes in its roof, nearly the entire length of the church.

I took Ben's hand again and led him further down the street, soon stopping in front of one of my most cherished places in the city. The windows were boarded up, their glass missing since 1940. Despite its lack of windows, the bookshop with its elegant black façade had survived and endured.

"This is Hatchards, the oldest bookshop in all of London," I said with a flourish. "Opened in 1797."

Ben smiled at the elegant gilded store name above the door and led the way inside. Bath had a lovely bookshop but nothing compared to the five floors of Hatchards. Many shelves had noticeable gaps, probably due to paper shortages and rationing.

Squeezing through the other browsing customers, we found the corner where all the Arthur Conan Doyle Sherlock Holmes mysteries were lined up neatly on shelves. His eyes warm, Ben trailed his fingers affectionately across their spines as his eyes ran over their titles.

"Thank you for bringing me here," he whispered before kissing the top of my head.

Biting my lip I slid a finger down one of the nearby Conan Doyle books. "What do you think of the name Arthur if it's a boy?"

Ben stared at me. "What?"

I guided his palm to my stomach. "Or perhaps Jane if it's a girl?"

He blinked hard at me, looked at my abdomen, and then back up at me. "Are you…?" Ben's eyes glistened with tears.

I nodded.

He cupped my face with both palms and looked directly into my eyes. "We're going to have a baby."

I nodded again, this time more enthusiastically. I choked out a little half sob as my joy caught up with me again.

Ben squeezed me in his arms, my feet lifting off the floor. I squealed and was soon silenced by his mouth firmly on mine. I gripped the front of his shirt, steadying myself as his lips slid across mine, making my heart thump wildly and my skin flame. I was dizzy with love for that man.

I had never known pure happiness until that moment—being kissed passionately by my future husband and the father of my child in a bookshop. It was perfect.

Caught up in the moment I reached for him but accidentally sent a stack of books toppling onto the floor.

"Oy, do you mind? This is place o' business," a shop girl said. "Get out."

Giggling and feigning embarrassment, we left the shop. Once out on the pavement, among the rush of busses and bicycles and cabs and shoppers, Ben took me in his arms, right there in the middle of all of it, and kissed me again. Even though this was our hundredth kiss, at least, every time our lips met created a new spark, igniting and spreading fire through my limbs, all the way down to the tips of my fingers—the same fingertips that would forever be reaching for him and wanting him near.

Would Jane Austen approve of my happy ending? Perhaps not. But it really wasn't even a happy ending. It was a happy beginning.

epilogue

Elsie

"Jane, dearest," I said from Vera's kitchen, "can you please set the table for dinner?"

Our oldest child, nearly nine years old, looked up from her book. "But I'm not done the chapter yet."

"It will still be there when you're done setting the table," I said.

She huffed and left her book on the rug next to her seven-year-old twin brothers, Christopher and Arthur, and her five-year-old sister, Emily. Dora, ever the doting grandmother, watched over them while Vera and I put the finishing touches on a birthday dinner for Herb.

Herb made it back from the war in one piece but with a severe limp. Herb and Ben's brother Walter worked on the farm with Ben, slowly transitioning Honeyfield from a dairy farm back to a sheep farm. The excellent quality of the wool from our flock was known around the county and it was in high demand thanks to clothing rationing ending in 1949–everyone was eager to freshen up their wardrobe after years of patching and mending. I knew Ben loved the cows but Honeyfield had been a sheep farm for generations. It was in Ben's blood. As we added more sheep to our flock we gradually sold our cattle to Amos, so they were never far away.

Vera cursed under her breath. "I was hoping to make a pie tomorrow but I'm low on sugar. Bloody rationing."

The war had ended seven years before and yet we still had to ration sugar, meat, butter, cheese, and even tea. Despite many, *many* lessons with Vera and Sheila, I remained an adequate cook at best with absolutely no hope of becoming a wizard in the kitchen like Vera. But I managed.

"I got a letter from June," Vera said as she checked the vegetables on the hob, a shadow of sadness passing over her eyes. "Her stepfather got a new job in London so they moved there. She said she planned to be at Buckingham right after the coronation. I hope she didn't get crushed by the crowd."

June returned to Manchester shortly after the war ended and only three months after learning her father had been killed on D-Day. Parting from June was tremendously painful for Vera after years of mothering the girl, but she did what we all did in those days: she swallowed back her tears, kept her chin up, and carried on. In Vera's case this meant seeing if any children made orphans by the war needed a home.

Arie, now a striking lad of sixteen, appeared at the door. "It smells great in here!" After six years in Fairbury and twelve in England, his words still had a tinge of a Dutch accent to them but it just made him more popular with the girls in the village.

Herb followed him in, followed by Ben.

My Ben.

My parents nearly had simultaneous heart attacks when they learned I was pregnant and that Ben and I would be marrying two weeks after we got engaged. They attended the small church wedding in Fairbury, scowling the entire time. Sheila, of course, was my bridesmaid and Amos served as Ben's best man. Archie and Percy couldn't make it to the wedding unfortunately but they more than made it up to me by coming home safe after the war.

Ben was right about one thing: Rosetta was *not* happy when she learned about our relationship. I couldn't tell if she was angrier about the "inexcusably inappropriate affiliation" between a land girl and her employer or the fact that I wasn't honest with her about who the baby's father was. I was quietly and unceremoniously removed from the Women's Land Army but continued to do the same work I had always done—that is until I was too pregnant to keep up. Thank goodness for Vera and Sheila, especially in those early days. I'm sure I would not have survived being a new mother without them.

Sheila was kind enough to wait until I wasn't pumpkin-shaped before asking me to be her bridesmaid when she married the very kind vet, Mr. Linden. I was completely gobsmacked when Ben told me Sheila admitted to seeing Mr. Linden secretly for months. I had no idea!

Ben squeezed into Vera's busy kitchen to give me a quick kiss on the cheek, his hand resting on my hip as he leaned in. Even now, almost ten years later, he still made my heart do backflips when we touched. His beard had a few grey whiskers in it now and I had early signs of crow's feet but we still could not keep our hands off one another.

"Ben, get out of the way or I'll beat you to death with a frying pan," Vera said, scooping food onto plates.

Ben put his hands up in the air, surrendering, before checking on the children and his mum. Everyone was soon beckoned into the small dining room and we dug into another one of Vera's magnificent meals.

Herb gazed adoringly at Vera across the table. "Thank you, sweetheart."

She smiled back at him. "Don't eat too much. I managed to get enough ingredients to make a cake. Don't ask me how. I could go to jail."

Ben had been eyeing me for a few minutes and I wondered what he was up to. Finally he took an envelope out of his back pocket. The top of it was already torn open.

"Are you giving me a bill at dinner?" I laughed. "How romantic." I frowned when I saw the return address. "Another rejection from a publisher."

He cocked a brow. "I guess you'll have to read it and see."

I snatched it out his hands and pulled the letter out.

In the tiny slivers of time between farm work, meal preparation, and raising children, Ben and I had worked on a project together. Inspired by Agatha Christie, we set about writing a mystery novel featuring a land girl who moves to a chocolate box village during the war and ends up investigating a murder. It took us ages to write it but we were intensely proud of our book—it was like our fifth child.

I hurriedly unfolded the letter, my eyes scanning the typed response. My hands quivering, I dropped it on my plate and slapped my palm over my mouth.

"What is it, Mummy?" Emily asked.

"What does it say?" Christopher added.

Dora plucked the letter from my plate as I stared at Ben.

"They want to publish the book next year," Dora read. "If sales do well, they hope to see more books featuring the same character."

"That's wonderful news!" Herb exclaimed. "Congratulations!"

"Does that mean people will be able to buy your book in a store?" Arthur said through a mouthful of food.

Ben laughed. "Yes, it does, but please close your mouth."

Wearing a huge grin Ben squeezed my hand under the table before bringing it to his lips to kiss lightly. I sniffed and swiped at a stray tear from the corner of my eye.

After everyone had their thin slice of birthday cake, we loaded our brood into the Hillman and returned home to Honeyfield. As I got out of the car and the children ran into the cottage ahead of us, Ben took my hand and I led us down to the front gate so I could check on how my lily garden was coming along.

"Oh, I see one," I said, pointing to a flaming orange bud.

Ben wrapped his arms around me and sighed as he rested his head on top of mine. "We really ought to take a swim in the lake one of these days."

I turned around in his arms and gazed up at him. "Perhaps tonight."

bonus scene

Elsie and Sheila went to the pub to treat Ben to a pint for his birthday but after almost coming to blows with a rude and intoxicated acquaintance, Ben stormed out and Elsie temporarily left the pub to go after him.

However, Sheila wasn't just sitting alone all that time. She ran into a gentleman friend, Mr. Linden.

Sign up at **jilly.ca/sheila**
for a bonus scene between Sheila and Mr. Linden.

Don't miss the other books in the Homefront Hearts WWII romance trilogy: *The Hobby Shop on Barnaby Street* and *The Seamstress on Cider Lane.*

Learn more at jilly.ca/homefront-hearts

acknowledgements

Thank you so much for reading *The Land Girl on Lily Road.*

If you enjoyed this book, I would appreciate it if you could take a few minutes and leave a review on whatever book retailer you purchased from.
Reviews are the easiest way to support authors.

If you would like to hear and get subscriber-only exclusivers, sign up to my monthly newsletter: **jilly.ca/subscribe**

Thank you to Colby, Mom, the rest of my family, Colleen, Geoff, and my lovely readers.

Extra shoutouts go out to Brodie MacBeath, Dr. Fabienne Uehlinger, Dr. Brian Short, and Francis Cleverdon of Hatchards Piccadilly.

Printed in Great Britain
by Amazon

41055538R00131